SHORT POURS

THE STAN CHRONICLES

CRIS HAMMOND

ISBN – 13: 978-0692863152
ISBN – 10: 069286315X

Cover by Starla Huchton
Interior formatting and typesetting by CL Foster

Short Pours is a work of fiction. Any resemblance to persons living or dead, is purely a coincidence.

To my lovely wife and wonderful daughters,
their husbands and the world's greatest
grandson, Daven.

Also, a special thanks to all
of those talented, and patient friends
in the Paris Writers Working Lunches Group.
This wouldn't be a book without you.

Cris Hammond

Table of Contents

Cris Hammond

Prologue

The flickering neon sign says, "Hotel Royale, Rooms." As he pushes the door open he's thinking, "Whoever named this place must have been on crack. There's no royalty living here, just juicers, hookers, and guys down on their luck, like my dad."

The surly little guy sitting behind the bulletproof glass in the entry hall is sucking ramen noodles through the holes in his teeth. Mike taps on the glass, "Is he in?"

"What do I look like, the fucking butler?"

"Hey, sorry, Alvin, I'm just asking if you've seen him."

"No, I ain't seen him. Stan and me, we keep different hours."

"Yeah, but you're here all day. You might'a seen him go past."

Alvin snorts out a sigh, then stabs the plastic spoon into the cup and aims his watery, encrusted eyes at Mike, "Look pal, I sit here every goddamn day and every night 'til three a.m., watching the girls dragging their clients up and down the stairs, and bugging the rest of those bums up there for last week's rent. Then, I go to bed. Okay?

At ten, I get up, drink my coffee, crap, and watch the news until noon. Then, I drag my ass back out here and sit and watch the world go to hell. Like I said, Stan and me, we got different hours."

"Still, you might'a seen him."

"Shit Mike, he's down the Teamsters hall by six in the morning. If he scored a job, you won't see him 'til five o'clock tonight. If he didn't, he's over at Mariano's, drinking his lunch."

"Thanks, Alvin. You've been a great help."

"Saved you the trouble of climbing the stairs, didn't I?"

"Yeah, you're a prince."

As Mike turns to leave, Alvin bangs on the glass and says, "Go to Mariano's. If he ain't there, he's on a job, and who knows when he'll be back."

"But, he's got an important meeting today. I gotta find him. Make sure he doesn't blow it."

"Go to Mariano's. Talk to Sal."

Short Pours

I'm at that point in a glass of whiskey where I begin coming up with reasons to have another. Thing is, I'm looking at the bottom of my third one and the reasons are getting to sound a little flimsy, though no less compelling.

I've already laid out some pretty good ones: "I'm finally starting to relax. One more oughta' do it." And, "Short pours in this place. Three drinks here are really only two anywhere else." And the clincher: "I got an hour before the interview, what the hell."

When I wave the glass in the air, Sal, pries his eyes off the television long enough to shove the bottle down the bar at me. "Take the rest, Stan," he says. "You get a bonus for being my best customer all morning."

It's raining outside. I don't have a hat and my car, Gladys, that piece of shit, wouldn't start this morning. Dead battery again. I'd parked her on a hill last night, just for that reason. I like to plan ahead. I thought I could get it rolling and pop the clutch and she'd start. But when I got to it this morning, I discovered that some joker musta' broke in and turned her around in the middle of the night and the goddamn thing was facing up the stupid hill.

So now, I'm gonna show up to this fricking job interview looking like I slept in the shower all night. I oughta have another drink... to ward off the cold.

I don't know why I'm going to this damn interview anyway. Don't get me wrong, I need the work, but they're never gonna hire a wreck like me. My kid, Mike, set it up. He told them his old man was a real pro. Then he started lying about how I was a manager and ran cargo terminals from Long Beach to Oakland. I never ran no warehouses. I could have. The guy who did was drunker than me most days, but he was Italian and I'm Irish, so, there you go.

Mike also forgot the part about how it was over twenty years ago and I wasn't no manager. I was a lumper, humping cargo by hand all day. Two years of that and I got a big promotion to forklift driver. That was my high point. Then I got drunk at lunch one epic payday, tipped my lift over and dumped a couple tons of Ripple wine on the foreman's car. Hot damn, was he pissed. The language he used was unique, even for the waterfront.

Then he started yelling and shoving me around. That's when it came to me that lumping and forklift driving were starting to get old, and the job had lost its appeal. So, I decked him. Knocked him out. The down side was that I broke my hand and had to apply for workman's comp, which the bastard denied. I still have two caved in knuckles on my right hand from it. Hurts like hell sometimes.

That there put an end to my warehousing career. My brother Teamsters gathered round me, but the union reps were drinking buddies with the port guys, so I disappeared. But Mike was almost twelve by then, and the old woman had taken off with the plumber, so, back to it. I still had my union card, so I bought a tractor with a loan, a cab-over Freightliner, and started hustling loads out of the Port of Oakland. A hundred fifty thousand miles a year, pushing that monster left me with a gimpy hip and mostly deaf in one ear, but it paid off the loan and bought Cheerios and TV dinners for the boy. That was 'til the DUI put me back on my ass.

I guess the kid's payin' me back now. Helpin' me find a job. Nice try. I can still stack boxes though, good as anyone I guess. They just gotta tell me where to stack 'em. As long as they do that and don't give me a lot of shit, I can do the work.

So, hell, I'll go to the damn interview. But I already know what's gonna happen. Some guy who's half my age and has never broken a sweat, will look me up and down and say, "Can I help you?" And I'll say, "I'm here for the job interview." Then he'll smirk or start laughing and, I swear to God, broken hand or not, I'll drop him.

And that, right there, is the best reason yet to have another whiskey.

Sal, the bartender is a big guy with dark, curly hair and a heavy brow over squinty blue eyes. He ties the strings of his apron underneath the many colored stains between his chin and the vast overhang that is his belly. Sal's feet went flat years ago, so he put wheels on a bar stool and scoots around on it when he's not parked at the end of the bar under the TV. At the moment, his eyes are glued to the set as he drags his fingers through a bowl of peanuts that's been sitting around for at least a week. He's been dropping shells all over the bar and onto the floor for several days now. They pile up down there until Saturday, which is the day he sweeps the place, whether it needs it or not. He looks so peaceful. I almost hate to disturb him. "Hey Sal, how about one more?"

"Did you leave any in the bottle?" He spins his stool to face me. "That there was the last of it." Then he twirls back around toward the television.

"There wasn't much in there. It's all gone. We need a fresh one."

"I gotta get it outta the back. Wait for the commercial," he says, as someone on the television screen throws a chair at his wife.

"Hey, what kinda bar is this anyway? I'm a paying customer."

"You are? When did that start? And anyway, Stan, what are you doing drinking three whiskeys at ten-thirty in the morning?" The wheels crunch on peanut shells as he turns to glare at me.

"I got a job interview at eleven-thirty. Thought I'd get loosened up for it."

"You have a job interview? In an hour? That does it. You're cut off."

"Hey, look. The commercial's on. You can go get-"

"You're cut off."

The door opens and a redheaded guy walks in. He's disheveled, wet and windblown, a victim of the weather. He's wearing a pair of baggy khaki's and a pale blue polo shirt with an emblem on the chest that looks like a penguin. His name is Jimmy, but I didn't find that out until later. He looks like a Jimmy though, or a Bobby, or Eddy, basically any grown man whose name ends with a "y."

This Jimmy says, "Does anyone know when the bus for downtown comes?"

"Isn't there a sign out there, in the bus stop?" I ask him.

"It's torn down."

Sal has rolled himself back behind the bar. "Yeah, the city puts them up and the kids in the neighborhood get a lot of laughs tearing them down. It usually comes every half hour, but they been off their schedule lately. In fact, I heard they were going to only stop in this neighborhood twice a day for a while. They don't even like to slow down around here anymore, let alone stop."

This is news to me. "Sal? You sayin' there's no bus? How'm I gonna get to my interview? It's way out on 150th avenue. Shit."

Sal looks at me for a second. "I guess you could drive. But I'd also guess you're over the limit."

Then Jimmy looks at me and says, "You got a car?"

"Yeah, I got a car, but…"

He sticks out his hand and says, "My name's Jimmy."

"I'm Stan, Stan O'Brian."

"Great to meet you, Stan. Say, I just had a thought." His eyebrows go up, showing me that he just had a thought. He says, "How about, I drive you to your interview and we just stop for a minute at the Starbuck's on 63rd and East 14th so I can meet my friend. I'll even buy you a coffee? Then I'll drive you out to 150th."

"I'd say that's a great idea, Jimmy. How are you at pushing cars?"

"This car needs to be pushed?" Jimmy's enthusiasm wilts.

"Just 'til I get up to speed, then I pop the clutch and, boom, off she goes."

"Dead battery?"

"It's temporary."

"Is this a big car?"

"Tiny. A Pinto. Two doors. Name's Gladys."

"A Ford Pinto? Named Gladys? Do they still make those?"

"They don't. She's a classic."

"Where is this Gladys?"

"Couple blocks over, on Poplar."

"Couple blocks?"

"Yeah, and she's on a hill. Pointing up. And it's raining. You want a ride or not?"

Jimmy turns out to be a natural at pushing cars. He had one or two smartass comments about how he's getting all wet and he'll have to wash his hands after, but he put his back into it and soon enough he's got me rolling downhill. It's time to warn him off. I yell out the window. "Alright, back off. Back off!" Jimmy falls behind and I let out the clutch. The tires chirp and a huge wad of black shit and smoke shoots out of the exhaust pipe as the engine fires. She's running, barely. I pull over and pump the gas while Jimmy catches up.

"Okay," he says, a little out of breath. "Great. She runs. So, slide over and I'll drive."

"No. You're the pusher. I'm the driver."

"But, I thought I was going to drive you."

"I drive. I'll take you to meet your friend and then we're done. Thanks for the push."

"But, you're drunk."

"No. I've been drinking. Drunk, and 'been drinking' are two different things. Besides, she's a little delicate. Not just anyone can keep this baby moving. Get in."

He listens to the squealing fan belt and the clatter of the engine popping away on three of its four cylinders. Then he shrugs his shoulders and trots around the car, pulls open the door and heaves himself into the seat before I can warn him. "Ow!" He yells. "Jesus Christ! What the hell?" He starts digging around under his butt.

"You okay?" I ask, filling my voice with sincere, caring tones.

"Jesus God! That hurt." He holds up a foot and a half of one-inch pipe. "What's this?"

"What's it look like?"

"A pipe. You a plumber?"

"No."

"Well then, what the hell?"

"I like pipes."

He touches the four-inch lag bolt welded across the end of it. "What's this for?"

"Luck. Give it to me before you hurt yourself." Now he's looking at me like I hurt his feelings or something. I put Mr. Pipe under my seat where he belongs and say, "Let's move. We gotta get all the way across town to, what? 63rd and East 14th?"

"Yeah. Starbuck's there."

"How much time we got?"

"Twenty minutes."

"Shit. Hold on." In a cloud of dust and a hearty "Hi-ho Pinto!" we're off.

Horns honk as we bust through a red light, but I've had just enough Jack Daniels not to care. I look across at Jimmy and ask, "So who's this friend we're risking our lives to meet? I'm guessing a lady."

"My girlfriend."

"You got a girlfriend?"

"Yes, I have a girlfriend." He sounds offended. Then he says, "Sort of."

"You either have one, or you don't. What's she call you? Jim, or Jimmy?"

"What difference does it make?"

"Big difference. What's this meeting about?" He's making me curious.

"I'm not sure exactly. She texted me a half hour ago to meet her at Starbuck's. It was kind of strange, really."

"Why strange?"

"I don't know. She usually doesn't drink coffee or hang out at Starbuck's. I tried to call her but she didn't answer. I texted her back, but same thing."

"Does she ever call you Jim?"

"Why?"

"Here we are." I pull up and double park in front of Starbuck's. "Here you go Jimmy. Good luck." He's looking out the window, searching for this girlfriend of his. "See her in there?"

"No." He looks at his watch. "Maybe she's late."

"Look, I gotta get going. So, goodbye and good luck."

"Just let me run in and see if she's in there, okay? I'll buy you a quick coffee. It'll help you, you know, with the interview, really. You could use a little coffee. It'll only take a minute."

By this time, I'm starting to feel a little bit sorry for Jimmy. Not sure why, but he doesn't seem to have the armor that most the guys I know wear. Kind of vulnerable. Maybe it's because I've been there one or two times myself, looking for a woman who never showed up.

Anyway, I figure two, three minutes ain't gonna make a real big difference in my job prospects. "Okay. I'll wait here. But make it quick. I like it black with two honeys, by the way."

He stops. "Honey?"

"Yeah, from bee's. Move!"

I watch him go into the place and look around. His red hair makes him easy to follow as he surveys the room. He doesn't seem to recognize anyone, so he moves over to the counter and orders the coffee, but he never stops scanning the room. I can tell by the set of his shoulders that she isn't there. She's either late or she's stood him up. I'm guessing the second one.

Then one of those big, ugly, SUV's, like a shiny black armored personnel carrier just back from a war zone, pulls up two inches behind me and flashes its lights. I'm sure G.I. Joe just wants to make friends, but I'm not interested, so I ignore him and turn my attention back to Jimmy. As the tank pulls out and crawls by me, a heavyset gorilla in the passenger seat gives me the evil eye. He's too ugly to look at, so I just rub my ear, with my middle finger. The SUV stops in front of me.

The two guys climb out and go into Starbuck's. I get some nasty looks, but I'm just an old geezer and they're moving like they have more important things to deal with than me, so nothing bad happens. I turn and look for Jimmy but I've lost him. He was at the counter just seconds ago, and now he's gone. Then I catch sight of him. He's under a table. He's tripped or something and people are helping him up.

No, they aren't. They're running away. The guy I thought was helping him up is holding him down. Now the SUV cowboys have arrived and are joining in. Shit, this is a mugging! Jimmy's crawled under a table and the thugs are trying to pull him out. Aw shit!

I tell myself I'm too old for this, then grab Mr. Pipe and drag my ass out of the car.

I'm holding my eighteen-inch friend against my leg as I come around the front of the Pinto. My gimpy hip is shooting pains up my back, telling me I really am being a fool. But then I figure, "At least I'll have the element of surprise. I'll sneak up on them. I mean, what's more invisible than an old man?"

I make it to the coffee shop door just as they bust through dragging Jimmy, who's struggling for all he's worth, but he's got about as much hope of getting away as a duck in a suitcase.

The bruiser in front stops short when he realizes there's somebody blocking the doorway. He's surprised and annoyed that anyone would be stupid enough to get in his way. He looks me square in the eye, and as he puts his hand on my chest, I say in my best old fart voice, "Pardon me, sir." His pressure hesitates for a second and I meekly go on, "Um, I was wondering…"

"What!" he shouts.

"What is that?" and I lightly touch the top button of his shirt. He looks down, like a dope, and gets the business end of Mr. Pipe stuffed right where his front teeth used to be. One down, two to go.

Now there's a big heap of writhing, bleeding and whimpering cowboy that the other two have to climb over, dragging Jimmy, who is thrashing around like a fish on a line. Their simple plan has just gotten complicated. Flopping and flailing and screaming like a pig stuck in a fence, Jimmy is becoming a real nuisance. Also, bad guy number one is rolling around, picking his teeth off the ground, blocking their escape. They've got some choices to make. These types aren't always the quickest of minds, I've found, and making decisions can give them pause.

I don't normally like to hit people on the head with my pipe. I'm not a killer. But I don't mind smashing up a knee or an elbow, or breaking a leg once in a while if a guy deserves it. In my opinion, these guys made the list.

The next one gets the worst of it. While he's chewing on his options, I go into a crouch and swing at his left knee. Even with my bad back, I put some heat into it and that nasty bolt welded to the end of Mr. Pipe actually buries itself an inch or so behind his kneecap. I have to wriggle and wrench it around to get it out. Two down.

The third guy, the hard-case, who gave me the stink eye from the SUV, gives me a look again. This time his expression is different. He looks like he's gonna puke as I'm jerking and twisting to yank the pipe out of his partner's kneecap. He looks at his backup, suffering on the sidewalk, then he drops his hold on Jimmy and takes off running.

Jimmy's suddenly free and he takes off too. The two punks are on the ground, screaming and crying. Blood's flowing. A crowd is gathering around, sipping lattes and gawking, and I'm beginning to hear sirens. It's time for me, and Mr. Pipe, to start backing out of the picture. Three steps into the crowd and I spin around and make for the Pinto at my fastest hobble.

Jimmy's crouching down behind the car, shaking and sweating, but otherwise, not too much worse for the wear. "Jimmy, get up! We gotta go." I grab his shirt and pull him to his feet.

"Right. Shit, let's get outta here," he cries and pulls open his door.

"Hey Jimmy, did you forget something?"

"What? No! Let's go."

"What's the first thing we have to do when we go for rides in the Pinto?"

"Oh, shit no."

"Oh yes. Now put your back into it. Ready. Set, Go-Go-Go-Go!!" Jimmy and his adrenaline get us up to speed in record time. She starts on the second pop and we lay down a regular Pinto smoke screen as we scream outta there.

"You gonna tell me who those guys were?" Jimmy's still shaking and sweating, but not as bad. It's time to get some things straightened out here. "Were they there for you, or did you just happen to start something with that first guy?"

"I never said a word to him. I was just standing there, waiting for your coffee.

"No idea who they could be?"

"Well…"

"Well, what?"

"The first guy? He said he had a message for me from Eileen. That's my girlfriend's name."

"Nice name. And what was the message? 'Eileen told us to kick your ass?' You think she sic'd those dogs on you?"

"No, she wouldn't do that." He said it, but he didn't sound like he quite believed it.

"Who then?"

"Might be friends of her husband."

"She's married?"

"Uh-huh." Now he's looking at his hands, folded in his lap.

"Who's she married to? Sonny-*Fucking*-Corleone? Is he some kind of gangster?"

"No, he's a baker."

"A baker. Like in a bakery?"

"Not exactly."

"Where exactly? A Wonder Bread factory?"

"He works in a prison."

"Not –"

"Yeah, San Quentin."

"Christ! You're messing around with the wife of the guy who bakes cookies for the meanest criminal motherfuckers in the country?"

"I was gonna break up with her."

"Gosh, why?"

"I think she might be cheating on me."

"Jimmy, has anyone ever told you that you are one sharp son-of-a-bitch?"

"No."

"Well, don't hold your breath."

I don't know where I'm going, but I'm going there too fast. All this action has given me a heavy foot and I need to back off some. I turn to Jimmy, "What time is it?" Jimmy holds up his wrist and shows me his watch. "Just tell me goddamn it! I can't read that thing from here."

"Eighteen after eleven."

"Shit, I'll never make that interview now. Great! Just great."

"Why don't you call them? Tell them you're running late."

"Yeah. Good idea. Better yet, you do it." I dig into my pocket for my phone. "Here. That's the number. You call 'em and ask for Hendricks. Tell 'em you're my assistant and I had an important meeting come up. I'll be late."

"Your assistant?"

"Just do it, okay? And try to sound like an assistant, will you?"

"I'll try." Jimmy gives me a look as he dials the number. "Hello, this is Mr. Greenglass, calling Mr. Hendricks on behalf of Mr. O'Brian. - Yes, would you please tell Mr. Hendricks that Mr. O'Brian would like to reschedule this morning's appointment? Something's come up in our New York office that requires his attention. Unavoidable, I'm afraid. – Yes, I know. Isn't it always? – Perhaps we could reschedule for some time later this afternoon? - Ah, that would be fine. Two o'clock then. I'll tell him. Thank you so much." Jimmy rings off and hands the phone back to me. "You're set for two o'clock."

"Jesus, Jimmy, that was good. When you aren't busy making bad decisions about your love life, what else do you do?"

"I'm a home appraiser. Or, used to be. The outfit I worked for is kind of under indictment right now. A little too much fooling around with home loans, so –"

"You're under indictment? And you've got a baker after you, and your girlfriend, who is married to that gangster baker, is cheating on you? How do you find the time?"

"It's my boss who should be indicted, not me. But he plays golf with the Assistant Attorney General, and he's in some posh men's club in the City with the guy from the SEC. So, he's sitting on something like eight hundred million bucks, and I'm fired, beat up, and riding around with a drunk, in a rusted-out wreck of a Pinto."

"Well, you could have taken the bus to meet your girlfriend, but I doubt the bus driver would have stuck around to save your shivering little white ass."

"Yeah," he sighed. "I owe you for that."

"Don't mention it. You know we just took a squirt on one big hornet's nest don't you. Now you not only got the baker after you, but you, no *we*, are on someone's nasty list for hurting those two guys."

"Shit, I hadn't thought of that."

"Well, think about it. We gotta do something to divert their attention for a while. Tell me about the baker's wife."

"Her name's Eileen."

"I know that. How'd you meet her?"

"My job. I went to appraise her house. "

"Did she answer the door wrapped in Saran Wrap?"

"No, a bathrobe."

"Love at first peek?"

"It was slightly open at the top, yeah. But she's very nice, and really cute."

"Oh Christ. She's cute? So, you went back for more 'appraisals' on a daily basis?"

"Not every day, no. Only two or three times a week, but not to her house."

"Your place?"

"No. She has this favorite motel out by the airport she likes."

"Did you just say she has a favorite motel?"

"Yeah, The Golden Palms Inn by the airport. It's real close to the runways."

"Okay, so while the baker's at work, at San Quentin, you're off humping his wife three days a week in a dive motel at the airport. Sounds like a Doris Day movie."

"I wasn't humping her. We made love. There's a difference, Stan."

"Right. So I've heard. Why the airport?

"She has this thing about jets. She gets off when they, like, fly right over her head when she's well, you know."

"Nothing strange about that. Big, jumbo jets?"

"Yeah. She can tell you if it's a 747, 787, or an Airbus, just by the sound."

"That's a gift. Does she scream, *'Fasten your seatbelts!!'* When she's coming?"

"You know, it's funny you should mention that."

"Really?"

"You asked me what she called me before."

"Yeah, Jimmy or Jim."

"Well, when we first started, she did call out my name, just when, you know, the jet was landing. But she doesn't anymore. Once, I thought she said, 'Eddie.' But I wasn't sure because of the jet. It was really loud. But since then she doesn't use my name at all. Now she just calls me Baby."

"As in, 'Oh baby! Oh baby?"

"Yeah."

"Count on it, Jimmy. She's cheatin' on you."

"Really?" He puts his face in his hands and says, "God damn it!"

"Who's Eddie?"

"I'm not sure. But it could be my boss, ex-boss. She came into the office a couple times and he seemed to take a special interest in her appraisal. His name's Edward."

"I take back what I said about a Doris Day movie. This is The Three Stooges."

"I just wish she'd call or text me, or something. I think it's time to confront her, actually find out, I mean before my legs get broken, or worse."

"Okay, listen up dummy. You got a text, from her phone, telling you to meet her at Starbucks. But it was a setup. It's obvious that either she wants you gone, or the baker has her phone. Could he have it without her knowing he's got it?"

"Only if -. Shit."

"What?"

"She always has it with her. It's like an addiction. She's checking it constantly, except, when we're at the Palms. She leaves it at home then. She thinks she can be tracked on its GPS."

"So, like I said, she's either in on it with her husband, or the baker has her phone because she's left it behind because she's someplace she doesn't want to be tracked on GPS."

Jimmy sagged in the seat. "Christ, now I need a drink."

"Hey, I know just the place. You ever been to Joey Nice Guy's Bar out on Hegenberger? It's a cruddy little place, but it's dark, and Joey gives you his personal attention and a solid pour." I slide my eyes over onto Jimmy. "It's right near the airport, not far from The Golden Palms. We can swing by. It's right on the way. Take a cruise through the parking lot. Poke our noses around a bit. Find out what's what."

"Alright, but-."

"But what?"

Well, if she's there, then she didn't set me up."

"So, that's a good thing."

"But she's still cheating on me, with my boss, or someone."

"Maybe not. Look on the bright side. "Maybe she just got a part time job. You know, cleaning rooms, making beds, to the sound of jets.

"She'd have her phone with her."

"Ah, right. So then, if she's there, she'll be cheating on you, and her husband, and God knows how many other fools. Is that better or worse than her trying to get you killed?"

"Good question."

"Think about it."

"But wait. How'd her husband get it, the phone I mean? He's at work."

"Oh, don't be an idiot. He probably suspects something and popped home to surprise her. Catch her with her feet up in the air. He doesn't find her, but he finds her phone. Goes through her calls and texts, then puts two and two together. Bingo. He let's the dogs loose on you."

"But why me? Why not my boss? Eddie? If she's with him, why am I the target?"

"Well, he probably sees calls going to him too, but they go to his office and a secretary answers. Legitimate business calls, about the refinance. But when he calls your number, it's just you. It's personal."

"So, my boss gets my girl, and I get fired and beat to a pulp."

"That's why it's always best to be the boss."

"I'm screwed."

"It ain't over yet, Jimmy. Let's drop by the airport. See if she's there."

The Golden Palms Inn at the Airport is a sagging outhouse of a motel, but it's right across the highway from the end of the main runways. Nobody in their right mind would rent a room there, unless they were broke, or Eileen, who doesn't go there to sleep. The management had decided to put the dumpsters at the back of the parking lot where they'd be the first things to take the hit if a jumbo jet missed the runway. Next to the dumpsters and on the second floor, is Eileen's favorite room, number 32B. It's closer to the jets. A brand new Lexus is parked in front of the faded pink door of 32A, on the ground floor.

The rest of the parking lot is empty except for a Chevy wagon from the 80's that someone must be living in, and a brand new Maserati, parked two slots up from the Lexus.

We're making our second slow cruise around the empty parking lot and the conversation is lagging. "The Lexus? It's hers?" I ask Jimmy, who's biting his lip.

"Yeah."

"And the Maserati?"

"His. Yeah."

"Nice car. Say, how about we sic the baker on the banker? Let the jilted gangster husband do the dirty work." I'm warming up to this now.

"How?"

"You can take pictures with that phone, right?"

"Sure."

"Hand me Mr. Pipe."

"No. I don't trust you with that thing. Are you going to hurt somebody?"

"Not unless I have to. What do you think I am, some kind of crazy baker? Unless of course, you want me to hurt someone?"

"No thanks. At least, I don't think so."

"Like I said, let's let the baker do the hurting." A cloud of belching exhaust rolls over the Maserati as I bring Gladys to a stop behind it. "Okay, jump out and get a picture of the Eddie's car and its license plate. Then get one of it sitting next to the Lexus. Both cars, and the sign, the Palms." Jimmy grabs his phone and climbs out of the car. I take my little friend and hobble round to stand by Jimmy. "Got the plate?"

"Yeah. What are you doing with that pipe? You're not going to attack him are you?"

"What kind of a drunk you think I am? Now move over there and aim your camera at the door to 32B." He does like he's told. "You ready?"

"I'm ready."

A Maserati is a beautiful car. The lines are something very special in the world of automotive design. Its only rival might be a Ferrari or a Lamborghini. They are all precious vehicles, much loved by their owners. And when you lock the doors, they automatically arm their burglar alarm systems. So, when you smash an eighteen inch steel pipe through their taillights, they let out a god-awful shriek. Oh yes they do.

The horn is blaring and I have to yell over it. "Okay, Jimmy, wait for it. Aim, five, four, three, two, one. Here they come!" The door to 32B bangs open and a naked, bald-headed man stands in the doorway. A second later, he's knocked aside by a disheveled brunette, dragging a sheet that almost covers one of her breasts.

Jimmy is clicking away as I flip Mr. Pipe into the air and catch him again like a juggler on Market Street. I smile at our tiny audience, then touch my forelock and bow deeply as the man, who I sure hope is Eddie, screams, "Hey you! You! What the hell are you doing? My car! You're smashing my car!!"

"James!" the woman yells. "What are you doing?"

I turn to Jimmy, "James? When the jets are landing it's 'Oh James! Oh James?' That's just weird."

"God damn it! I'm calling the cops!" The naked Eddie is yelling threats, while hopping from foot to foot and holding both hands over his privates, which makes him a lot less threatening than he thinks he is. But Eileen, one admittedly nice breast exposed, is making for the stairs. It's time to split.

I turn to Jimmy. "Let's go."

Diving into the Pinto, he's shouting, "Awayyy! Haha!! Did'ya see her?! Ha!!"

"Jimmy." I'm leaning in the window.

"What? Let's go. Go-go-go!" He's actually pounding on the dashboard.

"Jimmy, aren't you forgetting something?"

"What?"

"What do we have to do every time we make our getaway?"

"Aw shit."

"Right. Out, Rambo, and put your back into it. Eileen is coming."

Neither Joey nor his Nice Guy Bar has lost any of their charm. He's well over eighty now, and has a shaved head that is so pointed that you kind of picture it topped by a tiny clown hat with a plastic flower floating over it. He always wears some kind of beer-stained, t-shirt that hangs over a revolving collection of brightly patterned Bermuda shorts. He says it livens up the place and attracts the ladies. He's wrong though. Spotting a lady in Joey Nice Guy's is about as likely as pushing open the doors and finding that someone has booked the place for a wedding.

Joey is in the corner by the pay phone when we walk in. He's moving a gap-toothed broom back and forth over a spot on the floor. The place is blessedly dark so you could miss the dust that's been there since the Reagan administration. The booths that line the wall across from the bar are dark and worn, and showing their stuffing. Ten uneven bar stools stand in a row, like town drunks. They present themselves there, on their heavy oak legs, purposely too big to throw or swing over your head.

Joey walks over and recognizes me when he gets close. "Hey Stan, it's been a while. You still drinking the JD? He reaches for the Jack Daniels.

"Sounds good, and one for my friend here too. Joey, meet Jimmy. Jimmy, meet Joey Nice Guy." Joey gives Jimmy a nod and sticks out a broken, arthritic hand. He gives Jimmy a couple of pumps then puts the bottle on the table, slaps down two shot glasses and goes back to his broom.

Nice Guy and I were lumpers together on Pier Six back in the glory days. The walls are lined with old black and white photographs of prizefighters, some of him. He's an ex-light-heavyweight. He still has the arms and shoulders, and the nose, long since flattened into a shapeless lump. He breathes through his mouth. Joey ain't pretty, but he pours an honest drink.

Jimmy scans the room, turns to me and says, "This guy was a fighter, huh?"

"Yeah, he never made the big time, but he had his share of wins. He taught my kid to fight."

"Your son's a boxer?"

"No, he makes furniture. But when he was in high school, he needed a little straightening up. Nice Guy taught him some things I couldn't."

Jimmy mulls that over for a few seconds, then he grins and says, "I like this place."

"Hey, Nice Guy. Did you hear that? Jimmy likes your dive." I have to yell because Joey can only hear out of one ear. He popped an eardrum in a card fight thirty years ago in a smoker in Oakland. He shouldn't have been there. He was too old, but tell him that. He never got it fixed, but he's hung mirrors all over the place so he can see if people are talking or waving their glasses at him.

I'm yelling toward his good ear though, so he leans on his broom and answers me right away. "You ready for another one Stan?"

"Not me, but I think Jimmy's ready." I point a thumb at Jimmy. He's still got a half-inch in the bottom of his glass, but he looks at it, blinks a couple times, and nods to me. "Yup," I say. "Another Jack for my friend."

"That sure felt good back there." Jimmy is swirling a taste in his cheek. "Did you see the look on her face?"

"I wasn't really looking at her face."

"Oh yeah. Well, it was priceless. So, what do we do now? Blackmail her?"

"I'm thinking that we are into this mess about as deep as we should be, Jimmy. I say we fade out."

"What, run away to Mexico or something?"

"No Jimmy, Mexico won't do it." I watch Joey shuffle by and pour another Jack Daniels until it slops over the rim of Jimmy's glass. "We gotta get off the baker's shit list. I say you send those pictures to Eileen. Right now."

"What's that gonna do? She already knows we have them. What's she gonna do?"

"Sorry, I should have been more specific. I mean, send them to Eileen's phone."

"But she doesn't have - Oh."

"Right. Her husband has the phone. Sure, your number is on it, but that's legitimate. You're the home appraiser. They lure you out and catch you blatantly buying a coffee at Starbuck's. Colossal fuckup. They went after the wrong guy and got their asses whipped for their trouble. There's going to be a lot of hell to pay over that. But, once they get those pictures, maybe they can go to work on the right guy, and make amends. The baker doesn't want you. He wants the guy who's playing airplane with his beloved. The guy in those pictures."

"But, what'll they do to Edward?"

"Who cares? That's his problem. At least it will get that lunatic off our asses. So send them, goddamn it. Now!"

As Jimmy pulls out his phone, I look into my glass. There's still a little color left on the bottom. I should probably have another one. I've got that interview in an hour, and it's been a tough morning. I should loosen up a bit. Besides, Nice Guy pours 'em short. Four drinks here are like two anywhere else.

No Good Deed

It's after four o'clock and that bum still hasn't shown up. He was supposed to be here at three-thirty. My guys are at the bar, waiting; my neighbors Leo and Sonny Bouncer from the Hotel Royale, and even Elmer, who came all the way in from Walnut Creek for the show. Sal's tending bar. He's in the deal as the go-between, but he's firmly with the good guys. They have my back. That bastard's gonna want his money, and as much as I hate this, he'll get it. But, it'll be on my terms. Not his.

There's an old saying, "No good deed goes unpunished." I'm not in the habit of doing many good deeds, so I don't worry too much about suffering any punishment. But, when I saw old Eddie Furman, bedded down in his car out on West 18th street, I took pity on him.

Eddie's a house painter by trade. He's also a drinker by inclination. The one was getting the better of the other and he was having a hard time finding, or keeping, any paying work. He'd forget which colors went on which house, or show up on the wrong day or at the wrong place. Then he started falling off his ladder. It was beginning to get ugly.

I walked over and tapped on the window of the old Volvo and yelled. "Hey, Eddie, what's up my man? You all right in there?"

He fumbled around, found the window crank and rolled it down. The turpentine and chemical fumes that escaped burned my eyes and I had to turn away. The ancient station wagon was crammed to the roof with everything he owned. Most of it was just clothes and crap, but there were also a lot of paint cans, brushes, drop cloths and worst of all, leaking cans of enamel and paint thinner. It was a rolling toxic waste dump.

He broke into a short coughing fit, then wiped his eyes and wheezed, "Oh, hi, Stan. You got a cigarette?"

"No, Eddie. I don't smoke."

"Oh, I thought you did. You got a match?"

"No. Ain't got a match. Besides, man, if you lit a match in there I swear you'd blow up."

"Yeah, I guess so."

"How you doing these days, Eddie? Working at all?"

"Not much lately. But I got stuff lined up. Maybe gonna start up soon."

I took that with a grain of salt. He never was a smart dresser or a stickler for grooming, but his ragged, paint splattered jeans and worn out sweatshirt looked like he'd dragged them off the floor of a dog kennel. His stringy grey hair was matted and his beard was shaggy and infested with various bits of food that hadn't quite made it to his mouth over the past few days. He looked up at me through red-rimmed, watery eyes that seemed to focus and wander at random.

"Hey, Eddie, how long's it been since you had a shower?"

"Shit, I don't know. A while I guess. Why, do I stink?"

"Well, yeah, you're getting pretty ripe." I thought about it for a second. Then I figured, 'What the hell, won't cost me nothin' and it'll do him a world of good.' So I said, "Look, I'm taking care of a place across town, belongs to a friend of mine. Why don't you come with me and you can get yourself cleaned up."

"Hey!" I was banging on the door. "You still alive in there? Eddie, come on, time to get out." He'd been locked in the bathroom for half an hour, water running and steam blowing out from under the door. I was beginning to think the old man had died in there.

My friend, Miguel, wouldn't be at all happy if he came back from Alabama and found out that I let goddamn Eddie Furman die in his bathroom. Miguel was on his way to Oklahoma, hauling a double set of forty-foot containers out to Tulsa. From there he was picking up a load in Chicago and taking it down to Birmingham. He'd be gone two weeks.

Since the gangs had started roaming the neighborhood a couple years ago, he didn't like leaving the house empty when he was on these cross-country runs. He wasn't so much afraid of being robbed. The house was a pre-war, stucco wreck, with off street parking on the brown dirt patch that once was a front lawn… not a gleaming target. But he didn't want to come home and find a bunch of crack-heads camped around the fireplace. So he let me babysit, and enjoy the luxury of a hot shower whenever I felt like it, and use the washer/dryer.

Eddie's filthy rags were, at that moment, stuffed in the washing machine, waiting for him to drag his ass out of the shower so that I could turn it on and get him some clean clothes. In Miguel's house, you couldn't run the shower and turn on a faucet at the same time. If you did, the shower would fade to a pathetic, cold, dribble. But, it was time to find out if Eddie was dead, or alive. So, I went to the other bathroom, enjoyed a private smile, and then flushed the toilet.

It took about five seconds for the shouting to come down the hall. "Hey!!" he cried. "What happened? Shit! It's cold! Turn the water back on."

I pounded on the door again and said, "Time to come out, man." Two minutes later, and the sight of a naked Eddie Furman, bouncing from foot to foot while making a puddle in the hallway had burned itself into my mind forever.

I'm not much of a cook, so for dinner, we fired up old Gladys and went down to the Chinese take-out place next door to Mariano's and got us a bucket of Chow Mein. Then we went to see Sal for a little something to wash it down. He was serving a couple guys I didn't know down the bar, so we bellied up at the other end and started scarfing down the noodles. "Yo, Stan," Sal said as he scooted toward us on his rolling bar stool.

"Hi Sal," I said

"I'll give you guys two minutes to eat that shit or get it out of here. You're stinking up the place." Then he looked at Eddie. "Wow, am I looking at Eddie Furman? Jesus, did somebody wash him?"

"I took a shower, yeah," said Eddie. "Stan let me use the shower at his place."

Sal raised his eyebrows and gave me a look of disbelief. "I'm helping him out," I said. "Okay?"

"I guess that means you're buyin' the drinks too?"

"Might as well. I'll have a JD and he'll have the cheapest beer you got," I said.

Eddie raised a finger and said, "Um, I'll have a Jack Daniels too, Sal, on the rocks."

Sal's eyebrows went up again as he leaned on the bar and he rolled his eyes over to me. I said, "Okay, give him a Jack." Turning to Eddie, I said, "After that, we're done."

"Hey, I thought you were gonna let me stay at your house, man. It's cold out there," Eddie waved a hand vaguely toward the door.

"Look, you got a shower, and a shave. And I washed your rags for you. Plus, you're eating chow mien and drinking bourbon. So don't push your luck."

Then Sal put in, "He's right Eddie. You owe him big time. That's how you thank him? What are you gonna do for him?"

"I don't know. Shit, I'm a house painter. Want me to paint your house?"

"I ain't got a house, fool."

"What you got? I'll paint something for you."

"All I have is a car; piece of shit Pinto."

"Yeah, I saw it. It's a piece of shit all right. I helped push it, remember?"

"You leaned on it. I did all the pushing."

"Hell, if I really pushed it, my hand would go right through it. Goddamn rust bucket," he said.

"Hey," I said. "There's a few rust spots on the doors and stuff. That's it."

Then Sal delivered a couple JD's, slapped his hand on the bar and said, "That's it, Eddie! You can fix the rust spots on Stan's car. Sand 'em down, slap a little paint on and, bingo! That Pinto is just like new again, almost." Then he looked at me and said, "He could probably do that without doing too much damage. What do you think?"

"Alright, alright. He can sleep on the couch tonight, but tomorrow he fixes the rust spots on the car. Then, he goes. We're even."

Two days later, the doors and back hatch of my, once solid faded red, Pinto are smeared with drying blotches of blue house paint. It looked better with the rust, but at least Furman was gone, as were my urges to do any more good deeds.

The next few weeks went by like some kind of vacation from bullshit. I started getting pretty regular work out of the hiring hall and I landed six days of forklift driving at a warehouse south of San Francisco. Guy was going on vacation and he tagged me to be his replacement.

Miguel came back, but two days later he was gone again, so I was back to living for free at his place and even cooking sometimes. I had money coming in and not much going out, and I was, for the first time in a long time, putting a little aside. I was beginning to wonder if doing that good deed for Furman might have been paying off, karma-wise.

It was about a month since I'd last seen Eddie and I was settling myself onto my stool, when Sal rolled over to the cash register, picked up a wrinkled envelope, slapped it on the bar, and slid it under my nose.

"What's this?" I asked.

"It's for you. Furman came in yesterday and left it for you. I'm guessing he's thanking you, finally."

I picked it up and turned it over a couple times. "For Stan" was scrawled in pencil across the front. "Well, he spelled my name right. That, right there, is a surprise. Alright, let's see what this is." I tore it open and pulled out a piece of lined, binder paper, smudged with dirt, and showing pencil scratches stumbling across the top. The first word I recognized was "Invoice."

"What is it?"

"It's a fucking bill!" I said, hardly believing it myself. "It's an invoice for three thousand bucks! … For painting my car."

"Ha!! He's charging you? Amazing. What a prick."

"Oh, but wait. This is nice. He's giving me two weeks to pay without incurring a fucking late fee… ten percent."

"Oh, well, that is very generous. What are you gonna do?"

"My first impulse is to fold this four ways and shove it up his ass. But that would involve touching him." I looked at the grimy piece of lined paper. It had been creased a number of times and one corner was dog-eared. Then I noticed a scrawl along the bottom. It was barely legible, but I squinted down at it and it came into focus. I read it out loud. "Cash only, no checks. To be delivered to Sal, at Mariano's."

"Oh, that's swell," Sal said. "The little shit's puttin' me in the middle of this? Christ."

"This is crazy. He's nuts. Man, I don't know whether to tear it up, or frame it, like a masterpiece of stupid."

Two weeks and two days later, Sal greeted me with, "Guess what." Then he hands me another envelope. Seems old Furman was disappointed that I had neglected to get my payment in on time, so he scrawled out another invoice. This one showed the original balance owed, plus the ten percent late fee. So, now I owed him $3,300.00, payable in cash, in two weeks, unless I wanted to incur another late fee.

I tore it up and shoved the pieces back into the envelope. "Sal," I said. "If that son of a bitch comes in here again, give him that and tell him I said to go fuck himself. I ain't paying. Not a dime, period."

"I'll be happy to, Stan," he said.

From then on, I had Furman on my tail. He'd never actually get close enough for me to catch him, but there might be a note left on my car, or I'd look in the mirror behind the bar and see him, standing out on the street looking in the window at me. But by the time I'd get out there, he'd be gone. The whole thing was getting freaky. Every day I got more and more convinced that I should have just left that bum to rot in his car.

About four months into this circus, I was greeted at Mariano's with another goddamn gift from Furman. Sal poured me a shot of Jack then laid the grimy envelope gently on the bar in front of me. I just grabbed it and tore it up. Then, for no particular reason, I tossed the pieces into the air.

This caught the attention of a guy drinking a beer by himself at a table near the door. He got up and picked a few pieces off the floor, brought them over and set them on the bar in front of me and said, "You dropped these."

He was a broad-shouldered guy, with a shaved head, two-day beard, and a small silver skull stuck in his ear. He wore a light blue polo shirt under a dark blue blazer that was stretched tight around his arms. I caught the stale smell of old cigarettes. He turned and bent down and got some more pieces off the floor and brought them over, dropped them on the bar and said, "It's kind of like littering, don't you think? Tossing this shit all over the place."

Sal, by now was rolling towards us on his stool, preparing himself for an intervention. "Stan," he said. "We all cool here?"

The big guy said, "Your name's Stan?"

"Yeah."

"Stan O'Brian?"

"That's me."

Then he smiled, slid his hand inside his coat, brought out a folded piece of paper, set it across my drink and said, "You've been served."

God, I hate judges. I don't care if they're judging a dog show or a hula hoop competition, they're all of them, pompous sons-of-bitches. And there I was sitting in front of a purebred example of the breed. I was in Small Claims Court. Small fucking Claims Court! Sitting in an institutional green courtroom, on a hard, wooden bench, with two burly bailiffs at the front to make sure no fights broke out between the sixty bozos filling the place, half of us on one side of the room, glaring and snarling at our enemies across the aisle. A puffed-up balloon of a judge with an elaborately sprayed comb-over was sitting in his black robe up on his perch, looking down his nose at us, bored as shit. He was almost totally absorbed with chewing on what must have been a very tasty hangnail on his middle finger. I figured he must have really pissed someone off to draw this duty.

Small Claims, the Everyman's court; such a zoo. No lawyers allowed. Any fool can sue anyone he wants if he's got the dough to pay the fee. Furman was suing me for the maximum, five grand, the highest he could go for a fifty-dollar fee. So, there I was, a defendant, accused of defrauding the poor, innocent bastard out of his righteously earned three grand, plus late fees, and an extra thousand or so for pain and suffering.

I'd been there for more than an hour. The cases went from bounced checks and broken windows, to a guy who was suing his neighbor for stealing the affections of his cat. Seems the cat moved in with the neighbor because the food was better. He sues the guy for a grand. Wins two hundred bucks. Justice was served and the neighbor now has a two hundred dollar, gourmet cat.

By the time Furman's name was called, and we shuffled up to our places in front of the court, the judge was aggressively gnawing on the fingers of one hand and patting down his comb-over with the other one. He looked us up and down, rolled his eyes and barked, "What's this about?"

I raised a hand and pointed at Furman, "This guy's nuts. He wants me to pay him for painting my car."

"Are you the plaintiff?"

"No, I'm the defendant, O'Brian."

"The plaintiff goes first, sir," the judge rumbled. "Haven't you been paying attention? The plaintiff always goes first in my court." Then he pointed the business end of his gavel at Eddie and said, "What's this all about, plaintiff?"

"He won't pay me for painting his car."

The judge actually laid his forehead on his arms. Then he raised his head, looked over at me and asked, "Did plaintiff paint your car?"

"No. Well, yeah... sort of."

"He sort of painted your car?" He looked at the papers in front of him and went on, "It says here, he's asking three thousand dollars for the paint job, plus late fees because you didn't pay on time, and... nine hundred sixty dollars for pain and suffering?" He looked over at Furman and said, "We don't do pain and suffering here, sir. I'm striking that."

Then he looked at me again and said, "Three thousand dollars doesn't seem like an outrageous sum for painting a car. Why did you not pay?"

I wanted to say that I already paid the bastard with a shot of Jack Daniels and a bunk on the couch, but I thought this might not be the best place to start mouthing off. So, I bit my tongue and said, "Because he didn't to a complete paint job, your honor. He sanded down a couple spots of rust on the doors and trunk, and smeared house paint over them. That's not a real paint job."

"That's it? House paint over some rust spots?" He looked at Furman and asked, "Are you a painter, sir?"

"Yes, I am. I'm a professional and I deserve to get paid."

"A house painter?"

"Yeah."

Turning back to me again, the judge asked, "Sir, what kind of car are we talking about?"

"A 1974 Pinto."

"Jesus, a Pinto, with rust on it…"

Furman piped up, "I fixed the rust, and –"

The judge raised his hand, turned to me and asked, "Now that the rust is fixed, what's this Pinto worth?"

"Hard to say, sir. It's a classic… maybe a few hundred bucks." Then I stepped up and said, "But that's not the story. I helped him out. I gave him a shower, and washed his clothes. I bought him a drink and - "

"Did you just say, you gave him a shower? And bought him a drink?" He looked at both of us, picked up his gavel and pounded on his desk. "The court has heard enough. Giving a man a shower is not the same as paying him for work he's done for you." I opened my mouth, but the judge gave me a look that shut it again. Then he banged his hammer again and went on, "I find for the plaintiff…"

"Ha!" Furman shot his fist into the air.

"…in the amount of five hundred dollars."

"What? But, what about the late fees?"

The hammer came down three times in a row and he was going for a fourth when he stopped, gritted his teeth, closed his eyes, and said, "Five hundred. Defendant pays plaintiff. Now get out!"

I was going to appeal the verdict, but I got the feeling that if that judge saw my face again, he'd have found a way to put me in jail. All that work I'd been getting since doing my good deed had set me ahead just enough to pay the judgment and still have enough left over for a hamburger. My belief in karma had been seriously tested.

It's almost four-thirty now and I just caught a glimpse of Furman out on the sidewalk, getting up the courage to come inside. He's still avoiding any face-to-face communication with me, so we've agreed to make the payment in a public place, with witnesses around so he'll feel safe. Mariano's was tapped and Sal is the go-between. Sonny, Leo, and Elmer are witnesses.

So, we're playing this by Furman's rules, which are: 1. The payment is in cash, no checks and 2. Sal is holding the money.

I have decided to just be good and go along with it. So, I've given Sal the cash. He's got it in a box behind the bar, or maybe I should say he's got it in a crate behind the bar. Five hundred bucks weighs almost a hundred pounds, when it's all in nickels.

Between God and Stan

I don't need anybody telling me that having a few drinks before a job interview isn't such a good idea. I get it. Even switching from whiskey to rum hadn't helped me get to second base. A year and a half of looking for steady work and it was starting to sink in. My kid was right. I needed a new approach.

The meeting I'd had that day was a fiasco. 'Course, I was late. The stupid Pinto wouldn't start, as usual, and Leo from next door was too sick to help me push it. So, there I was, rolling it down Oak Street by myself, one hand shoving against the doorpost and the other holding on to my canned Mai-Tai. Finally, I got her up to speed and I threw myself in just in time to avoid flattening a kid going by on a bike. I cranked the wheel, hit the key, popped the clutch, and dumped the freaking Mai-Tai right in my lap.

I wasn't drunk, but I smelled like a goddamn Tiki lounge, and I looked like I'd wet my pants. It was a short interview. Five minutes, then he laid his pen down and said, "We'll call you." I ain't holding my breath.

So, there I was again, sitting on the ice chest that I used for a chair in my crappy room in the Hotel Royale, "Rooms to Let, by the Hour, Day, Week," wondering how the hell I was gonna come up with some cash so I didn't get thrown out. Thanks to Furman and his goddamn law suit, I'd had to borrow the last couple week's rent from Mikey "The Face" Fallon down on 7th Street and now I couldn't go near West 7th without the dough if I wanted to keep my kneecaps.

I also didn't want to get kicked out of the Royale. The place was a shit hole, and about six inches from the gutter, but it had been home for four months and I'd gotten used to knowing where I was gonna sleep from one night to the next. Me, and Leo, the guy next door, were the only long-term residents since Maurice jumped off the roof and broke his neck and the cops took Ricardo away for, well, being Ricardo, only in public. The rest of those poor bums on the first and second floors were some real down-and-out guys. At the Royale, Rule Number One was, never leave your room without your shoes on. You could step on some things in the hallways there that'd infect you with shit that would make you wish you only had Ebola.

I was back on hard times, but I still had a union card and wasn't a stranger to work. Those guys downstairs hadn't honestly earned a dollar in decades, except for the hookers. They were employed, hardworking, and relatively clean.

Life hadn't exactly been throwing me posies, but it could've been worse. I was broke, and the people down at the unemployment office were starting to call me "Him Again." But I had a roof over my head, 'til the end of the week, and I still had two cans of tomato juice in the ice chest, and some cheese crackers, stashed under the bed. I also had some luck on my side in my son, who I never leaned on, but I knew I could if I had to. He'd turned out to be a good man, despite growing up with his mother run off somewhere to Mexico, and a father who was out on the road, pushing freight six days a week for most of his life.

I hadn't had a drink since breakfast, which I think he would'a liked. I still had a hankering to go see Sal down at Mariano's for just one little pop, but my credit was strung out pretty thin down there so I was stayin' in until I could cover my tab.

Evenings at the Royale in those days weren't what you'd call "posh." The light bulb that hung from the ceiling in each room was attached to a coin meter in the wall: A buck an hour, quarters only, one at a time. There was a light in the entry hall, down on the first floor, but no chairs, or anything to sit on, and you'd better have a can of bug spray with you.

So, preferring the luxury of my own room, and lacking a sack full of quarters, I'd settled myself on my ice chest, in the flickering glow of the Royale's neon sign, to watch the street action and check out a couple paperbacks I'd found down by a dumpster. The first one went right back out the window. It was some Star Wars episode thing with half the pages stuck together and most of the rest covered with crayon scribbles. But the other one looked interesting, and it was in pretty good shape. It was about the Crusades. I like that stuff; swords, kings, blood and guts. The title was, *God's Battalions*.

"God's Battalions?" I said to myself. "Why does he - Hey, Leo," I pounded on the wall a couple times and called, "Leo! Why does God need battalions?"

All I got in reply was a couple anemic thumps and some muffled curse words that I took to mean he was wrapped around a bottle of Thunderbird and wouldn't be up to discussing literature, or God, until morning. Still, I couldn't help telling the wall, "He's God, for Christ's sake. What's he need battalions of soldiers for, anyway?"

Then, with a flash and a pop, the light bulb came alive and a blinding light filled the room that was so hot that I felt it flash across my face. It was like I'd put a whole dollar's worth of quarters in the meter at once. Then, I'll be damned if this voice didn't knife through my head, saying, "You're right, Stan. I don't."

I spun around on my ice chest, sloshing another Mai-Tai into my lap, and scanned the room to see who had broken in. The locks were flimsy in the Royale, but the table I'd shoved against the door was still there. Nothing had changed. I was still alone, but the air felt different. It seemed liquid, it came in waves, and shudders, then as quickly as it started, it went still again. And the voice, it was coming from inside my head, not through my ears. "What is this?" I said, quietly.

"It's me," the voice replied, more insistent this time.

I'd seen enough guys on the street who were hearing voices, and they didn't end up well. This was disturbing. I didn't want to ask, but I did. "What d'ya mean, me? Who's there?"

"Me. God."

I wasn't buying it. I was sitting in a ten by ten room with a sagging bed, a broken chair, an ice chest and a closet with no door. This was a flophouse, not Grace fucking Cathedral. Some guys in here heard voices from time to time, but not from God. But I was hearing one now, and it was damn clear. And I was definitely alone. I thought it might have been coming from out in the hall, so I got up and faced the door and called, "Come on, really, who's out there?"

The voice came back, "It's me alright. I'm God, and I'm right here. I know it's a bit unusual, Stan, but I'm here, talking to you."

"But, you can't be God," I said. "You can't."

"Why not?" The voice asked.

"Because, well –"

"Go on. Say it. It won't be the first time I've heard it."

"Well, um, it's just that –"

"What? You're surprised I'm a woman?"

"Well, yes. Okay? Everyone knows God's a man and –."

"Oh really? Everyone knows?"

"Well, all the books? The pictures? He's a man... he has a beard."

"Oh please," She said.

"Seriously... How about, 'God made man in his own image,' that kind of stuff?"

"Think about it for a second. If I were a man, and made men in my image, why would I put hair all over their faces to cover them up? And what comes out of men? Poop and violence! That's it. Women produce babies! And what about the whole foreskin thing?"

"Good point," I said. 'Christ,' I thought. 'This is turning into a goddamn conversation.'

Then She added, "And, also, don't forget the multiple orgasm. Who did I give that to?"

That one sunk it. "Holy shit, am I really talking to God?"

"Yup," She said.

"Why are you here? Talking to me? And where are you exactly? I can't -"

"I'm everywhere, don't bother looking, I rarely show myself. But you asked a good question. Rhetorical, but good."

"About the battalions? ...Why do you need battalions?"

"Yes.

"But, I was asking Leo."

"I know, but he's drunk right now, and it's not every day that somebody asks that question? Everyone just assumes that I need great, huge armies marching around, smiting the unbelievers or the infidels or whatever."

"Right. 'Smite them, hip and thigh!' I've heard that a lot," I said.

"Yeah," She said. "Always a man saying it, too. 'Smite this, smite that, smite, smite, smite...' Jeez, gets boring after a while."

"Um, you just said, Jeez."

"So?"

Cris Hammond

"Isn't that short for 'Jesus' as in, taking the Lord's name in vain?... Bad?"

"Oh, get over it. You hit your thumb with a hammer, what are you gonna say, Oh, *Apples*, that hurt!?"

"I see your point, and it brings up a few more questions I have. How much time you got?"

"Time is infinite. Mine especially. And I sense that you've got nothing pressing at the moment."

"True, I'm a touch short on funds right now, so I thought I'd just stay in and feed the cockroaches, instead of doing the town or going down to Mariano's to see Sal."

I sensed a smile in the voice when I heard, "Sal, one of my more successful creations. Lives with his mother. Takes good care of her."

"He does? Sal? He lives with his mother? Are we talking about the same guy?"

"Of course. Sal, the bartender. One of my better jobs, even if he is a man. But, do you still want to talk about my so-called battalions? I'm here," Her voice said.

"Sure, back to the battalions, so, you don't need them?"

"Think about it for a second. I made everything. I can unmake everything. Why do I need battalions, or armies for that matter? I don't really need to slaughter a bunch of people if I want to make a point. That's strictly the male influence."

"I guess you're right, but – "

Her voice suddenly dropped an octave and took on a mocking, guttural kind of tone. "So sorry, but we're slaughtering you all in His name." Then it shifted and She wasn't mocking. She was angry. "It's always the same. They're killing and murdering left and right and in the end, they stand there in the stench and ruin and whoever got the most heads, starts thanking the big, bearded

50

man in the sky, who they think is God. Well, it wasn't me, cheering them on and rejoicing in all that gore. He was there, and He was pleased, but it wasn't me."

"Who? Who was pleased?" I asked it, but as soon as I did, I knew the answer.

She went on as if she didn't hear me. "You humans always seem to remember the wrong things. You glorify all that nonsense and you take the really great stuff that I actually do for granted, like mountains, for example, and stars, and oceans…and ducks."

"Ducks?"

"Especially ducks. One of my best works. They swim, fly, walk on land, eat pond scum and stale bread. A perfect fit for their environment."

"When you put it that way, I guess you're right.

"Of course I'm right! I'm God, remember? I'm perfect and infallible."

"What about that 'quack' noise they make? Wouldn't they be better if they had some beautiful song or something?"

"I admit, the quack isn't all it could be, but it seemed right at the time. There was no one around to complain back then."

"So, ducks are perfect and infallible?" I asked.

"Exactly."

"Except the 'quack."

"Okay! Okay, the quack. Jeez. But like I said, the complaints came in later."

Now, at this point in the conversation, the idea that I might be going stark staring crazy and soon be talking to lampposts and potted plants, hadn't completely left my head. But the possibility that I might really be talking to God, or at least His Wife, was beginning to take root. If it was true, and I really had God there in my room, it could be a real opportunity. I mean, talk about your fairy godmother dropping in for a visit. Fairy godmothers are nothing compared to this, and I had a wish or two, so, I changed the subject.

"Say, God," I said. "Love the ducks, great work, but while I've got you, can I ask you something?"

"Sure."

"You know a guy named Mikey The Face Fallon? Down on 7th Street?"

"Yeah, I made him, poor guy."

"Poor guy? Are you kidding? He's one of the meanest motherfuckers on the planet."

"He's had some tough breaks."

"So have a lot of guys. But they didn't turn out like him. What possible reason could you have for making him?"

"He has his uses. You needed money, right? He was there, for you. I did that. You could give a little credit here. Think of it as Divine Intervention."

"Divine Intervention? Mikey, The Face?"

"Yeah."

"And how about the idea of 25% interest, compounded weekly? Did you put that in his head too?

"If it's there, I made it. Why? You'd prefer free money? I should make it grow on trees?"

"God, now you're sounding like my mother!"

"Made her too. Maybe you should have listened."

"Yeah, like she never reminded me of that. Look, when you made Mikey, did he come complete with his 280-pound pal, Little Harry, hovering over his shoulder?"

"If he's there, I made him. Tell the truth, sometimes I lose track." She said with what sounded almost like a little wistful pride creeping into her voice.

"You lose track? How can you lose track? You made that sadistic prick, Little Harry, but you don't quite remember it?"

"Well, every once in a while, I take a little time off. Stuff happens while I'm away, you know?"

"Now you're really freaking me out. Look, I didn't believe in you all that much before you showed up here, you know? Now, you're just starting to get me falling for it, and then you tell me that you take the occasional vacation from being God, and shit happens? Like what? Hitler?"

"Okay, my bad, alright?" She was suddenly sounding quite defensive, but she wasn't backing off either. "I took my eye off the ball and let my assistant run the show for a while. Shouldn't have done it, I know, but really, I needed some R and R after the First World War. It seemed like the perfect time to take a break. I mean, who'd 'a thought they'd come up with a Second one?"

"So, let me get this straight. While you're off relaxing, the world is going to shit. You didn't notice the Blitzkrieg?"

"I noticed. I couldn't believe it, frankly. But I thought, just maybe, another World War might finally teach them a lesson."

"And how'd that work out?"

"Don't get me started."

"So," I asked, "are you saying everything you do isn't always exactly perfect and infallible after all?"

"They start out that way, it's just that every once in a while, they can go a little haywire."

"And why can't you just wave a magic wand and undo them?"

"Oh, I can, if I want to, but I don't very often. Sometimes it's kind of interesting to see where it'll all end up... Adds a little spice."

"A little spice? World War II?"

"Look, you have no idea how many millions of things I deal with every day. Just while we've been talking there's been an absolute flood of stuff, mostly crap. Like this, just now. Listen to this." Her voice changed to a hysterical teenager. "Oh-my-God! Oh-My-God, please make this zit go away before tonight! - See? Am I supposed to just drop everything and go cure a zit?"

"It's a zit," I said. "How tough can that be?"

"Right. It sounds simple, but first I have to go out and find this little twit and locate the zit. And by tonight? Who knows what time zone she's in?"

"It's just a zit," I said.

"It's another one of those 'OMG' calls. I swear. I'm so sorry I created that. You know, I'm usually in control of my temper, but sometimes, the stress, it starts to get to me. You know?"

"Yeah, I know stress. Look around. I know stress."

"See? You know how I feel sometimes," she said. "Really, I should just undo things once in a while. Make it like they never happened, and solve things quietly."

"You can do that, right? Un-make things? You can un-make your creations, if you want to?"

"I'm God. I can do anything I want," She said. "I thought I made that clear."

"Okay, good, while we're on the subject, can we get back to Mikey and Little Harry? I'd consider it a huge favor, if you could maybe, please, could you un-make the two of them? Just for me?"

Short Pours

"Well, of course I could. I'm God. But why should I undo them? Hell, I didn't un-make Hitler. Why would I undo those two?"

"As a favor to me? I'd really appreciate it. Please, God?"

"Oh, don't start with the 'Please, God' stuff, please." And then she actually sighed. Yes, God sighed.

"Okay, look. Just hear me out," I said. "I'm into your perfect and infallible loan shark and his leg breaker for three weeks rent and a couple horses that didn't come home. I can't pay them and I still don't have next week's rent. So, you do the math, and you'll see the squeeze I'm sitting in here. I need some help or I'm out on the street, sleeping on cardboard, and pissing in bus shelters, not to mention landing on The Face's shit list."

"I don't know…"

"Hey look, you're God, so if you won't un-make them, how about letting me find a fat wallet, or giving me some lottery numbers, and I swear to, You, I'll be a good boy, stop drinking, get a job, and help old ladies across the street."

"You'll stop drinking?"

"Sure, no problem."

"You forget, Stan, I made you." Now She was gloating.

"Alright, but I'll get a job, and the old lady thing too," I said. I was rapidly coming to the conclusion that this was a lot of blab and it wasn't getting me anywhere. I didn't have a lot on my plate right then, but I still didn't appreciate people wasting my time. I mean, God was an interesting conversationalist, but so are a lot of people. Mikey The Face will talk your ear off, mostly bullshit, granted, but he actually takes action once in a while, which isn't always a good thing, but it's as real as a heart attack when he does.

This God character was beginning to sound like she was just running her mouth. She claimed to have made everything, and

55

since she made it, it was all just fine and dandy and didn't need any maintenance. Well, I didn't have to look very far out the window to see that if she made a lot of the shit I was looking at, she should be ashamed of herself.

Leo, next door, for example, he didn't start out being a juice freak. He was probably just some cute kid, like anybody else. Bad breaks, criminal friends, broken heart, broken wallet, and bingo, he's a drunk. She might'a stepped in somewhere along the way. Might'a helped out. Little Leo, the kid, didn't deserve to end up the shaking wreck that was passed out in room 3B of the Hotel Royale in East Oakland.

"You know, I hear your thoughts, Stan. For your information, I gave Leo freedom of choice. He didn't have to make some of those bad choices that set him on his path." Then She added, "It's called Free Will, and I'm pretty proud of it, since I created it."

That's when I lost it. "Now you're starting to piss me off. Free Will? His choices? Did he choose his parents? Did he choose a wife-beating, vicious animal drunk for an old man? He flunked out of school because he couldn't read. Did you know that? He didn't choose not to read. No, he can't read because he has double vision and he's deaf in one ear, because his old man used to hit him in the head with a book whenever he felt like it. And you want to guess what book it was?"

"And glasses? The old bastard drank the money for glasses… and for the rent. Little Leo could have used a little help. And where were you? Off fixing zits?"

"I can see you're upset, Stan. But I also gave you Freedom of Choice. You didn't have to go to a loan shark for money."

She was sounding more ignorant by the minute. "Oh sure," I said. "I could have gone to any bank, with a Smith and Wesson and a ski mask." Then I cut to the chase. "Look, God, why are you here anyway?"

"You asked a question, an interesting one. You weren't just another 'Oh My God' gimme this, gimme that. You weren't asking for anything… at least not at first. But now you want me to un-make a couple of guys for you."

"It's not just for me." I said. "Think about it. You'd be doing a huge favor for a whole lot of folks who are down on their luck right now." She didn't reply. I thought I might be getting to her, so I went on. "One little un-making job, and there'd be so many happy, smiling faces all over West 7th Street in the morning. It'd be like Christmas, in July."

"Don't you think you're laying it on a little thick? Happy smiling faces? Christmas on West 7th Street?"

"Okay, I admit, I went a little overboard. But think about it God, those guys are vile, vicious, stinking scum. You made them. Not your best work. Take a little responsibility for Christ sake. You could do something here. Getting rid of them would make the world a better place. Just think about it, will you?"

She was quiet for longer than usual. I was beginning to think I might have run her off, asking for a favor like that. But then she came back. Her voice seemed different when she said, "Let's go down and see them."

I'm not going to go into how useless God is at pushing a car. Let's just leave it at, she's full of advice, but doesn't want to get her hands dirty. So, we're running stop signs and nursing the dying clutch, past the crack dealers and low riders, heading down to Toni's Collision and Glass Repair shop on West 7th, where Mikey keeps his office.

God was quiet for most of the trip, and I was beginning to worry that she had dumped me and gone on another vacation. The closer we got, the more nervous I was getting. I didn't want to be going face to face with Little Harry with only my mouth, and no backup, so I called her. "Hey, you still there? Talk to me."

The silence lasted a few minutes more. Then she came back. "I don't like it here. He's close."

"I know. His shop is down on West 7th. It's about three blocks away," I said.

Then Her voice became more brittle, more like a rasp on wood. She said, "Stan, do you know what's happening here?"

"Yeah, we're going down and get Mikey off my back. I'm gonna introduce you to him. He's gonna think I'm crazy at first. But, then you pipe up and start talking to him. Convince him you're really God, and tell him to cancel out my debt, or you'll un-make him. Basically, scare the shit out of him."

"No, Stan. That's not it. We're getting too close."

She was silent for a while and I thought she might have left me again. Then the voice came back, but it was even worse, still brittle, but dark and deep, as if it was distorted, and echoing from a distance. It wasn't the same voice. "Stan, how do you suggest I get rid of them?"

"Any way you want. Use your imagination."

You don't park on the street at night down on 7th. If you do, it's best you just lie down under the seat until daylight and hope nobody breaks in. But Tony's Collision and Glass Repair did most of its business in the wee hours, so I rolled the Pinto right into the brightly lit shop and let her die there.

There wasn't any collision repair going on, but a few guys were drinking beer and leaning on the hood of an old Pontiac, playing cards. They all looked up as the Pinto coughed into silence. Then the dealer, the big one with the Marine Corps haircut and the prison tats creeping up his neck, threw down his cards and straightened up. Little Harry spit on the ground, and walked over. I had just lifted the handle when he jerked the door open and spilled me out onto the shop floor. So much for dignity.

"Well, if it ain't Stan," he said, looking down at me. "It's so nice of you to drop in." Then he bent down close and said, "I'm guessing you're here to pay up?"

"I'm here to have a talk with Mikey," I said. "Not you." I was doing my best to sound like I wasn't on my knees, struggling to lift myself to my feet while crammed between the Pinto and Harry's boulder-sized calves.

Harry shook his head and said, "Stan, oh Stan." He sounded disappointed. "Mikey is kinda busy right now, he's getting a haircut."

"Mikey doesn't have any hair."

"Yeah, well she ain't no barber either. You talk to me."

"I'm here to talk to the boss, Harry, not the help." Harry never did like being called "the help." It didn't improve his mood.

"You got the money, you give it to me. We're done. You get to walk," he said. "You don't got the money, I take you out back and tie your ass to the car hoist, rack you up and break a knee, or two. We don't need to disturb Mikey."

"I want to see Mikey. I brought a friend."

His hand shot out and grabbed a fistful of shirt and chest hair. "I heard about your little friend. Big piece of steel pipe you keep in the Pinto, right?" He jammed his face so close to mine I could smell the mold between his teeth. "Just so you know, I got a friend too." He pulled open his jacket, flashed the gun in his belt, and said, "Mr. Beretta."

Then he turned to the three guys who were sitting fumbling with their cards and stacking their chips, pretending that nothing was happening. "You guys, get lost. Beat it!" And like roaches hearing a light switch, they vanished.

Frankly, I was beginning to wonder if I really did have a friend with me. If she'd split, I was talking myself into one hell of a shit storm. I softened my pitch a touch. "Look, Harry. I don't want any trouble with you, okay?" He was twisting my shirt front and cutting off my air. "My friend wants to talk to Mikey, just talk is all."

Harry's hand went to the Beretta and was closing on it, when the door to the office opened and a tall, expensive, Hispanic woman emerged. She was gazing into a small hand mirror and touching up her lipstick, rolling her lips around to get an even spread. When it was just right, she tossed her thick black hair and shifted the mirror up to check her eyes. She batted her eyelashes and I swear I felt the breeze.

Harry put me down and turned to stare at her. She was definitely high rent, and Mikey was paying retail. She had on a sheer, see-through blouse, high heel shoes, and bare legs that disappeared into a skirt that was a lot tighter than it was long. She strode past us without even turning her head.

That's when I should have made my move, but I was as distracted as Harry.

Within seconds, I was choking again. Then Mikey stepped into the open doorway. He was tying a bathrobe around himself. "What's going on out here? Can't a guy get a-," then he saw me dangling from Harry's fist. "- a haircut, in peace around here?"

"Mikey, call him off. We gotta talk," I croaked.

"Stan? Is that you?" He took a few steps into the shop and squinted his eye at me. He only had one eye. The story on the street was that his mother was a meth freak. She was cooking up a batch in their kitchen one night when little Mikey, who was about nine at the time, ran through, chasing a cat. He ran into her, just as she was pouring a hot batch through the strainer. She dumped the whole bucket on the kid and boiled half his face away, including one eye. Guys called him "The Face" after that, but never actually to his face. He grew up mean, and stayed that way.

"Mikey, yeah, it's me," I coughed. "We gotta talk. Make him put me down."

"You got the money you owe me?" he asked, the words slurring through his grotesquely deformed mouth.

"No, but I got a friend, wants to talk to you." At that point, I was only hoping I had a friend with me. Maybe the whole thing was something I'd cooked up in my dreams. But this shit going down was definitely real, and it was bad. My only hope was to get Mikey alone. I could handle Mikey, but not the two of them.

"Does your friend have my money?" Mikey slurred.

"Sure, plenty of money," I said. "Just not here."

"Yeah? Where, Stan? Where is this friend? I don't see any friend." He turned to Harry, "Harry? You see his friend? Maybe he's invisible."

Harry said, "He ain't got no friends. He's full of shit."

Mikey's eye landed on me again. "Looky here Stan. You got the money, give it here. You don't, you're wasting my time." He held out a hand about as clean as a drip pan, and all I could do was look at it. Then he turned to Harry, "He's wasting my time. Break something. Make an impression. But don't kill him. I want my money." Then he cinched up his bathrobe and turned to leave.

Harry's fist was cutting off my wind again as he started dragging me toward the tool bench at the back of the shop. I did not want to go there. Harry was known to have a way with tools.

"Mikey! Wait!" I choked. "I brought a friend, She can fix your face!" I was panicking. My only hope now was for some serious help from God, but there was nothing from Her. I was alone.

Then, suddenly, Harry's grip loosens. He set me on my feet, but he still held me in a pair of hands the size of frying pans. I thought to myself, "She's here. He put me down. She didn't leave me. She's here." But when I turned around, it wasn't God who had stepped in. It was Mikey.

Mikey's tongue was moving in and out of his mouth, bubbles sliding down his twisted chin. His rotten breath came over me in stinking waves. He said, "My face? Is there something wrong with my face, Stan?" Then Harry's fingers crushed into me and Mikey leaned close, stuck out his putrid tongue and slowly licked my face, from my jaw up into my hair. I wanted to puke.

"You shouldn't have said that about my face, Stan. Nobody talks about my face." Then he turned to Harry, "Take him over to the work bench, and soften him up. I'll bring the doors down."

The next second, my right arm was twisted up behind my back, tearing my shoulder at the socket and bending me over the workbench. Struggling was useless. I tried to twist and kick. I dug my feet in and flailed with my one loose arm, but Harry had me by a hundred pounds and twenty years. I was wrapped up. His knee was grinding into my back, pressing me down. My face was being mashed onto a broken, steel vice, clamped to the edge of the metal table. I smelled black, rancid grease, and something else. An electrical fire, it's pungent fumes filled my head and sparks flashed across my eyes.

Time slowed. Sounds receded into the distance and pain took over my senses. I looked up at the wall behind the table, where Harry hung his tools. I was surprised at how clean and orderly it was. Each tool had its own place. Little silhouettes, in white paint, indicated where every tool would hang. The channel-locks, were hanging neatly in their place, in front of the picture of channel-locks. So were a whole set of screwdrivers, socket wrenches, and what looked like a wheel-puller. All of them had a place, and all of them were in their place, except for the crescent wrench. It wasn't in its place.

Then Little Harry grabbed my hair, jerked me around and twisted my head to grind my ear against the vice. It was almost as if he wanted me to see what was lying there, on the bench, just a few inches from my free hand. Eighteen inches of case hardened, polished steel, at least eight pounds, with a serrated, non-slip handle, the missing crescent wrench.

I don't know how it got into my hand, but it was there. I swung it. I felt the crunch of bones, and Harry's arm slid from my neck. I was free.

Spinning around, I saw he was on his knees, his hands covering his face and blood flowing through his fingers into a pool on the floor. He choked and spit. Bile hung in strings from his mouth. I watched from somewhere else, as my arm came up and then the wrench slammed down behind his ear. It swung again, but he had slumped down to his side and it missed.

I could feel it now, my feet planted and the warm wrench, nestled in my hand. I was hitting him again. I hit him for Leo's pain, and Maurice. I hit him for my mother, who dumped me, crying, in a liquor store parking lot when I was ten, and for Sidewalk Alice who lives without her teeth, in a box on Oak Street, and for so many others. I don't know how many times I struck. Bone splinters flew and mixed with blood and snot and tears, flowing down my face. Gasping for breath, I was crying and sobbing, watching through a red haze as I buried that wrench in his brain. Then, just as it came, the rage was gone. I left the wrench buried there, and stepped back.

I looked at what I had done. Blood was everywhere. Blood, brains, and hair covered my fist and arm. It soaked my shirt. My face was dripping. The floor was awash in it. Harry's head was all but gone and he lay in his own waste. It was then that I heard the voice again. It was far away, and it was laughing.

"Oh Shit!" I cried. "Shit, fuck, shit! I killed him! Why did you let me? "Where'd you go? It wasn't supposed to be like this. Oh God. Where are you?"

A dark, bitter voice rumbled, "She's gone. But she'll be back. I'm done here."

I turned and saw Mikey walking toward me. "Shit! Mikey! I killed him. I'm sorry. I don't know what happened. I couldn't stop! Shit! Shit, I'm sorry."

Mikey looked puzzled. "What are you talking about, Stan? Who'd you kill?"

"Harry! Little Harry, goddamn it! I killed him. What am I gonna do?"

"Who's this Harry you say you killed?" Mikey turned, so his eye bored into me. It held no expression, but then, it never did. I expected anger, horror, revenge, anything but this indifference. I'd just beaten a man's head into mush. I'd killed Little Harry, right in front of him, and he was acting like nothing happened.

"Him!! I killed him, Harry." I turned and pointed at the corpse lying on the ground at my feet.

But, there was no corpse.

There was no blood splattered on the walls or pooling along the floor. My hands were clean, my shirt, freshly pressed.

I looked at the workbench. Everything was neat and tidy. The crescent wrench was polished bright and hanging in its place in front of its little white outline on the wall. Mikey tapped me on the shoulder and said, "Stan, you wanna sit down or something? You don't look too good."

I was starting to hyperventilate. Stars sparkled at the edges of my sight. I just wanted to get out of there. I said, "I'm okay, Mikey. Thanks. Can I go? I'll get you your money somehow. I'll pay you. I swear."

"Aw, forget it Stan. It was nothing."

"Forget it? You're saying forget it?"

"Yeah, it was nothing. You don't owe me nothing."

"I don't?"

"Naw, ten minutes, that's all it took. Your battery wasn't dead. It was just the terminals were all corroded. So, I wire brushed them and dipped the contacts in acid to clean 'em up. Tightened up the ground cable. She starts fine now. Took ten minutes, is all. Forget it."

I was starting to shake, so he took my arm and walked me to the Pinto and lowered me in. I turned the key. It started. First try. It was like a miracle. I put the car into reverse and started backing her out. When I was on the street, I looked back and saw Mikey. He was standing in the middle of the shop. He was alone there, but I could see that he was talking to someone. Maybe it was the wall.

Cris Hammond

Elmer's Revenge

When I saw it, I knew one of us was crazy. I hoped like hell it wasn't me. But, there it was, hidden under the bed. I was looking at it. It was real, and it had no business being there. It'd been a few days since I had visited him. But this thing wasn't new. It had been there a while.

Elmer was eighty-one years old. He had been a merchant seaman and a short haul trucker in his prime. He was way past that now. Age was hitting him hard. He was mostly deaf and losing his eyesight. His knees were gone from years of hard work, and his hips were no better. But his mind was mostly still there, and his sense of humor was intact. So was his fierce sense of independence. He'd rather stay inside and rot, than go out and be seen using a cane or a walker. And he wouldn't give up driving. I had to take his keys away after he missed a red light and ran his old Chevy into a beer truck. Didn't stop him, though. The next day he hot-wired his car and drove it to Safeway, then forgot where he'd parked it. I finally had to take the distributor cap and coil wire.

I'd known Elmer for over forty years. I met him when I was working day jobs out of the Teamster's hiring hall in San Leandro. Union rules said that any truck that needed loading or unloading had to have a union helper come out to work with the driver to handle the cargo. Drivers had to call the hall and ask for a lumper to be sent out whenever they had to move a load. That's how I met him. We unloaded forty thousand pounds of Coca-Cola one day on Pier 6, in Oakland. It was hot, ugly work. We tossed eighty pound crates of Coke for seven hours, and laughed most of the time. We were friends after that day. From then on, whenever he called the hiring hall, he asked for me. You could say Elmer looked out for me.

Now, life had come full circle. It was time for me to start looking out for him. He didn't have any living family. His wife had died and most of his old friends were gone or in homes. I would drop by his run down little studio apartment in the East Bay at least once a week. I'd take him out for groceries, and to the doctor when he needed it. We'd always go out for hot dogs and milk shakes at Olivia's Café, then finish up with a small tot of whiskey back at this place. He was keeping his spirits up, but I was beginning to worry about him, living alone.

Not that he was alone all that much. He had girlfriends. Walnut Creek Manor was an apartment complex that had a lot of elderly tenants. Most of Elmer's neighbors were single women, widows. Elmer, being Elmer, saw opportunity. First thing he did was join The Ladies That Hike. Three times a week, a small crowd of the ladies of the Manor would gather for a hike through the fields next to the complex. Within a couple of weeks, they were calling him "Scout" and he was leading them along trails, through creeks and out to the horse pasture, where they'd feed sugar and carrots to Blackie, the old swaybacked mare that had retired there.

This wasn't destined to be a long-term gig though. His bad hips and knees couldn't take it, so after a couple years he had to give it up. Also, about six months ago, a big construction project had begun tearing up the fields. They'd put a chain link fence around the whole thing so the morning hikers had to do most of their hiking on sidewalks. Blackie was still in her pasture though, so every couple of weeks, The Ladies That Hike still made their way out there. Only now, in addition to sugar and carrots, they carried scones or cookies and dropped them off for Scout at his apartment.

Being fed cookies while sitting around laid up with bum knees wasn't Elmer's style. He liked the attention, but he didn't want it for being crippled. He was still good with his hands, so he printed up some business cards that proclaimed him to be "The Happy Handyman." The ladies loved it. They would ask him to come over to oil a squeaky cabinet hinge or fix a broken toaster.

Sometimes he'd do a little watering and weeding in the tiny patch of garden at the front of each apartment. He'd always end up with an invitation to stay for lunch. There was inevitably a fresh roast or extra pork chop on the stove when he came by. He rarely refused. He'd charge them six bucks an hour whether he was pulling weeds or enjoying lasagna, but they never complained and he was always booked up. He'd often come out his front door and step in a warm casserole or on a tray of fresh baked banana bread that had been left on the step, with a nice note saying something like, "Dear Scout, we were baking today and thought of you. Hope you enjoy, Marion… or Agnes, or Dorothy."

I could hear the guy talking before I could see him. He sounded angry and threatening. As I came around the corner from the parking lot, I saw a tall, broad man, with a gut, short grey hair and wearing a blue sport coat over a pink shirt. He was standing on Elmer's front step.

"If you don't shape up, you're outta here!" he said. "I don't have to put up with this crap from you. Shape up!"

"What's going on?" I stepped in front of him. "Who are you?"

"I'm Settleman. I'm his landlord. Who are you?"

"I'm Stan, his friend."

"Well, Stan, if you're his friend, tell him to shape up or he's out on his ass."

"I already heard the shape up part. I asked you what he did."

"He flooded the place, again!" he said. "He left the water on in the kitchen all night and it overflowed the sink. It ruined the carpet."

"You mean the thirty-year-old carpet that you could see through?" This guy was beginning to irritate me. "That carpet?"

"You saying my building isn't – look, if he doesn't like this place, he can clear out."

"He's staying," I said and folded my arms across my chest.

"We'll see about that. I'm remodeling around here and building a whole new complex next door. Might just have to get rid of a few people. We'll see."

"Thanks for the update. Now, his rent is paid, so if there's nothing more, he'd like to enjoy his apartment in peace. Good bye." I walked past him, took Elmer inside and closed the door.

I turned to Elmer. "Did you flood the kit – What happened to your face?" Elmer had a split and swollen lip. "Did he do that?"

"What?" He didn't have his hearing aid in.

I pointed at his face and said, louder, "That. Did that guy do that to you?"

"No."

"What happened then?" Now I noticed a bump on his forehead.

"I fell."

"Oh shit, Elmer. When? You okay?"

"Beg your pardon?"

I raised my voice again. "Where's your hearing aid?"

"What? Oh, I took it out when I saw Settleman coming. I don't need to hear anything he has to say."

"Well, put it back in. He's gone." This resulted in a thorough search of the whole apartment until we finally found it in the butter dish on the sink.

"Okay, now, when did you fall down?"

"Couple days ago. My hip gave out and I came down on the coffee table. I guess I knocked myself out. Then I got stuck."

That's when I took a fresh look around Elmer's apartment. It's a studio, as I mentioned. Everything is in one room with an alcove kitchen, and a bathroom at the back. A quick glance around confirmed that Elmer had run out of drawer, closet, cupboard, nook, shelf and counter space in the early spring of 2001. Since then things have piled up.

The only place that's really safe to sit is his old overstuffed rocker in front of the television. When I come over, I try to clear a space on the couch, which is easier said than done. The coffee table in front of the couch doubles as his workshop table. It's nearly collapsing under the weight of boxes filled with plumbing gear, engine parts and a constantly changing assortment of dismantled tools and equipment from his handyman business. He likes to keep his hedge trimmer handy, poking out from under the couch. He also was afraid of getting his lawn mower stolen, so he brought it in every night and parked it next to his chair.

It's not that he's a hoarder. He just has lots of interests and no place left to keep things. There's a combination toaster/coffee maker, spread out in parts on his kitchen table for repair, an exercise bike by the bathroom and an eight-foot ladder hanging from the ceiling. He also likes to read. His collection of Reader's Digest, Large Print Editions, is extensive. Even the ladies of Walnut Creek Manor have had no luck in bringing order to Elmer's private sanctuary.

He was still talking, "I couldn't get up. I was stuck between the couch and the table."

"For how long?"

"Couple days. I got out this morning." Then he added, sheepishly, "Kinda made a mess on the floor."

"Jesus Elmer. That's not good."

"I cleaned it up. I'm fine."

"Yeah, this time. You were lucky this time my friend. What if you fall again and break something? What if you're really out of it? This is serious."

"If you're gonna start talking about putting me in a home, I'm taking my hearing aid out and flushing it down the toilet!"

"But maybe-"

"I ain't going in no damn old folk's home. Nope!"

"Okay. No damn home. But -"

"No 'buts.' I'm not going into no home."

"Wait a minute. I got an idea," I said. He put his fists on his hips and shot me a suspicious look. "I saw this thing on TV the other night. It's kind of a security alert thing. Vital-matic, or something."

"What are you talking about?"

"It's a thing. You wear it around your neck, like a Saint Christopher medal. If you fall and can't get up, you push a button on it and it calls for help. Secure-Alert. Something like that."

"I wear it?"

"Yeah. Around your neck."

"You think I'm gonna wear a necklace around in my own house? Damnit, I might as well be in a home if some electronic gizmo is tracking me all around. I don't like it."

"Elmer, what if you fall down again?"

"I ain't gonna fall down."

"What if you do and you're laying there for a couple days again? What if Dorothy or Marge comes in here and finds you lying in your own poo? Wouldn't you rather just push a button and have someone show up and help you out?"

"Jeez, you got a gruesome way with words."

"It's a gift. Can I call them?"

Two days later we were waiting for the Secure-Alert salesman. We had an appointment set for 5:30 in the afternoon at Elmer's apartment. We heard him before we saw him. A squeaking, sort of squealing, dragging sound was coming toward us from the direction of the parking lot at Walnut Creek Manor. When I looked out the front window, I saw, coming around the fence, a short, rotund, bald guy, wearing thick glasses and heading for Elmer's front door. As he got closer, I could see that he was struggling with a battered, black, sample box, about the size of a small suitcase. Most of the corners had been knocked off and the thin vinyl surface was peeling back, exposing its cardboard inner walls. He was dragging it along by an extended handle, like a piece of luggage, but one of the wheels had fallen off and the other one had picked up a rock and wouldn't roll.

The man from Secure-Alert looked at the number on the fence, stepped up and presented himself at the front door. "Hello there. My name's Billy. Billy Jeffery." He stuck out his hand to shake. "You can call me Billy. From Secure-Alert? Am I speaking to Elmer?"

"No, I'm Stan. Elmer's inside. Come on in."

I don't know what I had expected really, maybe someone in a white lab coat, or a shirt with a tie, even one of those polyester short sleeve shirts from Walmart, and a clip-on; I would have felt, well, secure. But that, apparently, was not Billy's style, if style is a word that applies here. "Sloppy" comes to mind.

"Elmer! Put your hearing aide in. The Secure-Alert guy's here." I called.

"Please, call me Billy," Billy said, again. He had on a blue and grey striped polyester shirt under a yellow cardigan that he'd buttoned up wrong. His brown slacks had been ironed, about a year ago, and his loafers were scuffed and worn where his big toe pressed up from the inside. His glasses were smeared with fingerprints.

"Okay. Elmer! Billy's here."

"Who?" He was coming forward, fiddling with the on/off switch on his hearing aide.

"The Secure-Alert guy. He want's to be called Billy."

"Jeez." He looked Billy up and down, raised his eyebrows at me, stuck out his hand and said, "Aren't you a little old to be called Billy?"

Billy's mouth opened, but he closed it again. Then he coughed and said, "Well, shall we begin?" Then he started tugging his sample case into the apartment. "Where would you like to-?" He stopped and looked around. His face literally fell. He got a sort of pleading look and said, "We usually like to have the Senior sitting somewhere where I can, well, lay out the whole Secure-Alert system so they can see it in its – um." His face literally fell.

"He likes to sit in his rocker mainly. Will that do?" I said.

"Am I the Senior in this?" Elmer's hearing aid was apparently working.

"You're the customer," I said.

"Perhaps we could clear a space on the coffee table and you two could just sit on the couch there?" Billy said.

"How big a space do you need?" I asked.

"Not much, maybe we could move that thing. What is that?"

"A cylinder head, from a lawn mower." I dragged it onto the floor, leaving a thin trail of oil and grease across the table. "There. How's that?"

"That'll be fine. I'll just-" He moved an empty fish bowl to the side of the table. "There. That's better. Thank you. Um, if you two just want to get comfortable while I get my things."

Elmer and I cleared a space and sank into the couch.

The first hurdle he faced was opening his case. The latch holding the top flap seemed to have jammed. After a few jabs at it, and a firm twist, Billy simply grabbed the edge of it and, with a growl, ripped the flap completely off. "God dammit," he said under his breath. Then he went into his spiel.

"With the new Secure-Alert, Senior Security System, from Secure-Alert, you will know a total sense of security, knowing your loved one is constantly being watched over." Just as he got to the part about their guaranteed rapid response times, he looked down and noticed this finger was dripping blood. "Oh shit," he said again.

"Do you need a Band-Aid?" I asked.

"No, I'm fine," he said and jammed his injured finger into his mouth.

"Whiskey! He needs a shot, for the pain." Elmer got up and grabbed a bottle of bourbon off the kitchen counter. He had poured a shot before either of us could object. Then he drank it in one go, grabbed a couple more glasses and said, "Stan, you'll have one too I assume."

The glasses went around as Billy, still sucking on his finger, dug out a slightly battered cardboard box about the size of a shoebox. Inside was our whole Secure-Alert system. A small, faux-wood, plastic box with speaker holes drilled along the top, a couple knobs and lights at the front, two phone jacks and a USB port on the side was the heart of the system. There was a power cord, a long phone cord and a small, plastic, antennae that screwed on at the side. A separate little box held the Secure-Alert Fob, with a lightweight neck chain attached.

With this display finally laid out among the lawnmower parts and oil, Billy pulled out a sheaf of well-worn papers and brochures and looked around for a place to sit. It was obvious that he was out of his depth in Elmer's world, so I got up, cleared a pile of laundry off of a kitchen chair and brought it over.

He pulled his finger from his mouth and said, "Thank you, Stan. Now, let's see how this whole thing works, shall we?"

"Does anyone else want another little nip?" Elmer asked. "I'm just gonna have one more little one while Billy's getting set up."

"Don't you get up, Elmer," I said. "I'll get it. Billy, do you want another one? For the pain?" Billy took his finger out of his mouth, looked at Elmer who was smacking his lips and beaming, sighed and nodded. I came back from the kitchen and poured another round.

Glasses drained, and the blood no longer flowing, Billy started in with the first part of the demonstration, the Audio Alarm Test. Dangling the fob from its chain, he said, "This is the Secure-Alert Fob. The Senior wears it around his, or her, neck at all times." Then he handed it to me so that I could feel the heft of the thing. "If there is a fall, or some other emergency, the Senior simply pushes the button in the center of the fob and an audible alarm is emitted."

"Very nice," I said, and handed it to Elmer who looked at it suspiciously.

"In addition to the audible alarm, that fob also connects wirelessly to the Secure-Alert control box, which will instantly send a message to our Secure Alert Specialists, letting them know there's a problem."

Billy donned a proud smile and said, "So, Elmer, if you would like to just push that button on the fob, you'll hear for yourself the audio alarm. But be ready. It's pretty loud." He sat back and nodded, "Go ahead."

We all braced ourselves and Elmer pushed the button. The silence was deafening. "Did you push it?" Billy asked.

"Yeah, I pushed it. I know I'm a little deaf, but, it didn't do anything."

"Are you sure you pushed it?" Billy was getting concerned. "Push it again."

"I pushed it. Nothing happened," Elmer said.

"What's it supposed to do?" I asked.

"It's supposed to go Akk-Akk-Akk." Billy said. Then he turned to Elmer. "Push it again."

"I pushed it again. It didn't go Akk-Akk. It doesn't work."

Billy reached for it. "Give me that thing." He took it off Elmer and held it up in front of his finger-smeared glasses. "It's supposed to go Akk-Akk-Akk, for thirty seconds." Then he shook it and tapped it with his finger. "Maybe the battery's dead. It takes those little things, like in your hearing aide. I have some in the car. I'll go get one." Then he grabbed the fob and ran out the door.

Elmer looked at me and said, "What do you want to bet he gets lost and we never see him again?"

A few moments later, from the parking lot I heard a very distinct, "Akk-Akk-Akk." Moments after that, Billy was back. He was beaming. "Okay, now, it works. Just changed the battery." He pushed the button and we were all treated to thirty seconds of Akk-Akk-Akk-ing.

"Isn't that neat?" he said.

"Sure is," I said. "It's loud."

"When it works," Elmer said.

"So, when this goes off, it shoots a signal directly into the control box, which automatically phones our control center and alerts them. Let's set it up and I'll show you." He started unbundling the power cable and the phone line from his case. "I'll need a plug, and a phone jack."

While Billy went looking for a plug, I followed the phone line from the back of the answering machine into the kitchen, around the corner and down behind the dresser. From there it disappeared under a pile of old suitcases, two folding lawn chairs and a stack of ancient National Geographic's, then it disappeared under the bed. I dragged the bed away from the wall and looked. I instantly shoved it back again.

"Did you find it?" Billy asked.

"I'm not sure," I said. "Did you say you have more batteries in your car?"

"Yeah, why?"

"I think Elmer's hearing aid is dying. I just heard it beeping." I turned to Elmer. "Hey, Elmer, did you hear that beep?"

"What beep?"

"See? Billy, would you mind going and getting another battery? It might work in his hearing aide. He's deaf and hopeless without it. I don't want him to miss the rest of your demo." Elmer was starting to say something, but I reached behind him and pinched his arm.

"Okay, sure," Billy said. "I'll go get what I have. No guarantee it will fit, but might as well try." He turned and left.

Elmer looked at me. "What the hell was that all about?"

As I jerked the bed out again, I said, "Elmer, tell me fast, 'cause he's coming back, what the hell's that thing doing under your bed?"

"What thing?"

I reached behind the bed, put a couple fingers through an eye socket and pulled out a human skull. "What's this doing there?"

"Oh, that's where it is. I thought I'd lost it."

"Elmer! It's a goddamn human skull. Why is it hidden under your bed? Where did it come from?"

"It's not hidden. It's just… misplaced."

"Whose skull is it Elmer?"

"It's Lily's."

"What? Your wife's? This is her skull? Why do you have her skull?"

"She died, I wanted to keep it. Reminds me of her."

The door burst open and Billy rushed in yelling, "My car's gone! It's gone!" Then he stopped. "What's that?" He said, pointing at the skull dangling from my finger.

"It's probably towed," Elmer said.

"No. What? Towed?" Billy cried. Then he turned back to me, "Why do you have a skull? Is it real? Is that what was under the bed?"

"Where did you park it?" Elmer asked him.

"Just in front. Across from the dumpsters."

"Yup. Towed."

"Why is it towed? There's no sign. This sucks!"

"It's Settleman," Elmer said. "He loves to have cars towed, the bastard. The tow truck driver gives him a kickback."

"What'll I do? It's got all my stuff in it. My boss is gonna have a shit fit."

"You can get it back, later tonight. But it'll cost you." Elmer said.

"Yeah, it'll cost me, like, my job. My boss is a – He won't pay for it." Billy cried plaintively. "God, I hate this job. I hate the damn Secure-Alert B.S. doesn't work anyway. It's a load of crap! He can fire me and who cares?"

"Whoa, so that means you aren't going to put the big 'final close' on us?" Elmer said.

Billy stopped his rant. "Hey, your hearing aids working again."

"Oh, yeah. I banged it on the table a couple times. It's happened before."

"I gotta get my car. Shit! Isn't there a number I should call?"

"You can call it, but he won't answer until about seven or eight o'clock, when he gets back to the warehouse. Then, I think it's a couple hundred bucks to get it back."

"Shit! Shit-shit-shit! I don't have two hundred bucks. How'm I gonna get home? Shit!" Billy sat down on the wobbly kitchen chair and looked around. Then he turned to me. "What are you guys doing with a skull?"

"It's Elmer's," I said. "Well, actually, it's his wife's."

"What? What'd he do, chop her head off?" Then he turned to Elmer. "Keeping her skull is a little strange, I'm just sayin'. I mean, lots of our Seniors have keepsakes, but somebody hiding his wife's head-"

"I didn't hide it! I just lost track of it for a while." Elmer shouted. "Christ, I need a drink." He looked at me. "Stan, will you just put a little color in that glass for me?"

"All around?" I handed Lily's skull to Elmer as I went into the kitchen. "Billy?"

Billy picked up his glass and handed it to me. "Sure. Why not? My life's going to hell anyway. Might as well get shitfaced." Then he turned to Elmer, "I don't think people are supposed to have their dead wives' skulls under their beds is all. People could get the wrong idea."

"Like what?" Elmer took his first sip.

"Well, like the rest of her is buried in the garden maybe?"

"Have you seen my garden? Christ, I couldn't bury a canary in there."

"Maybe if it was in little pieces you could."

I thought it was time to jump in. "Hold on now. Let's not get carried away. I'm sure there's a perfect explanation for why Elmer has his wife's head."

"It's not her head, idiot." Elmer drained his glass, then held it out to me. "It's her skull. Her head is with the rest of her." He turned to Billy. "And not in the garden either, smart ass."

"Where then?" Billy asked.

"In an urn at the crematorium columbarium, in Oakland."

"All of her?"

"All of her."

"Then how'd you get her skull out of her head so you've still got her skull and not her skin and brains and stuff?"

"Well, you boil it of course. Takes hours." Elmer turned to me. "Stan, one more sip, please. This fool is getting tiresome."

"Now, I'm calling the cops!" Billy exclaimed, and started pawing around his pockets for his phone.

"Okay, relax," Elmer shot back. "It's not her head, okay? It's her skull. She's had it since she was a kid and she kept it on a shelf all her life. Her uncle gave it to her when she was a girl." He folded his arms. "God, look at you two. You look like a couple of scared old women."

I put the bottle down. "Why didn't you say so? Wait, can you prove that?"

81

"No. I never had to. It's just been her skull. What's the big deal?"

"Elmer, having someone's skull under your bed is something that some people might find alarming. Do you have any idea the shit storm you'd be facing if the Settelman came in here and found it?"

"What? Why?"

"Christ, he'd have every cop in town looking up missing persons cases and opening unsolved murders. They'd be on your ass like stripes on a skunk."

"Whoa, whoa. Calm down, man. It's an Indian."

"What does that mean?" I asked.

"It's an Indian. Like a Navajo or an Apache or something."

"Um," Billy sat up and put his glass down. "I think you meant to say, Native American."

Elmer shifted on the couch and looked at Billy, "Ya know, if I was fifty years younger, I'd take you outside and beat your ass. Drink your drink, Billy, and listen for a second." Then he turned back to me. "My Lily's uncle found it on his ranch and gave it to her when she was a kid. He also gave her a bunch of arrowheads and stuff that he'd found. They're in that little sack over there. She kept it all her life. She died. I kept the head. Now you two just keep your pants on."

"So, it's an Indian skull?" I asked again.

"Yeah. Once we took it up to Cal, at Davis, to see if they could tell us anything about it. Big mistake."

"Why?"

"When the Indians found out about it, they went berserk." Elmer turned to Billy. "Excuse me, the Native Americans went berserk.

"Like how?" I asked.

"Like they had to know where it came from. Where did we get it? Was it buried? Who dug it up? Were there other bones? Did we disturb an old Indian burial site? They were itching to find out where it came from so they could go out there and turn the place into a huge archeological, Indian burial ground, holy site, shit storm disaster. Her uncle's ranch would be theirs forever. So, we grabbed the head and skedaddled. Believe me, you don't want those people after you. They can take over your land and tie it up for years."

We all jumped when a sudden pounding shook the front door. "Who the hell's that now?" Elmer said, and started to get up.

"Stay put. I'll get it." I stood up and looked out the window. "Oh shit. It's Settleman. Hide the head." Elmer tossed it to Billy who juggled it for a second, then dropped it and rolled it under the bed.

Settleman was still banging on the door when I opened it. "Oh, it's you," he said. "Where's Elmer? I got something for him." He waved an envelope in my face.

"What is it?" I said.

"Just get him. I'm gonna give it directly to him." He folded his arms across his belly.

Elmer was on his feet and he stepped to the door. "Give it here. What is it?"

"It's your official warning. You got no more slack. You're warned, in writing. I'm upgrading around here and guys like you won't be welcome. Any more flooded kitchens or anything I don't like, and you're outta here. So, shape up!" He turned to go, but then stopped, turned back and said, "And that includes parking in the wrong spot." A nasty smirk flashed across his face, and he said, "Have a nice day." Then he walked off.

I turned and saw Billy by the couch, bouncing from toe to toe. He said, "That's the guy? That's the bastard had my car towed? What a prick." Billy had been brooding, now he was reacting. "How'd he like it if I had his car towed for no reason? What an asshole. And he's trying to evict you? What's he got against you?"

"He want's me out so he can get some dot com rich guy in here and jack up the rent."

"He thinks Elmer is a low-class tenant." I said. "He wants to upgrade this place and get rid of all the old people. He's building that whole new complex next door and wants to fill it with Facebook and Google employees, who'll pay three times the rent."

"That big hole in the ground is his project?" Billy asked.

"Yeah," Elmer said. "The bastard bulldozed that beautiful field and when he's done, we'll all have to look at a big parking lot and three stories of stucco apartments.

I looked at Elmer. "Elmer, it's time you got rid of Lily's skull. You can't keep that thing around here anymore. If Settleman ever gets wind of it, he'd make your life a living hell, and he'd love every minute of it."

"Yeah, you're probably right, but where? I can't just drop it in a dumpster. That wouldn't be right. I oughta give it back to the Indians, but I don't want to get involved in all that crap again.

"The way I see it, we've got two things that we have to do," I said.

"What's that?" Billy asked.

"We gotta get your car back, and we gotta give Elmer's head back to the Indians."

"Wait a minute. Why do you say we gotta give back the head? That's not my business," Billy said.

"Right, it's not exactly your business, strictly speaking. You just need to get your car."

"Right."

"The car that that rat bastard Settleman had towed and will cost you two hundred bucks to get back."

"That asshole!"

"So, I just thought that, on the way to get your car, you might want to help us get rid of the head, do the right thing, and have a little fun at the same time."

I looked at Elmer. He was starting to smile. I said, "We'll need your ladder, and a flashlight."

"With pleasure," he said. Then he turned to Billy, "You coming?"

The next morning, I was at Elmer's place when The Ladies That Hike stopped by to check in and bring him some freshly baked peanut butter cookies. They were surprised to find him in his full hiking rig, including a pair of very long shorts, very old Nikes and a t-shirt that said, "John 'The Wad' Holmes" across the front. He shoved me forward, planted his walking stick and announced, "Good morning ladies. This here's my friend Stan. I been telling him about you guys. He's a great hiker and we been talking about getting out there again. So, let's go."

"Oh, Elmer, we're all so happy that you're feeling well again." Dorothy exclaimed." Then she turned to me and said, "Any friend of Scout is a friend of ours. Welcome, Stan."

Elmer shot me a smile and stepped forward with only a tiny wince and a small hitch to his giddy-up, and said, "Let's go ladies. This is going to be fun!" Then he set off toward the fields with me and The Ladies That Hike falling joyfully in behind.

We were just passing the big oak tree that marked the beginning of the old field when Scout stopped the group, pointed through the chain link fence into the construction site and said in a voice that rang clearly and strongly enough for even the most deaf of the ladies to hear, "Oh my god! What's that?" He was pointing through the fence at something white, half buried in the dirt at the edge of a large excavated ditch. "It looks like a skull!"

Beatrice got out her birding binoculars and focused them on the object. "Oh my gosh. It is. It's a skull! Somebody call 911!"

Marge was pointing at it now and exclaiming, "It was buried, and it's poking through. It must have come up when they were digging! What if it's a grave?"

I pointed at a small pile of disturbed earth, just a few feet inside the fence. "Look, arrowheads," I said. Then I looked to the left and cried, "Oh, hey! There's more. Look, and some beads too!"

"This must be a sacred Native American burial site," Elmer said. "Nobody touch anything! We need to call the authorities!"

"Yes, yes!" said Dorothy. "Who do we call?"

"That would be the Native American Burial Sites Protection Agency at the Department of Archeology and Historic Preservation," he said. "Here's their number." He handed it to Dorothy and smiled as she started dialing.

Boom-Boom's Gloves

When I was growing up I knew kids whose dads took them to ball games. Their fathers were engineers, or executives or something. They went fishing on weekends, or camping. They'd even go to the movies with their dads, or skiing. My old man drove a truck until he got the DUI. Then he loaded freight and sold used cars. He took me to repo auctions.

Down at the dirty end of West 7th Street in Oakland, dreary, corrugated iron warehouses loom over cracked, weed encrusted sidewalks, surrounded by fields of garbage, broken furniture and lean-to cardboard shacks. Every two or three weeks, I'd go with the old man down to the last warehouse on the right, next to the railroad yard.

Locked up and guarded by the pickpockets and car thieves who made up the repo team of United California Bank, the most recent harvest of repossessed cars were packed in rows at the back of the cold, dimly lit cavern, the sorry flotsam of hard times and bad luck. They sat there awaiting our inspection. We were vultures. We were there to scavenge something cheap, looking to make some money off all that misery. That's where I found Boom-boom's car. I knew he'd been down. I didn't know how far.

Tony "Boom-boom" Torres was the only guy who ever knocked me out. He didn't mean to. He just lost it one time. Truth is, it really wasn't his fault. Joey Nice Guy, my coach, told me to pepper him around the nose and eyes. It was pointless to go to his body. He wouldn't feel it. He really didn't feel much in his face anymore either, but it made him blink, and that put him off his rhythm. It also tended to annoy him. Boom-boom was a welterweight. I was a junior in high school. Yeah, he knocked me out.

Nice Guy was in his late fifties when I started working out with him. He told stories of when he was a young light-heavyweight, fighting in a stable of fighters along with Jack Dempsey. Now, he worked in a tire store and trained fighters. He trained Torres and me. Well, he was training Boom-boom for pro fights and smokers. He was giving me boxing lessons. There's a difference.

Boom-boom weighed about 170 pounds, most of it in his chest and shoulders. He had close cropped, black hair and a stubbly beard so coarse it left red welts on my arms when I grazed his jaw. He wasn't what anyone would call a polished fighter. He didn't have footwork and he only knew two or three combinations. But he had a head like an anvil and fists like four-pound hammers. He was a slugger. He'd just walk through whatever was coming at him and then wail away until he connected with something. He fought almost every Saturday night. I'd spar with him on Fridays and get him worked up. Then, when I'd see him on Monday I could tell how he did by the way he looked. He was always banged up, with black eyes, cuts, and bruises on his head, and swollen hands. His nose had long since lost its shape. But it was the set of his shoulders and arms that told me if he'd won or lost. If his shoulders swayed when he walked and his arms hung down loose and swung heavy hands, he won. If he was tight, it was best to walk quietly and move slowly in his presence.

Joey was trying hard to teach him a little style. He'd put us to work together on the speed bag and the heavy bags. Torres would hold the big bag steady while I put everything I had into pounding it mercilessly. Joey calling out the combinations, "One-two. Step back! Again, one-two. Step back. Jab-hook-cross! Good!" He'd call them out until I couldn't hold my arms up anymore.

Then we'd switch. I'd hold the bag for Boom-boom. Joey would call them again, "Jab-jab-jab! Good. One-two. No. I said, One-two! Good. Again. Now, jab! Step back. BB, just pretend someone's trying to hit you back, will ya? Step back!" Boom-boom would stick with this for a few minutes longer, then, he'd shake his head and explode with a flurry of body shots, uppercuts and hooks that would knock the bag clean out of my arms and set it dancing on its chain. That was a sign for Joey to break the mood with pushups. "Alright you bums. On the ground. I want a hundred pushups!"

Shoulders burning, sweat puddling on the mat beneath us, the great Boom-boom Torres would look over to me at around pushup number seventy-five and say sheepishly, "Sorry, Chico." My name is Mike, but he called me "Kid Chico." He figured I needed a ring-name.

In our Friday sparring sessions, Joey would put me in the ring with Boom-boom and tell me to just go at him. Nice Guy figured that Boom-boom was taking way too much punishment in the ring. He knew BB needed to learn to do some blocking, dodging, and slipping, maybe even step back once in a while. He knew that if B didn't' learn to duck, in a year he'd be so punch drunk he'd be talking to parking meters.

I was fast and didn't have the power of a pro, so he'd send me out there to throw everything I had at Boom-boom's head. The idea being that this would encourage him to learn how to block a punch. Joey made it very clear to Boom-boom, and to me, that this was training and he was not supposed to hit me back. And he didn't, until he forgot, and unloaded a left-right-hook combination, which I never saw.

I woke up on my back with Joey squeezing a wet sponge on my head and holding his hand in front of my face. "How many fingers you see?" he said. "How many fingers?"

"Three." I said.

"Good. What town are we in? Do you know where you are?"

"Yeah, get back."

"Where are you?"

"In the gym. Oakland."

"Good." He said and turned to Boom-boom. "He's okay B. He'll be fine."

I looked past Joey and saw Boom-boom behind him, bouncing on his toes, and smashing his gloves together. He was crying.

He moved closer and said, "I'm sorry Chico. I'm sorry."

I raised a glove to him.

We were standing on the street later with our gear bags and Boom-boom turned to me, "Hey, Chico, you want a ride to the bus?"

The bus was only four blocks away, but I could tell he really wanted to give me a lift, so I nodded "yes" and he pointed with his chin towards a two-tone '63 Thunderbird parked down the block. "That's your car? The T-Bird?" I asked.

"Yeah."

"Wow, Boom-boom. Nice ride." I said.

"Thanks. Just got it a couple weeks ago."

"You been winning lately?"

"I did okay last month, but a guy I know got me a loan for it. I gotta make payments, but-." He shifted his gym bag and puffed his chest. "Come on. I'll take you to the bus."

The first thing I noticed as I slid into the seat was an old, faded and cracked photograph of a young woman wearing a flowered dress and standing next to a beat up pickup truck from the 40's. "Who's that?"

"That's my mama."

"She's pretty."

"She was, yeah. That was a long time ago, Kid. In Mexico."

"When'd you come over?"

"After she died, when I was about ten."

"Oh, your dad brought you?"

"Ain't got no dad."

"Oh."

"Hey, you want a hot pepper? There's some in the glove box."

"Oh man, I can't eat those thi-" Just then, something brown and hairy jumped over my food and disappeared under the seat. "Holy shit! Boom-boom. There's a rat!" I could still hear it scurrying around under his seat.

Boom-boom was smiling. "That ain't no rat, Chico. That's Pedro. He lives here."

"What? What's a Pedro? It lives in your car?"

"Not all the time. But I don't like to leave him at home too long. He gets lonely. That's his box on the back seat."

"What is it?"

"Guinea pig. Hey Pedro! Pedro, tk-tk-tk." The little thing climbed up his leg and onto his lap. "Ain't he cute?" He gently laid one huge hand on its head and began to stroke it.

"Yeah. Jesus, he scared the shit out of me. I thought it was a rat."

"Naw. I don't like rats. Neither does Pedro. Right little guy? That's why I don't leave him in my room. The rats in that dump..." He ruffled Pedro's hair. "Hey, Pedro, say hi to Kid Chico. He's a fighter too." He picked it up and showed me its face. I have to admit, it was cute. "Here, pet him." He handed it to me. "Careful though, he's awful little."

Pedro snuggled into my lap as Boom-boom started the T-Bird and we headed off to the bus station.

Two weeks later, on a Monday, Boom-boom was tense and tight. The fight on Saturday hadn't gone well and Joey said it was best to leave him alone for a while. It was a smoker at a private club in San Francisco. He'd been up against a guy from L.A. who was fast and strong and had the moves. He'd hurt Boom-boom bad in one eye. By the third round, he was as good as blind on his left side and he took a lot of pounding. He lasted the full five rounds, but he was messed up. The eye was worse that next Monday. He was totally blind on the left. Joey was telling him to go to a doctor, but Boom-boom didn't like doctors. So, he pounded the heavy bag in the corner by himself.

He didn't come in on Wednesday. "He's taking some time off." Joey said. "His eye is really messed up. I think it's a detached retina, plus the bone around his eye, the socket, got some kind of problem. It's all mushy when you push on it."

"Did he go to the doctor?"

"Not yet. He's waiting to see if it goes away."

"It won't just go away." I said.

"I know. I told him. But he's stubborn you know. He figures a doctor's gonna tell him he can't fight."

"But he can't." I said. "He's blind. They'll tear him apart."

"Well, I'm not setting him up with anything while he's like this." Joey said. "But he needs the money and there are other guys who might book him."

Two weeks later, Boom-boom still hadn't been in for a workout. He told Joey he was resting his eye, but Joey thought he might be working out somewhere else. I was still working the bags and shadow boxing with Joey, but I couldn't help thinking about Boom-boom, worrying.

Once in a while, I'd work out with a guy from San Diego who trained with Joey when he had a fight lined up in the Bay Area. He was lighter than Boom-boom, but still strong. He called himself "Spider." Where Boom-boom was a slugger, this guy was a counter puncher. Both are dangerous, but in different ways. Counter punchers will throw a counter punch the instant they see you throwing one. They think your guard will be down while your arm is out there, and they can sneak something in and tap you on the chin.

That was Spider's style. I didn't like it. Every time I'd throw something, Spider's fist would be in my face. Joey thought I needed the practice, so he set us up for three rounds of full sparring. We had headgear on and mouthpieces, but that's not where I was open.

I had wrapped my hands myself and I must have gotten sloppy. My thumbs were too loose and they stuck out too far. When I threw a jab, Spider threw a right hand and our fists crossed midway. His glove hooked my left thumb, drove it back and broke it. It hurt like hell, but I didn't know it was broken. Sprained maybe. So, I kept fighting, but I threw fewer lefts and more right hands. So, it was my right thumb that got broken in the next round. I put up my hands and stopped the fight.

That's when I took a break from boxing. My hands were broken, my friend was blind, and I wasn't eighteen years old yet. I didn't see a future in it. I would still work out with guys sometimes at night and on weekends, in parking lots mainly. But I quit going downtown to work out with Joey. I lost touch.

Four months later, my dad and I were standing in a dingy warehouse in Oakland, looking at a familiar two-tone '63 T-Bird. I didn't like the feelings I was having. "Dad, that T-Bird down there, it looks like Boom-boom's."

"The guy you spar with?"

"Yeah, but—"

He put his hand on my back and said, "You better go check it out."

I had to climb over a couple cars to get to it, but once I was close enough to look in the window, I knew it was his. The door was unlocked, so I squeezed inside. His gym bag was on the floor. His bag gloves were there, on top of his own ten-ounce gloves that I had written "L" and "R" on one time when I was being smart. I also found his trunks, his shoes, and his sleeveless sweatshirt with "Boom-boom" scrawled in marker across the front. And Pedro's box was there too. Pedro was in it, curled up and dead.

Holding that little thing, I think it was the first time in my life that I felt real, overwhelming, paralyzing fear. Boom-boom loved that guinea pig. He wouldn't have left him. Sitting there, looking at poor little Pedro, I knew that something bad had happened to Boom-boom. I was terrified of finding out what it was. I grabbed the gym bag, climbed out of the car and held it up to show my dad.

"Oh no. His?" he asked.

"Yeah. Dad, can we go see Joey? Something's wrong."

"He'll be at the gym. Let's go."

Joey Nice Guy was standing over a couple young guys doing pushups on the floor of the ring. He didn't hear us come in and jumped when I tapped him on the shoulder. It took a half second for him to recognize us. He looked at my dad, broke into a smile and said, "Hey, Stan, how you doing? And how's Kid Chico, Mr. Fast Hands?" Then, his smile vanished when he saw Boom-boom's bag. He put a hand on it. "Where'd you get his bag, kid?"

"It was in his car."

"In his car? Where's his car?"

"It's in a bank warehouse on 7th Street. It's repo'd. We were down there looking for deals and I saw it. Joey, what happened?"

"He's gone, kid."

"What do you mean, 'gone'? Where? What happened?"

"I told him to go to a doctor. He wouldn't listen. He went fighting again. It killed him, three months ago."

My legs went soft and I had to sit down. I put my arm around his bag. "Joey, what? He's dead? I can't believe--."

Joey turned to the two guys who had stopped their pushups. "You two bums go take a leak or something." He turned to me. "It was in San Leandro. I wasn't there, but a guy I know said he was taking it to the head pretty bad, his left side you know. Got knocked down. They stopped the fight. Next day he couldn't get outta bed. His neighbor called an ambulance and they took him to the hospital. He died there."

"Holy shit. Why was he fighting? He shouldn't have been-" I had to stop.

"I told him. But he needed the money, right?"

I couldn't help it. I was trying like hell not to cry. Not here, I told myself. Not in front of Joey and my dad. Not in the gym. "His stuff. What should I do with it?"

My dad said, "You should keep it, son. Joey, can he keep it?"

"Hell yes, Stan. He'd want you to have it. He liked you a lot, kid. He was really sorry about knocking you out that time. You keep it."

All that was a very long time ago. I kept Boom-boom's kit with me for almost thirty years. It had found a place under my tool bench, between the band saw and the lathe. His bag gloves were hanging from a nail above the workbench, covered with sawdust. I had a little business struggling along, making furniture, mostly chairs. To pay the bills, I was putting together Ikea furniture for people who couldn't figure it out themselves. But what I liked most was making chairs.

My shop was in a shed, stuck behind a duplex south of San Francisco. I lived upstairs, in a one-bedroom apartment. The landlord called it "vintage" because nothing had been updated or fixed since the '60's.

I was down in the shop wearing ear protectors while running some mahogany through a jointer, so I didn't hear the kid walk in. When I turned around to grab another board, I saw him standing in the corner. He was about fifteen, thin, and wearing a dark hoodie sweatshirt, hood up. "Hey," I said. "I didn't see you there. What are you doing?"

"Nothing. Just watching." His voice hadn't fully cracked yet. He spoke softly and stuffed his hands in his pockets. "Is it okay?"

"Sure. Come on in. You know anything about this stuff?"

"No. What's that thing?" He pointed at the lathe on the table next to him.

"It's a lathe. Hey, I know you. You live in the apartment up front."

"Yeah. We moved in last month."

"Live with your mom, right?"

"Yeah."

"Shouldn't you be in school?"

"It's a holiday."

"No, it's not. How come you're not in school?"

"I don't like school. I gotta go." He turned to leave.

"Wait a minute. Where you going?"

"Nowhere. I don't know. I just heard you working in here and thought I'd come see what you're doing. I'll go. I'll go."

"Hold on. I won't bug you about school anymore. Stick around. I'm about to use that lathe next. Might interest you. What's your name?"

"Tony. Tony Mullen."

"Hi Tony. I'm Mike," I said. "Yeah, I didn't like school much either. Is your mom at work?"

"Yeah. She always is."

"Don't you think she'll be mad at you if she finds out you cut school?"

"You gonna tell her?"

"Probably not. Do you cut often?"

"No. It's just that, this morning – never mind." He turned toward the wall. "What are those?" He was pointing at Boom-boom's gloves.

"Bag gloves. Used to belong to a friend of mine."

"What are bag gloves?"

"They're leather gloves that protect your hands when you're working out on a punching bag. You ever hit a heavy bag?"

"No. What's a heavy bag?"

"That's one over there." I pointed into the next room where I had a big Everlast bag hanging from a chain. There was also a speed bag, hanging from a rack in the corner. It had been hanging there, unused, so long that it had grown a pretty thick shroud of sawdust draped spider webs. I walked over and wiped them away then gave it a straight right hand that set it spinning and bouncing against its frame. It felt good.

"Oh, I've seen those things before. Are you a boxer?"

"I did a little, a long time ago."

"Were you any good?"

"World famous. They called me Kid Chico."

"Why'd they call you that?"

"I don't know. Guy I used to fight with just started calling me that one day. It's a ring name."

"Cool."

"You can just call me Mike, though."

"You still box?"

"No, I just like to whack the bags sometimes. Feels good. You want to try it?"

"Can I?"

"Sure. Go ahead. Just don't break 'em." He cracked a smirk, then went over and stood in front of the big bag. He gave it a shove. As it swung back towards him, he balled his hand into a fist and drove it into the middle of the bag with a satisfying pop.

He did it again, and then again, harder. In seconds, he was whaling away at it with both hands and the bag was spinning and swaying on its chain.

"Stop for a second, Rocky," I said and walked over. "I'll hold it for you." Then I braced myself behind the bag. "Okay, go!" He lit into it again. "Whoa, whoa, hold it. That's enough for now." I said. "Look at your hands." He spread his fingers and looked down at his bloody knuckles. "See? Bag gloves."

"Ouch," he said. Then he laughed. "Jeez, that hurts."

"Feels good though too, huh?"

"Yeah."

"There's a sink over there. Go wash your hands and I'll drive you to school."

"But, I don't want -."

"You're going to school. After school, you can come back here and work out on that bag all you want. But you gotta go to school. Okay?"

"Okay."

"I'll get you some bag gloves."

"Really?"

"If you promise to quit cutting school, I'll get you some gloves and I'll show you how to work on the speed bag too."

"Okay."

"Let's go."

Tony was a regular at the shop after that. He was coming in almost every day for a while and working up a sweat. I got him doing pushups between rounds and he was starting to grow some shoulders. I rigged up a pipe at the top of the doorway so he could do pull-ups from it, and I filled two buckets with water and made him lift them with each arm. He seemed to be enjoying himself, but there was something off.

One day I asked him, "Hey Tony. Why are you coming in here every day? Don't you have any friends to hang out with?"

"Sure. I got friends. It's just – I like this. It's fun."

"Maybe you oughta do something else once in a while. How's school? You liking it anymore?"

"No. I don't cut anymore, but I don't like it."

"What don't you like? You're doing your homework, right?"

"It's not that." He looked down. "There's just these guys-"

"Guys?"

"They don't like me."

"Oh." I didn't like the picture that flashed across my mind, of "guys," nasty, loud, mean, guys. Guys who like to push people around. I got up, picked up his bag gloves and said, "Hey, you've been slugging that bag long enough, I think it's time you learned some combinations."

"What are combinations?"

"Combinations of different punches. Like, jabs and hooks, and upper-cuts. One-two, jab-hook-cross, two hooks-cross. You throw them in combinations."

"That sounds interesting."

"Yeah, it'll give you a little finesse. You don't want to just be some dumb slugger."

I got a pair of punch mitts for myself so I could catch his punches and combinations and the next day I started teaching him some style. After he'd worked up a sweat on the heavy bag, I pulled him aside and got him started on the simple stuff, like his stance. "Tony, put your hands up like you're going to hit me."

He squared his shoulders to me and put his gloves up in front of his face. "Like this?"

"No. Watch." I put a hand on his chest and gave him a little shove. It pushed him back a step and put him off balance. "Okay, now drop your right foot back and twist your left shoulder toward me." He shifted his weight. I gave him another shove. He didn't move. "See?"

"Yeah. Wow."

"Okay, now, hands up." He put both hands up in front of his face again. "Now, put your right hand next to your chin and your left hand out toward me." He was ready. "That's your stance. Okay, in slow motion, swing your shoulders to the left and then to the right. When you're coming back to the right, straighten out your left arm. Good. You just threw a jab. Bring it back and step back." Then I put on the mitts and held up my right hand. "Alright, now do it again, full speed, and aim at the glove." I waved the mitt. He swung his shoulders and shot out his left. It smacked into the mitt with a sharp pop. "That's good. You got some snap. But remember to step back." I raised the mitts again. "Let's try throwing a right cross." We spent the rest of the day going from slow motion to full speed, lefts and rights. "This time, I want you to aim six inches past the mitt. Okay? Punch through the glove." Smack! "Good. That's power."

By the end of the day, Tony had developed a little form. He could throw a sharp jab and was showing some power with his right hand. He could shoot out a one-two combination and pop back to his ready stance, set to throw it again.

"Okay, one more and I want twenty-five pushups," I said. He threw the combination and the second he was back in his stance, I shot out a left and popped him on the side of his head with the mitt. "Hey, don't look so surprised kid. You ain't alone. Tomorrow we're gonna work on blocking."

For the next week, I had to make him stop at six o'clock and go home for dinner. One night, his mother appeared with a plate of cookies. I was at my table, sketching designs for a chair when I heard her light footsteps as she made her way through the shop. I spun around in my chair just as she stepped up to my worktable. She wore pressed slacks and a loose sweater that didn't give any clues. Her hair clung to her forehead and her eyes seemed more lined and tired than they should have been at her age. I looked at the cookies and said, "Hey, those for me?"

"They're chocolate chip. I hope you like chocolate chip."

"My favorite. You're Tony's mom, right?"

She put the plate down and stuck out her hand. "Carolyn."

Her hand was small and cool and her grip was gentle. "Hi Carolyn. I'm Mike. It's nice to finally meet you."

"I know. I should have come back here sooner. You've been so nice to Tony. He loves hanging out with you. He really has been needing some father influence…" She stopped for a second and covered her mouth. "I'm sorry. I don't know if that sounded right."

"I take it his father's not involved?"

"No."

"His loss. He's a good kid," I said, and stood up. She was taller than I had thought, but I still had a couple inches on her. "He helps me around the shop sometimes. He sweeps up and keeps things put away. This place would be a mess without him."

"Well, he's much happier than he's been in a long time. He's eating again, and he even does pushups and sit-ups before bed each night. I'm amazed. He's even been doing his homework without a fight." She pushed a strand of hair behind her ear and said, "Thank you for that, Mike, and here." She put the plate of cookies in my hand.

"Wow, thank you. Really, I like having him around. Reminds me of my son. Say, you want some coffee? I could make some. I might even have a cup around here without sawdust in it."

"Thanks, but no. I have work to do. But thanks again. You have a son?"

"I did. He died." The plate of cookies went onto the table.

"Oh, that's horrible."

"It was a while ago. My wife was driving. There was an accident."

"Was she-?"

"Drunk."

"Oh my god. I'm so sorry."

"Don't be. Having Tony around kind of reminds me of the good times, before all that."

"I'm so sorry, Mike. But, truly, I want you to know, Tony really looks up to you. He loves the boxing and the things you're teaching him."

"That's good. He's a natural. And I think it's helping him get through some stuff."

Her eyes took an edge and looked into mine. "What stuff? Is there something I should know about?"

"No, no, just the usual kind of thing, being the new kid at school. He's gotta figure out who are his friends and who aren't. We're working on confidence." I picked up a cookie and took a bite, very casually.

"I guess you're right. I hated having to move and take him out of his school and away from his friends. But I had no choice. I'm so glad he's found you and you're helping him through this. He wouldn't talk to me about this kind of thing."

"He's being a guy. He'll get through it. New kids get picked on in the beginning, but it's nothing a couple of lefts, and a good right hand can't fix."

"You're kidding me, right?"

"Of course."

A couple weeks later, Tony showed up at the shop with a friend. "Hey slugger," I said. "Who's your pal?"

"His name's Ernie."

"Hi, Ernie." I stuck out my hand to shake. Ernie jumped and took a step back. "Any friend of Tony's is welcome around here." I said. Ernie was shorter than Tony and still waiting for his testosterone to kick in. He had curly blonde hair, one lazy eye, and a fat lip. "What happened to you Ernie?" I asked, squinting to get a closer look.

"He got hit," Tony said. "Some guys, they were trying to take his lunch money, and he wouldn't give it to them, so this butt-head hit him."

"At school?"

"Yeah."

"Were there teachers around?"

"No. They wouldn't do anything anyway. Those guys get away with everything. I hate those guys."

"Are these the same guys who don't like you?"

"Yeah. There's this one guy, Jason, who's the worst. He picks on Ernie and when I try to stop him, he starts shoving me around, saying he's gonna kick my ass."

"I see. You know, that's not likely to happen. Right?"

"Yes, it is. He took a couple swings at me today, but I blocked him. But I didn't hit back. Now he's telling everyone I'm a chicken and he's going to beat me up, this Friday night. If I don't show up, everyone in school will think I'm afraid and a coward. I don't want to fight. Maybe I am a chicken."

"You're not a chicken, Tony," Ernie said. Then he turned to me. "He's not."

"I know he's not, Ernie. Tony, you just know that if you unload on him the way you been taught, you might really hurt him bad, or worse."

"But, what'll I do? They're gonna keep it up. They keep picking on Ernie to get to me. He's my friend. I wanna just quit that school."

"Me too," Ernie said.

"They want a fight this Friday night you say?"

"Yeah in the parking lot behind the library. That's where they go to hang out."

"Well, there's a couple ways to play this. Do they know anything about what we've been doing here? The boxing?"

"No. I don't talk to them, ever."

"Good. We got three days. This will be good. Okay. Listen up. Tomorrow, I'm going to pick you up in front of the school. I'll get there early. Where's a good place to meet you where the most people will see us?"

I was there ten minutes early. I rolled up in my truck with the toolboxes in the bed and the lumber rack over the roof. I parked it right in front of the school where everyone had to pass around it to get to their cars and the buses. I wore dirty sweat pants, a sweatshirt with the arms cut out, and a headband. I had my hands taped, Tony's leather bag gloves hanging around my neck, and Boom-boom's ancient gym bag in my hand. As I stepped down from the cab, I caught a glimpse of myself in the mirror. For a second I thought I was looking at old Joey Nice Guy, ready for a workout.

I heard the school bell ring and in seconds the place was overflowing with hurrying, laughing, chattering kids. They were pouring out of doorways and halls, all seemingly headed right for me. I went to work. "Hey, any of you kids know where Boom-boom Mullen is? I'm looking for Mullen, Tony Boom-boom Mullen? We gotta get to San Jose for the fight. Any of you seen Boom-boom?"

A group of four girls, clutching books and dragging backpacks, stopped in front of me. "Do you mean Tony Mullen?"

"Yeah, Tony, the fighter. We call him Boom-boom down at the gym." A small crowd was forming around me now, so I raised one of my taped fists and said to them, "Mullen's fighting Spider Morales tonight in San Jose. He's in the finals and we gotta get going. Golden Gloves, you know. Can't be late." The crowd was getting bigger.

I kept this up until Tony and Ernie pushed their way through to the front. "Hey, Boom-boom! Come on slugger, we gotta haul ass." I tossed him his gloves and the beat-up old gym bag with "Boom-boom" written across it. "I gotta wrap your hands, man. Come on! Let's move." Tony and Ernie looked around at the growing crowd, smiled and jumped into the truck.

"You're crazy, you know," Tony said. Ernie was still grinning.

"You just noticed that? Come on, we have some work to do." I put the truck in gear and we pulled out.

Back at the shop, I said, "Listen, kid, from now on, you're Boom-boom Mullen. Got it?"

"I like it."

"It's a proud name. Now look, we're going to work on combinations, blocking, and footwork 'til you're sick of it, for the next three days. Hopefully you won't need it, but by Friday night, you're going to be ready. Ernie, I want you holding the heavy bag when Boom-boom is working on it. I'll call combinations." Ernie still hadn't said a word, but he was beaming and practically hopping. "There's something else we're gonna work on."

"Sure, what?" Tony asked.

"Attitude and swagger."

"What?"

"Watch this and do what I do. This is important." I lifted my shoulders up toward my ears and then rolled them back and down. "Roll your shoulders like that." He did it. "Good. Now, roll your shoulders again and toss your head from side to side. Like this. Good. I want you to practice that move. Try doing it while slapping your gloves together. Excellent! You look like Jake LaMotta. Now try doing just one shoulder, toss your head and shoot your arms down and out." He was doing a perfect impression of George Foreman, standing in his corner before the bell.

"Okay, I want you to practice that move until you're doing it in your sleep. On Thursday, I want you to start doing it in the halls at school. Also, I want you to throw in some shadow boxing combinations. Ernie, you put up your hands and Tony will strike. Do it somewhere out of the way, but visible. Got it?"

"Yeah, got it."

"Also, there's 'the walk,'" I said.

"The walk?"

"You need to float a little more when you walk. Swing your shoulders and sway your upper torso, just a touch. And I want your arms to swing, like your hands weighed four pounds. Heavy hands. Like this." I walked across the shop trying my best to look like Boom-boom Torres after a win. "Do you think you can do that?"

"Like this?" He lowered his shoulders, shook out his arms, and did a perfect strut. It was amazing.

"That's excellent! Do it again." He had the walk down as if he'd been doing it his whole life. It changed him. He moved like he owned the ground under him and nobody would dare try to push him off. He seemed taller, heavier, and dangerous. "I want you walking like that for the next three days."

"Okay." He rolled his shoulders and tossed his head.

"You're a natural, Boom-boom."

"Boom-boom? Now, you're Boom-boom?" The three of us spun around and saw Carolyn standing, hands on hips, glaring at us. "What's going on here?"

"Nothing mom. We're just practicing the, um, the walk?"

"Yes, I saw the walk. Very impressive. But why are you walking like that and why are you Boom-boom?" She stepped further into the shop.

I stepped up and put a hand on her arm. "Boom-boom is just his ring name. Like "Sugar Ray" Leonard, or "Hitman" Hearns, like that. It strikes fear into his opponents."

"What opponents?" She turned to Tony and pointed a finger. "You aren't going into a boxing match, are you?"

Tony opened his mouth, but nothing came out. I took a breath, stepped in front of him and said to Carolyn, "Tony and his best friend, Ernie here, are going to do what needs to be done to get a bully at school to go jump in a lake. This guy thinks that because Tony is new at school, and Ernie is, well, not big, he can get away with pushing them around and picking on them."

"Tony, you never told me," Carolyn cried.

"Mom, I couldn't tell you. You'd freak out and there's nothing you can do. I gotta take care of this. Mike is helping me, and so is Ernie."

"What are you talking about?" Carolyn's cheeks were beginning to flush pink.

"Mom, these guys were pushing Ernie around and I stepped in to stop them so they ganged up on me too. We tried to walk away, but they started shoving and calling us chicken. So, now I gotta fight this guy, Jason, Friday night or -."

"You're not going!" she cried.

"Carolyn, listen to me," I said. "If he doesn't go, those guys will make his life a living hell at school. We're working on this and, believe me, Tony's gonna be alright."

"What, you think because he can hit a punching bag, he's suddenly a street fighter?"

"What would you say if I told you that Tony is a Golden Gloves welter weight? And that he's in the finals after beating Spider Morales last Wednesday night in San Jose?"

"I'd say you're all crazy."

"Well, maybe we are, a little. But that's the story that this Jason kid is starting to hear around school."

"What are you talking about?"

Ernie piped in, "It's true Mrs. Mullen. At school, they think he's Boom-boom now. It's really cool."

"Are you guys serious?" Carolyn asked.

"As a heart attack," I said. "This Friday night, Tony, sorry, Boom-boom will show up behind the library and we're betting that punk Jason will be home with a sudden tummy ache."

"What if he isn't home with a tummy ache? What if he shows up? Are they going to fight?"

"If there's a fight, Tony will take him out in a matter of seconds."

"Tony, you can't go. You can't go be in a street fight."

"Mom, I have to go. If I don't, I might as well quit that school. Me and Ernie will be picked on forever."

"But Tony, what if you get hurt?"

"Mom, I get hurt every day."

I touched her hand and said, "Carolyn, take a second and just watch this." I turned to Ernie. "Ernie, brace the heavy bag. Tony, take your stance." In seconds, he was ready, rocking and swaying, shifting his weight as he moved slowly and purposefully in front of the bag. Then I began calling combinations. "One-two! Jab. Two Jabs. Jab-hook-cross! Good. One-two. Step back." The bag popped and jumped as Tony laid into it with the speed, power and pinpoint accuracy that he'd developed over the months. The muscles in his neck and arms flexed and extended and a glow of perspiration appeared on his shoulders. "Do it again!" I cried. "Two jabs-cross! Good. Cover your chin. Tuck your shoulder. Good."

I looked over at Carolyn and her mouth was agape. One hand was at her chin, and her eyes were wide and staring. She turned to me, blinked, and said, "He's a man."

"He's getting there."

"Will he be okay?"

"Look, this thing tomorrow is something that happens a lot with kids this age. Tony is prepared and he's ready to put an end to the shit he's been taking from those guys. "Plus, I'll be there, and I swear, I won't let anything happen to this kid. I swear."

"I'm going to trust you guys, but I'm not going to watch." Then she kissed us all, and went home.

Friday night came soon enough. It was a moonless night and behind the library, there was an ominous feel to the yellow glow of a street lamp that cast shadows through a dying old oak and across the hoods and roofs of about a dozen parked cars. Interior dome lights flicked on and off as kids scurried around, popping beer cans and crushing empties. At least two radios added confused background noise that scraped across the asphalt.

The cars were parked in a half circle, facing in. I'd seen this before in vacant lots and back alleys. "Not much changes," I thought to myself. I parked the truck across from the circle and left the parking lights on. Heads turned as Boom-boom and Ernie climbed out. Boom-boom did the shoulder roll and head toss then bounced a couple times on his toes. I tossed him the gym bag.

Tony was wearing jeans and Boom-boom Torres' old, sleeveless sweatshirt, stained with sweat and blood. I fished the hand wraps out of the bag and start taping his hands. BB did the shoulder roll and head toss again, then bounced a few more times for effect. With his hands wrapped, I helped him pull the thin leather bag gloves on.

Across the circle, Jason and his friends were watching. It was the first time I'd seen Jason. He was bigger and older than Boom-boom, with a tattoo on his right forearm that I couldn't make out. He looked like he might have been in a scrape or two, but I was pretty sure it was all street stuff.

His friends were milling around the cars, drinking beers and trying to look cool for the girls, who were huddled in tiny, select groups, giggling and screaming. Everyone seemed to be parading for each other. They all were looking forward to a real fun time.

"Alright," I said. "Boom-boom, we're going to do a little quick work with the punch mitts, loosen you up. Got it?"

"Okay, I guess." He looked every bit the fighter, but his eyes told the truth: he didn't want to go out there.

"I'm gonna call some combinations and you're gonna throw them. I want the pop of your blows to carry across this parking lot. Okay?" I held up the mitts and started calling them. I turned to Ernie. "What are they doing over there?"

"Wow, they all just kinda stopped. They're watching us."

"Jason too?"

"Yeah."

"Excellent. Boom-boom, pay attention! Give me some jabs! Now a hook. Good."

Then Ernie spoke up. "Hey, he's walking out in front of the cars. They're starting to turn on the lights."

Kids started chanting, "Fight! Fight!" and "Kill him!" Only a couple voices were yelling for Jason but I heard several crying, "Boom-boom! Boom-boom!"

I said, "Sounds like you got some fans out there, kid. You ready to go? Are you alright?"

Tony looked across at Jason, standing in the lighted circle. Then he turned to me. "I don't want to do this, but I guess I will. Thanks Mike, for helping me. I--."

"Just do like I taught you. Take your time. Throw a few fakes to see what he does. Does he block? Does he cover? I'm betting he'll drop his guard and you can just go to town. Throw your punches fast and step back, then throw some more. Remember to aim six inches past your target. Watch for him to drop his hands. He will. Stick him. Keep your eyes open and don't forget to block and slip. You'll take him inside thirty seconds."

"You'll kill that ass-wipe," Ernie said, and punched him on the shoulder.

Tony laid a hand on his arm, "Thanks, pal." Then he took a deep breath and turned and walked out to face Jason.

Kids were yelling, "Fight! Fight!"

He did the walk, just like Boom-boom Torres after a win. He went face up with Jason, then took one step back and went into his stance. He started to sway and feint, moving slowly to his left, watching how Jason would react. Jason's motions were jerky and off balance. He looked scared. When Tony faked a left jab, Jason crossed his hands in front of his face and closed his eyes. Yeah, he was scared.

Then Jason dropped his hands and Boom-boom shot out a solid left jab that snapped his head back. Jason launched a looping right hand that went wild and Boom-boom countered with another jab-hook combination that landed on Jason's ear and sent him flailing and staggering to the right. As he fought to regain his balance, Boom-boom connected with a solid right hand straight to the nose.

Jason took three steps back and sat down. His nose was bleeding and his eyes were watering so that he could barely see. He raised one hand, palm up. It was over. Two of his friends helped him to stand. Then they walked him back into the darkness.

Tony and Ernie had no more problems after that. They made friends, went to parties and even went out for sports. Turns out, Ernie was a terrific long distance runner on the track team, and Tony learned to ski. I went with him a couple times on school sponsored ski trips when his mother had to work. We even went fishing a couple times. When he turned sixteen, I took him to a repo auction in Oakland and got him a great deal on a pickup truck. It needed brakes and a clutch, but I lent him the tools and he worked on it in the back yard. Had it running in a week.

The punching bags grew beards of cobwebs and sawdust again, as the after-school boxing sessions came to an end. But Carolyn came by more often. She brought her famous cookies, and one night she also brought a bottle of wine. Turns out, she's a great kisser.

Van Bo's Christmas List

I'd never seen Bo do his drinking indoors before. As long as I'd known him, he was strictly a sidewalk, brown-paper-bag man. But there he was, taking up two spaces along the bar at Mariano's. He turned when I walked in and rumbled, "Morning Stan. Want a drink? Sal's pouring a very nice Chardonnay." I didn't know what surprised me more, the offer of a drink, seeing Bo inside, or the Santa Claus hat he was wearing. I'd seen plenty of black Santa's, but not in September. And Bo, sipping "a very nice" Chardonnay, out of a glass? But then again, this wasn't Bo. This was Van Bo.

I first met Bo when he was in the business of not washing cars. He'd lounge on the street by a cash machine waiting for some poor sinner to roll up and park. Before the door was open, Bo'd be rapping on the window, saying, "Hey brother, how about I wash your car for ten bucks?" One look at Bo and his bucket, and most guys knew it would be better all-around if they just gave him ten bucks and asked him to please *not* wash their car.

Nobody really knew where Bo went at night. I've never seen him sleeping in any doorways, but I've seen evidence of campsites and burrows dug under the heavy junipers on the edge of the park. Despite what some people think, he doesn't wear all his clothes at the same time, so I figured he must have been stashing his winter sweatshirts and extra jackets in the bushes. In the wintertime, he doesn't mind doing an overnight in jail once or twice a month, so he can use the showers.

Bo isn't the violent type, but he is about as big as a double door refrigerator and he can get a bit frisky after eight or ten hours of drinking. He played football until his knees gave out, and he boxed until he woke up on his back one night with a couple guys in his face saying, "Oh good. He's not dead." That's when he announced his retirement.

Then, he claims, he was a porn star, going by the name of "Captain Black Snake." He'd lost his good looks, but he still had his bulk. Usually, he would have *not* washed enough cars by noon for a couple bottles of something red and cheap, and a six-pack, so he'd knock off for the day and rest his bones.

But a couple months back, Nickels Furman died, and that sad event inspired Bo to change his act.

Nickels was known for his stash of nickels, buried someplace under all the junk inside his car. He had been a house painter, but lately he was mostly a drinker. He was working on a house one day, when he fell off his ladder and broke his ankle and a couple ribs. He went downhill from there fast. The nickels ran out, he couldn't work, and whenever he was forced to choose between solid and liquid nourishment, he went for the juice. He died one night in his ancient Volvo, parked in the lot near Bo's bench. Besides the skinny remains of old Nickels and a case of empties, the car was packed with about twenty assorted colors of house paint, a pile of stiff brushes and rollers, and a crusty and cruddy drop cloth.

By the time the fire department rolled the late Nickels into the ambulance, the paint and brushes had grown legs and walked off. The next day, Bo was on the street, sitting on his bucket by the liquor store, painting pictures of the Golden Gate Bridge on scraps of plywood he'd pulled out of a dumpster. Bo had become an artist.

Bo made up for his lack of any actual skill or talent, with output. By the end of the first day he had decorated the sidewalk and himself with splashes, footprints, and puddles of paint, and surrounded his bucket with five completed views of the Golden Gate Bridge, done in a combination of house and finger paint.

Propped against his paint-splattered knee, was a sign that said, "Pantins by Van Bo, ten bucks."

So, now, he's Van Bo.

Seeing Bo lounging around in my favorite breakfast bar, piqued my curiosity, so I walked over and pulled up the stool next to him. "You buying?" I asked.

"Actually, he's not," Sal put in. "I am." Sal was rubbing fingerprints off the shot glasses with a rag that looked a lot greasier than the fingerprints.

"You're buying? What's the occasion? I know it ain't Christmas, despite the hat."

"No occasion," he replied. "Bo just needed a little cheering up. I thought the hat might help. You want a glass of wine or what?"

"I don't usually drink wine in the morning," I said. "You pouring any Jack?"

"I can pour it, but you'll be paying for it," he said, and put his fists on his hips.

I looked over to Bo and said, "Christ, wine in the morning."

"Technically, it ain't morning in Thailand, Stan," Bo said, squinting at me through the Scotch tape holding the broken lenses of his glasses together. Then he turned and asked, "Hey Sal, can I keep the hat? Feels good."

"It's yours, Bo," Sal said. Then he put down his rag, reached for the Jack Daniels bottle and said, "Alright, one JD on the house. But don't bother asking for more."

"You are a prince," I said. But something about all this just didn't seem right. Bo's drinking Chardonnay? Inside? Sal's giving me a drink? … I had to ask, "Alright, you guys, what's going on?"

Sal leaned his belly into the bar as he scooped a couple ice cubes into my glass. "There's been a big art heist," he said.

Without lifting his head, Bo said, "Some bastard stole about ten or twenty of my paintings. Took most of my paint too. Wiped me out. Van Bo may be done."

Although this was not a huge loss to the art world, to Bo, it was big. "Jesus, man. How'd they get them? Where were they?"

"I had 'em stashed round the neighborhood. Down the park mostly, under the junipers and out behind the lawn mower pen. They're all gone. They took a couple bags of my clothes too. Bastards."

"Did you look in the dumpsters? Might have been the park people, you know, cleaning up the place?"

"What are you talking about, man? They was my paintings. My Van Bo's. My name was on 'em. They ain't in no dumpsters."

"Okay, sorry," I said. "Did you call the cops?"

They both stopped and looked at me like stupid had just walked in. "I just thought, you know, maybe you could get a police report."

"What the hell good's that gonna do?" Bo asked.

"I don't know, insurance?" Bo blinked, shook his head and drained his glass. Then he held it up for a refill.

Sal reached for the bottle and said, "Earth calling Stan, come in please. It's earth calling."

"I know, I know. That was dumb," I said. "Maybe it's the hat, but my Christmas list just flashed into my head."

"That won't work here, Stan," Sal said.

Bo looked up. "What's your Christmas list?"

Sal stopped degreasing another glass and said, "Every year he sits in here and makes out a list of what he wants for Christmas.

He does it on a claim form from his insurance company. Seems, each year, just before Christmas, his car just happens to get broken into. And 'boo-hoo,' all kinds of cool stuff gets stolen. Last year, his "Insurance Santa" brought him a Nikon camera, some Ray-Bans, and a laptop. Right Stan?"

"I really liked those Ray-Bans,"

Bo turned on his stool. "You got insurance?"

"Yeah, sure, on the car. I have to."

"So, like, if the paintings were in your car, and they got ripped off, you could get paid by the insurance company?"

"I don't know if they'd cover your paintings," I said. "I've never tried it with other peoples' stuff, before."

"But, what if they were yours? They cover your stuff, right?" Bo was leaning into me now.

"But they ain't mine. They're yours… were yours, sorry."

"What if I just sold them to you? Then they're yours, right? Your car gets broke into, the insurance company's gotta pay up?"

"That's the deal."

"So, if you bought them for like, ten grand, they'd have to give you ten grand back for them?" Now, his hand was on my arm.

"Well, there's the deductible, of course. But, where'd I get ten grand to buy 'em in the first place?"

"Where'd you get a Nikon camera and a laptop last year?"

"Hey, a Nikon ain't costing no ten grand, man."

"Okay, okay. I'll sell 'em to you for eight. So, they get stolen out of your car and the insurance pays you back. You keep four, and I keep four. Not bad, huh?"

"Put it that way, what do I even need you for? I've been doing all right with my Christmas list on my own."

"I'm the artist, man. Van Bo, that's me. I'm the witness says you bought 'em in the first place.

"I'd need receipts."

"No problem. I'll give you a receipt. What does it have to say?" Then he turned to Sal, "Hey Sal, you got some paper and a pencil?"

"Sure," he said. Then he went to the cash register and found a pad of paper, brought it over and dropped a pen on it.

"Okay, Stan, what's it gotta say?"

"Well, start with the titles of each one, maybe the size, and the price. How many paintings were there?"

"I don't remember. Maybe ten. Make it eight, that's easier." He said and started writing on the pad. "Is it okay if they're all the same title? They were all the same thing, the bridge and a sailboat."

"I don't know. Maybe you oughta mix 'em up, you know. Why would I buy eight paintings, all the same?"

"But that's all I paint, man, the bridge," he said.

"Still – "

"Hey," he said. "How about we make it just one big painting? It's of the bridge with the boat, but it's a big one. That'd be more expensive, right? Like eight grand."

"Uh, Bo, no offense, but who'd ever believe I bought one of your paintings for eight grand? I mean, you can't hardly give 'em away for ten bucks."

"Shit man, hey! I'm selling like crazy. I'm sold outta the fuckers. Ten bucks, shit. I was about to raise my prices when this, this, theft happened." He looked at me, scowled over his glasses, flipped the pom-pom on his hat, and pointed the pen. "I'm giving you this bunch for a deal man, 'cause you supposed to be my friend."

Suddenly, we heard a loud "Pop!" from the end of the bar. We both looked over and there was Sal, holding a foaming bottle of champagne. This was another first in Mariano's. Champagne that popped when it opened was as rare in this joint as caviar blinis. "What are you doing, Sal?" I blurted out.

He came over with three chilled glasses, set them on the bar and started to pour. "What's up?" I asked.

"Gentlemen, this is a moment I don't want to forget. It calls for champagne." He poured slowly, letting the bubbles settle as each glass filled to the brim. He raised one up, smiled and said, "A toast, to Stanley and Dumb-Bo. I'm in awe. I feel like right here, in my bar, I'm watching history in the making. This must be how old President Harry Truman musta felt, watching Albert Einstein and What's-his-name Oppenhouser, hatching their brilliant plan to make that atom bomb."

Bo picked up his glass, gave it a swirl and said, "I think you mean, Oppenheimer, Sal."

He was just taking his first sip, when the door burst open and a short, bald headed guy in a raggedy jacket barged in. He planted his feet, squinted into the dimness of the bar and shouted, "Hey, does one of you guys own a red Ford out there?"

"I own a Pinto," I said.

"Yeah, that's it," he said. "A Pinto."

"What about it?" I asked.

"It's on fire."

"Oh no!" Cried Bo, "My paintings are in there!"

Cris Hammond

The Rose

Why the hell would such a gorgeous woman go and do that to herself? I didn't know what it was at first, maybe some horrible cancerous growth or a festering bruise. But then she settled a couple bar stools down, and there it was, staring at me, a goddamn puking skull.

Her boyfriend had tattoos too, but nothing quite so creative. He just had the normal, everyday spider web on his elbow, a snake poking up from his collar and Maori patterns on his calf, even though he sure as hell wasn't no damn Maori.

Normally I got nothing against tattoos, but lately, they're everywhere. Christ, they're getting to be like earrings or sunglasses. They used to mean something. My old man had a fouled anchor on his shoulder, over the names of his ships; General Edwin D. Patrick, S.S. Missoula and S.S. Dauntless.

Mine just says Rose. Messing around with her got me the closest I've ever been to stone, cold dead.

I've been through some shit before, but I've never been more terrified than that night in a gale, twenty miles off the coast of California at Point Conception. It was in December and Sal still calls me a fool for being there. But it was a job, and I needed the money.

It was about twenty years ago, I think. Every once in a while, when lumping cargo on the waterfront in Oakland got too stupid or the goddamn Freightliner was busted down, sometimes I'd polish up some of the tricks my old man taught me from years wasted as a merchant seaman, and go see if I could pick up a delivery job, moving private yachts around the Pacific. There was always work. The Frisco Bay was full of yacht club admirals who'd never poked their noses outside the Gate. I'd also done deliveries for a few yacht brokers off the coast. I had a hundred-ton license that was only about five years expired, so I could call myself a skipper, if I held my thumb over the date, and flashed it fast enough.

That time, I was delivering Compass Rose, a sixty-foot schooner, from La Paz, up to a guy in San Francisco who'd bought it on a whim. He liked the pictures of her that he'd seen in a magazine. The pictures showed her lying at anchor somewhere in the tropics with the setting sun glowing through palm trees silhouetted in the background. He'd never actually set eyes on the boat, or sailed her, but I had to agree, the photos did look sexy.

Over the years, I had worked with some pretty solid guys I could call on when I needed crew. Dick McCready was one of those guys. He had six weeks free, so he signed on and came down with me to Mexico to pick up the boat. He was an ex-crabber from Alaska and could handle just about anything the California coast could dream up for you. We'd done most of the Pacific and a lot of the Caribbean together over the years and I knew him to be a good man. I could trust him to stay on course and not go dumb shit on me while I'm below in the middle of the night, trying to get some sleep.

What we found when we got to La Paz was indeed a pretty vessel. Compass Rose was built in 1917, in Vancouver for the sealing trade. Her legend said that she'd been around the world a few times and she had even run guns up the Yangtze River to Chiang Kai-Shek. Old boats attract those kinds of tales. True or not, who knows? She had nice, classic lines, though, and looked like she could sail. What we discovered on closer inspection, unfortunately, was that her rigging was rotten and, simply put, she wasn't safe to take to sea. Dick and I spent a month re-rigging her in a boatyard south of La Paz. That put us way behind schedule and used up most of Dick's free time.

He stayed with me out of Mexico and as far north as Long Beach, but then he had to jump ship. I thought about going on alone, but it was a month deeper into the season than I wanted to be. The weather could get hard in December, and at sixty-feet, the schooner would be a lot to handle by myself.

I asked the harbormaster at Land's End Marina if he knew of any handy, sober, guys hanging about who knew the pointy end of a boat from the square end, and who might be available for a crew position to San Francisco.

"Sober?" he asked. "Not really, but there's Larry. He was in the Navy."

Larry showed up at the boat the next morning. He might have been sober, technically, but he was definitely suffering from a doozy of a hangover. He was under six feet and skinny. He wore threadbare jeans, a saggy wool sweater and rubber deck boots. He looked like the ragged remains of what was once a sailor. He had both arms and legs though, and a duffle with his own set of foul weather gear. I asked him if he could tell me the names of all the sails on a schooner.

"Um, yeah." He said.

"Well, go ahead. Tell me."

"Um, well, there's the main sail, the foresail, and, oh, top sails for both of them."

"Good. Go on."

"Then you got your head sails, the jib and, looks like she's got a flying jib too? Off the bowsprit?"

"Yeah, she's got one. I don't know if we'll need it, or the topsails. You left out the fore-staysail, but you're close enough. You ever done this trip to 'Frisco before?"

"Yeah, sure. Lots of times."

"Where do you prefer to stop, San Simeon or Moro Bay?"

He thought for a moment. "They're both cool."

"Jesus," I thought to myself. "I'm screwed." Then I shrugged and said, "Oh alright. What the hell. Stow your stuff. We're leaving in twenty minutes. You can call me Stan." I took him because winter was coming fast, and I didn't have time to hang around Long Beach waiting for goddamn Ishmael to come wandering down the dock.

Larry was a farmer when he went into the Navy, and he was a farmer when he came out. Turns out he'd never set foot on a ship. He was sober though, until mid-afternoon, although it was hard to tell, since he was seasick five minutes after we hit the ocean swells outside the harbor breakwater. He emptied his stomach over the side, then slithered below to his bunk, where he downed the rest of the half pint of rum he'd smuggled aboard. Then he passed out. He stayed that way most of the voyage.

With Larry staggering and puking and being useless, I was resigned to operating as if I were single-handing the boat. I set a course northwest from Long Beach, through the Channel Islands, to reach Point Conception after midnight, on the second night out. It was a pretty straight shot and if my luck held, I figured I'd round the point, and make for Morro Bay, where I could stop and trade Larry in for a puppy, or a box of rocks.

Point Conception has a reputation as the "Cape Horn of the Pacific." The winds there build up speed and power as they howl from the northwest down the coast of California to Conception, where the coastline cuts suddenly eastward and the winds spin around in a vortex that's rattled sailors for centuries. It's pretty normal for the winds and seas to be too high to get a sailing vessel around the point without two or three days of misery. When that happens, you tuck your tail between your legs and duck into Cojo Cove or head out to sea.

With my crew immobilized below, I wasn't looking forward to the Point, and when the wall of black clouds started building to the north, the thought of turning and running for Santa Barbara began to look like a good idea. Instead, I put my life jacket on, then got up and dropped the headsails and reefed everything else. I should have double reefed them. I should have run for Santa Barbara.

By 1 a.m., the wind was blowing close to fifty miles per hour, whipping a horizontal rain and slashing the tops off the black waves, driving tons of water over the foredeck and slamming it against the cabin sides. The sound was like an angry freight train, chasing a howling banshee through the rigging. I'd already dropped the mainsail completely and was down to just the reefed foresail and fore-staysail. The Rose was doing her best to behave, but the wind was knocking her down and the waves were bowling her over. From the trough of a fourteen-foot wave, she'd point her bowsprit to the dark sky, claw her way to the crest until she burst through at the top, and for a moment, hang her forefoot in midair. High up on the crest, she'd catch again the full punch of the gale. The wheel would spin as she crested the wave and her rudder broke clear of the water, doing its best to jerk free of my grip. She'd buck like an angry stallion, then go careening down the other side.

I was covered head to toe in foul weather gear and still I was soaked to the skin. The rain stung my eyes and filled my mouth and nose so that I had to turn my head away to breathe. Through all this, from the crest of the waves, I could just make out the lighthouse beacon at Point Conception to the east. The Rose was taking a beating, I was exhausted, wet, and frozen, and I was alone. I knew if I tacked the schooner, I could run east, get under the lee of the point, and make for the protection of Cojo Cove, where I could drop anchor, and wait it out. If I kept my present course, I could keep fighting like this for the next ten or twelve hours and still not make the turning. I swung the helm over and went for the tack.

When you tack a sailboat, the bow passes through the eye of the storm, and you end up with the wind hitting the opposite side of the vessel. When this happens, the sails are pushed across the boat and have to be set up and trimmed in their new positions on the lee side. With just the foresail and the fore-staysail up, this should have been only a major inconvenience. They were self-tending, meaning they slid across on tracks and would set up on the other side without a fuss. They'd need trimming for the new course, but I could do that without leaving the cockpit.

I put the helm over and her bowsprit slowly started to swing, coming into the wind, but she wasn't liking it. Slowly, painfully slowly, she came up into the eye of the storm and started across. Those few moments in the eye are when you worry. If she doesn't have enough momentum to come through and cross onto the other side, you can have problems. I held my breath as she swung. She passed. "Yes, thank you, you lovely darling thing." I yelled into the storm. Then I took it all back.

She had come across, yes, but the fore-staysail had jammed on its track and was stuck, struggling, still on the windward side of the boat. I tried to release the sheet to flog the sail, but it wouldn't free up. We were being rapidly pushed way too far around. Soon, she'd be broadside to the waves and things would really start getting ugly. The strain on the rigging could bring down a mast, or worse. From there it's straight to hell. I had no choice. I had to go forward to free it, fast. I grabbed a winch handle, said a few, *"oh shits,"* snapped on my lifeline, and climbed out of the cockpit.

I put my boot down through black salt water until it found the deck. I clutched the grab rails on the cabin top and started toward the bow. She was thrashing and rolling and it was all I could do to hold on and keep inching forward. I knew I should have gone up the other side, the windward side of the boat, but the spray and the attacking waves were making that route a wet and dangerous path, so I crouched down behind the cabin and continued up the lee side.

Without the protection of the cabin, the foredeck was open to the unchallenged rage of the storm, its waves rolling across like stampeding wild boar. In the darkness, I could barely make out the jammed traveler block, just nine feet across the deck, and oh so far away. I got on my hands and knees and started crawling up the steeply inclined deck. I was hoping to get close enough to give it a good kick, or a whack with the winch handle, the classic solution for this type of emergency.

I was just two feet from it when the ship jumped, a wave hit the sail, and with a loud bang, the traveler broke free, slammed across the deck and knocked my ass clean off the boat.

The first thing I felt was the breathtaking shock of the icy water. The first thing I saw was the blackness of it all. I was disoriented, running out of air, and starting to shake. I began thrashing, lashing out against its grip, trying to fight my way through to the surface, but in the dark, I couldn't tell which way was up.

It's true. Your life does flash before your eyes. I thought, "I wanna see my kid again. Shit, I forgot his birthday." Then the CO_2 cartridge in my life vest blew and it filled with air. I popped to the surface in time to catch a mouthful of salt water, and to see the Rose, sailing away.

I tried to swim after the boat, but my arms were like lead and the shivering was taking over my whole body. I screamed for Larry, but the words were torn away by the wind. I was alone with my spitting, choking cries, when suddenly my lifeline gave a tug and a jerk and it jumped up, a taut, dripping white line shooting from the clip on my lifejacket to the deck of the boat. Rose was taking me with her.

I watched my hands, frozen and numb, close around the line and I willed my arms to pull, but the water fought me, clutching and dragging me back. I got as far as ten feet from the boat when the cold took over and my strength gave out. I held on and called for Larry again. I blew the whistle that hung from my lifejacket. My shouts and screams were getting weaker, and still Larry didn't appear. I shouted until I had no more strength, then I tied the line off and passed out.

Larry saved my life that night. Not because he was on his toes. Not because he was a stout hand, knew there was trouble and came running. No. He climbed out of bed because he had to take a leak. On his way to the head, he happened to look into the cockpit and notice that nobody was at the helm. He poked his head out and saw my lifeline trailing taut, behind the boat. He figured that wasn't right, so he followed it and looked over the side. I owe my life to Larry's bladder.

It's Karma

I am just settling in for a little pick-me-up at Mariano's when one of my neighbors walks in and takes the stool next to me. He's known around the place as Sonny Bouncer. Sonny isn't your normal sort of bouncer. He achieved that title early one morning about a year ago when he was having a conversation with a pigeon outside his room down at the Hotel Royale, and he fell off the fire escape. He went down three floors and landed on a Volkswagen that was parked in the alley. He bounced. Twice. Left him with one shoulder higher than the other, and a lump on the side of his head that makes his eye bug out and want to roll to the side. Guys started calling him Igor but it seemed to hurt his feelings, so now it's just Sunny Bouncer.

We are about to flip a coin to see who gets the next round when the door opens up and a blind guy steps in and says to the place, "Hey, anybody want to buy a nice truck, cheap?"

I've been needing a set of wheels ever since the Pinto burned up, and 'cheap' had a nice ring to it, so I call him over. Following his white cane through the tables and chairs of the room, he makes his way up to the bar and stands there with his sunglasses turned vaguely in my direction.

"How cheap?" I ask him.

"Four hundred," he says.

"What is it, and what's wrong with it?"

"'95 Toyota, SR5. It could use some tires. But it runs good."

Now, four hundred for a '95 Toyota would be a good deal, if he ain't lying about how it runs. I got a Teamsters pension check that Sal doesn't know about yet, so this could happen. I inquire further, "Where is it? Can I take a look at it?"

"Outside, up the block. I'll show you. The name's Kingsbury by the way."

"I'm Stan." I put my hand out to shake, but I forget, he can't see it. He just nods, turns and starts tapping a path toward the door. At the same time, Bouncer nudges me on the shoulder and points at something he's written on his bar napkin. "Things worth at least $900 if it's good." I nod. He smiles, rolls his eye, and says, "Hey, I'll come with you." He climbs off his stool and we both follow the guy out the door.

On the street, Mr. Kingsbury points his cane up the block and says, "It's the red one," and he starts walking toward it. Just when I'm trying to decide whether I should take his arm or something, he says, "Tell me when I get there."

"Almost there," I say.

Meanwhile, Bouncer is walking alongside me, nudging, winking, and making faces like he's on an adventure ride at Play Land by the Beach.

Dirty green and sitting on four bald tires, it has one turn signal hanging out of its socket by a wire. But the rest of it looks pretty good. It has a couple dents around the edges, but I can see that it's no four-hundred-dollar truck. If it runs like he says, it's worth at least nine hundred bucks, maybe more. The paint job's in good shape too, so I'm thinking I can buy it and then maybe sell it for a grand. Make a profit and get me something with good tires on it. So, I say, "Can I start it up?"

"Sure," he says. Then he fishes around in his pocket and hands me the keys.

I climb in and check out the rest of the details. Heater, air, stereo/CD player, ripped seam on the passenger side, nothing big. I turn the key and it fires up instantly, sweet.

I'm sitting at the wheel, revving the engine and checking out the pedals, when I hear Bouncer say, "Wow, she smokes pretty bad." I look in the rearview mirror and I don't see any smoke. I rev it again and she's smooth and clean. No smoke. I turn to Bouncer who's standing by the door. He touches me on the shoulder and puts his finger to his lips.

"That's white smoke, like steam or something," he says. "I think that means she might have a cracked block or a blown head gasket maybe."

By now, I've climbed out and I'm looking around and I still don't see any smoke, white or black. "What are you…"

Bouncer waves his hand again. He mouths, "Shut up. I'll handle this."

Then he says to Kingsbury, "Car smoking like that pal, it's got engine trouble. You said it's in good shape. You trying to pull something?" Then he looks at me, winks, and flashes a big, shit-eating grin.

Kingsbury is looking around now, definitely off balance and getting confused. Bouncer is making little coughing noises, saying "…probably a head gasket, yeah, head gasket." I'm still looking for the smoke, when Bouncer goes on, "If it's a head gasket, I can fix that. I'll give you two hundred for it, as is. You don't have to take it, but I wouldn't drive it anywhere until you get that fixed. Could crack your block and then you got nothing but a junkyard in your future."

Kingsbury starts nervously waving his cane back and forth and looking like he just wants to get out of there, when I finally get into the act. "Hey, Bouncer. Back outa this. I can handle this myself," I say. "How 'bout you go back inside huh? Order us a round. I'll pop for it when I get there. I'll take it from here."

Bouncer's happy face falls, but he doesn't argue. "Okay, suit yourself, Stan. Just trying to help." Then he rolls his wandering eye, turns and slumps back toward Mariano's.

Cris Hammond

Half hour later I'm looking at a fresh JD and sitting next to a pouting Sonny Bouncer. "So, you bought it, huh?" he says, stirring his drink with his finger.

"Yeah, I did. It's a sweet running little truck, and it doesn't smoke either."

"How's he gonna know that, Stan? He can't see it. Jesus man, I had him going there. Just helping you out. Christ, what'd you end up paying him?"

"Four fifty."

"Four fifty? Are you nuts? He was only asking four. What's a matter with you?"

"Sonny, I saw you trying to rip him off; a blind guy, for Christ sake. Shit man, sometimes you got no class at all. Guy needs the money. He's blind, okay? You start pulling the wool over his eyes, tryin' to rip him off. Like he ain't got enough trouble. That kind of shit just brings bad stuff down on you. So, yeah, I paid four fifty. Makin' up for you, mostly. Anyway, it's still worth a grand, easy."

Sonny Bouncer swirls his drink a couple more times, watching the ice, and pouting. Then Sal leans across the bar and says, "Stan, you ever wonder what a blind guy's doing with a truck for sale?"

The next day is shaping up to be a nice Friday morning, so I park my new truck up the street and walk down to say 'hi' to Sal, and the only other guy in the place, Sonny damn Bouncer. He turns around when he sees me in the mirror, coming through the door. "Well, hey, it's the king of 'Let's Make a Deal.' How's that new truck, Stan?"

"It's alright. The front end could use some tightening up, but it still ain't smoking, and I stuck that turn signal back in place with some crazy glue and duct tape. I think it might be ready to sell. You watch, Sonny, I'm gonna do all right with that little truck. Oh, and look what I found under the seat." I pull a nice, green and red, snap-brim hat from my back pocket. It's one of those things made of wool that you see on Irishmen sometimes. "It's a good one too. Look at the label. Hand made in some shop up on Nob Hill."

"You paid fifty bucks more than he was asking, but that's okay, because you got a hat. You are slick, Stan. Why aren't you wearing that fifty-dollar hat?"

"Gentlemen don't wear hats indoors, right Sal?"

"That's why we have hat racks," Sal says as he pushes himself toward us on his rolling barstool.

"Plus, it doesn't actually fit. At the moment, it's too big. But Sal's got a big head. Here," I toss him the hat. "Put it against my tab."

Sal stands there looking at the hat and shaking his head. Then he turns toward the cash register, picks up a slip of paper and puts it down in front of me. "I'll knock four bucks off your tab for the hat, which is ugly as a mud fence." Then he points at a phone number jotted across the paper and says, "This guy called here last night. I think he might want to talk to you. Said his name's Carl."

A few minutes later, I've got this Carl on the phone and he asks me, did I buy a Toyota pickup from a guy named Kingsbury? "Yeah," I say, "Bought it yesterday."

"Damn!" he says. "I really wanted that truck. He showed it to me, but I just didn't act fast enough. I used to have one just like it when I got married. My son's turning sixteen in a couple days, and I wanted to buy it for him-for his birthday. Surprise him. He and I could work on it, fix it up. You know? He's a good kid but I need to spend more time with him. He'll be sixteen."

"Yeah, well, she's a sweet running little truck."

"Say, you wouldn't be willing to sell it, would you?"

"Jeez, I don't know, man. I'm kinda attached to it."

"I'll give you eight hundred bucks."

"Well, like I said, I'm pretty...."

"Nine."

"Okay, done."

"Just one thing though."

"What?"

"Can I take it to my mechanic, have it checked out? My kid and I can fix little things, but I'd hate to disappoint him with something's got real problems. You know..."

"Sure. The car's parked out front of Mariano's Lounge on Telegraph. You know where that is?"

"Yeah, I know the place, it's perfect. My mechanic's just about four blocks away. I'll take it for a short test drive around the block and stop by his shop for a quick check up. That sound okay with you?"

"That's fine. I'll be inside. Ask for Stan. When do you want to come by?"

"I'll be there in ten minutes."

I hand the phone back to Sal and turn to Bouncer, who's been listening to this whole thing and say, "You hear that? That guy's coming over to look at the truck, and if he likes it, he'll give me nine hundred bucks for it. Buyin' it for his kid. See, that's the way I like to do it, Bouncer, double my money, in one day."

"Stan, you're just a financial genius. Yes, you are. You're also about the luckiest bastard I seen in a long time."

"That ain't luck, my friend. That's karma. You do good stuff for people, you get good Karma. You tell lies and try to rip off blind guys, you get the bad Karma. See, if I'd gone along with you and tried to screw that poor blind guy, I'd be getting the bad Karma, and that truck would probably have blown up on me by now."

"Call it what you want, but I'd say you're just in the right place at the right time."

"Believe me, B, it's karma."

"Whatever you say. When's he coming over?"

"He'll be here in ten minutes."

A half hour later we're still sitting there. Sal's just poured us a fresh round and wandered off into the back room and I'm beginning to think this car guy's a flake when the door is shoved open and a stringy looking fella in a pair of ragged coveralls comes in. He sees us sitting at the bar, so he walks over and sticks out his hand. "Hi," he says. "I'm Carl. Lookin' for Stan, the guy with the truck for sale?"

"That's me," I say and take his hand. For a second I think we're going to have one of those goddamn squeezing contests, but then he relaxes his grip and smiles. I force a grin in return and say, "It's right outside."

"Yeah, I saw it coming in. So, can I take it for a quick spin? Check it out? I'll run it by my mechanic for a look, and if all's good, we have a deal. I'll stop by the bank on the way back and get your money for you."

"Sounds good, Carl. Here," I toss him the keys. "Knock yourself out."

He catches them, weighs them in his palm for a second and heads for the door. "Be right back," he says as the door closes behind him.

"That the guy's gonna pay nine hundred?" Sonny Bouncer says.

"You heard him. If it checks out, it looks like we'll have us a deal."

"I only want the best for you, Stan. But if it works out, you are one lucky son of a bitch."

"Luck's got nothing to do with it. Hey Sal, guess what."

Sal's just coming in from the back room with a couple of six packs dangling from his fingers. He shoves them into the ice and, without looking up, says, "Luck's got nothing to do with what?"

"I just sold that truck."

Now he's looking at me. "No shit? To that guy who called? That was quick."

"Yeah, man, nine hundred bucks. Not bad for a day's work, huh?"

"That's great. You're rich! You can take a vacation. Go on a world cruise or something."

"I only paid four-fifty for it. That's like, a hundred percent return, in just two days. I keep investing like that and I'll be set."

"Yeah, you're a genius. Hey, I hate to bring this up Stan, but this might be a good time. Uh, you got a bit of a tab running here. Want to lay something on the bar, since you're so flush?"

"I'll be happy to Sal, my friend. Just as soon as the guy comes back with the money."

"You ain't got the money?"

"Not yet."

"I hate to pop your bubble, Stan, but you ain't got the money, you ain't sold the truck."

"I'll get it. The guy's just taking it to his mechanic for a checkup. It's fine. He'll be back in an hour with the dough."

"You gave him the truck?"

"Yeah, to have it checked out, by his mechanic."

"So, you ain't got the money, and you ain't got the truck either?"

"He don't need the truck or the money," Bouncer says. "He's got his karma."

Three hours and two drinks later, I'm wondering about my goddamn karma. "Hey Sal, you know of any garages or mechanics around here? Like four blocks from here?"

"He stole your truck, Stan."

"You don't know that. It might still be at the garage, being checked out."

Sonny Bouncer pipes in, "It's a four banger Toyota pickup. It don't take three hours to check out a wreck like that. He's halfway to L.A. by now."

"Shit. Hand me the phone. I'm calling him. Find out what the hell's going on."

The phone only rings twice before a man growls in my ear, "Hello, Atlas Auto Wreckers, what can we do for you?"

"Atlas Auto Wreckers? Who is Atlas Auto Wreckers?"

"Who wants to know?"

"Me. I want to talk to Carl."

"This is Carl. You the guy had the pickup?"

"Goddamn right I am. Where's my truck?"

"It's not your truck. It's mine. Kingsbury owed me money and he promised the truck to me to settle up."

"That's bullshit. I bought it from him. I have the pink slip. It's my truck and I want it back, now! Understand?"

"Uh-uh. It's mine. And I have the pink, signed by Billy Kingsbury himself. You left it in the glove box."

"Oh shit! I left it -?"

"Yup. Thanks."

"But god dammit, I bought it from the son of a bitch yesterday."

"You got screwed, pal."

"What the hell are you talking about?"

"I'm telling you, he signed a note giving me the car, to pay off what he owed me. But then he took off with it. I heard from a couple used car guys I know that he was taking it around, trying to sell it. They wouldn't touch it. I tracked him to you, and retrieved my car."

"That's bullshit. How could a blind guy take his car around town, showing it to used car dealers?"

"That would be hard, for a blind guy. But Billy Kingsbury, he ain't blind."

"He's not?"

"Nope. He plays blind sometimes. When it suits him."

"But he had a cane."

"He stole it, from a blind guy."

"Son of a bitch!"

"You got that right. He's a slippery little bastard. And he ripped you off. But I'll tell you what. You find him, turn him upside down and see what falls out of his pockets. If he's short your four fifty, bring him around to me. I'll make up the difference, and bump you a hundred for your trouble."

"So, what happens to him?"

"That's my business, pal. Your beef is with Kingsbury. So is mine."

Now, Sal and Bouncer are both looking at me sitting here, staring into a dead phone, saying, "Ho-ly shit." Sal slowly reaches over and takes the receiver from my hand and hangs it up. Then he says, "Did I hear you say that that blind guy wasn't blind after all?"

"That's right."

"It was a con?" Now Bouncer is snickering into his drink.

"Yeah, fine. You guys laugh all you want. But I'm out four hundred fifty bucks."

"Whoa, Stan," Bouncer says, "I ain't laughing at you. I'm just a bit confused by the whole Karma thing. Is this the good Karma you been talkin' about? Payin' you back? Or the bad one? Just enlighten me will ya, Oh Wise One?"

"You know, you're on thin ice Bouncer. I'm in no mood right now for this shit. We're gonna go find Blind Billy Kingsbury and get my money back. Out of his hide if we have to."

"We? I seem to remember you telling me to back off. Now it's we?"

"Well, this particular job might require somebody with a car. You got one, piece of shit that it is, but it'll have to do. So, your services would be appreciated, if you're not too busy and you wouldn't mind a little kick ass adventure this afternoon."

"You make it sound like fun. You got any idea where we gonna start looking for this asshole?"

"Yeah, I do. Sal, give me that hat back."

The label in the hat says it was custom made at La Maison Chapeaux Blanc, and gives an address up on Nob Hill in San Francisco. We don't bother looking for a parking place around there. There hasn't been a spot on the street for anything that wasn't made in Germany for about fifteen years. So, Bouncer drops me off and proceeds to lay a smoke screen around the block while I push my way into the precious little hat shop.

If one part of Kingsbury's life put him dodging guys who tossed raw meat to Pit Bulls in wrecking yards, La Maison Chapeaux Blanc was the part where his sweet old auntie Bea baked him cookies and petit fours. The shop is filled with handmade hats for men and women. The ones for men all look like Humphrey Bogart or John Wayne should be wearing them. The women's section looks like the aftermath of an explosion in a lace factory that was full of peacocks at the time.

The look she gives me when I come through the door is saying, "You go 'round the back," until she sees the handmade hat sliding down around my ears. The old doll, who's embroidered name tag says, Maryanne, works up a smile and says, "Oh, my goodness. That looks like one of our "Quiet American, John Houston" caps. My sister, Lillian, made that one for a gentleman from Carmel, but, well…. Are you here to have it sized? We can take it in for you. Have it ready in a week."

"Tell the truth, um, Maryanne, it isn't mine. I found it, on the street, over in Oakland. I saw your label and thought maybe you could help me find its owner. I'd really like to return it to the guy. I'm sure he's just sick about losing it."

"Oh, well, the gentleman who ordered it, well, he found it not to his liking. So, he didn't take it in the end. Rather a difficult man as I recall."

"How dreadful, Maryanne. I bet Lillian must have been crushed."

"Well, not everyone is as nice a gentleman as you, um, Mr.?"

"Oh, please, call me Stan."

Now, she's beaming and starting to get a little flushed. "I wonder, Maryanne, if you could help me find the lucky fella who ended up with it? I just wouldn't feel right if I didn't try to get it back to him."

"Well, actually, nobody bought it, at least, not from us. We discontinued the Houston line a while back. I think that one, and a number of others, were part of a donation we made to the auction at the opening gala of the opera last season. Raising funds for the homeless you see. We donate every year."

"You mean somebody who was at the opening of the Opera last year might have bought this hat there?" This is not sounding like Billy Kingsbury.

"Oh no. Oh my no. We donated the chapeaux's to the auction as a lot. The money they raised went to the shelters, and the headwear went to the Salvation Army. They sell them in their shops, and raise even more. It's a wonderful event. We do it every year."

Okay, now we're getting back into Kingsbury land. "I see. So the guy who lost the hat might have bought it in one of those Salvation Army shops, huh?"

"I would think so, yes."

"You got any idea which shops ended up with the hats, or chapeaus?"

"You say you found it in Oakland?"

The good citizens of Nob Hill must be thinking it is just the afternoon fog coming in through the Golden Gate that's laying a pall over their neighborhood as Sonny Bouncer's well-worn Chevy leaves a layer of pollution in its wake as we head back across the Bay. "We're going back to Oakland," I say. "Going to the Salvation Army store on," I check my notes. "Webster and Oak." Then I make the mistake of saying, "And step on it!" which he does and promptly-stalls the piece of junk. So, we're popping the clutch all the way down California Street to get it started again.

It's a half hour before we pull up in front of the Salvation Army store in East Oakland. "This looks more like our boy's territory, B. You wanna take a chance on turning this thing off and coming in with me, or what?"

"I'll wait here. What are you gonna do in there?"

"I'm just gonna see if anyone remembers the hat. Might get lucky. It's ugly enough. If anyone does, at least we might have the right neighborhood."

It only took me a few minutes to find that nobody working in the place had been there for more than a couple months. And since they sold clothes by the pound, nobody gave a shit about the hat. So, I was not feeling all that positive when I climbed back into the Chevy. But then Bouncer's showing me that grin of his, and he says, "Stan, I think today is your day to buy a lotto ticket. You can't lose."

"Yeah, well I just did in there, big time."

"While you were playing Dick Tracy, your man Sonny here was on stake-out. Check out that coffee shop across the street."

"What."

"Wait for it…. There," Sonny points at the guy coming out of the shop. He has a cup of coffee in one hand and is stirring it with the other. Under his arm, he's got a white cane. He even has a pair of sunglasses pushed up on his head.

"Christ! It's him," I say. "That son of a bitch is walking around, spending my money like a goddamn sailor."

"What do you want to do?"

"Okay, I gave him cash, right. I'm guessing he's still got it on him, what's left of it. So, let's not spook him."

"There he goes."

"Alright, drive around the corner. Go on past him up to the end of the block. We'll wait 'til he gets close, then I'll get out, have a talk with him."

We chug past without raising a flutter from the not-so-blind Billy Kingsbury. I watch him in the side mirror as he comes closer, sipping his coffee and twirling his cane. When he's past a point where he could run, I step out of the car, cross the sidewalk and get real interested in the front window of a hardware store. In the reflection, I'm watching him coming. It takes him a few moments to recognize me, but when he does, he acts quick. The coffees tossed, the glasses are down, the white cane is in the proper position and he's starting to turn around.

"Hey! Hey Billy," I call out. "Is that you?" He slows, but doesn't stop. So, I trot up behind him. "Hey, it's Billy, right? It's me, Stan. I bought your truck yesterday." I put a hand on his shoulder and turn him around.

"Man, I'm loving that truck my friend. She's a sweetheart. All I can say is Thanks!"

He's rolling his head around, turning his ear toward me and waving the cane. I have to admit, he makes a very convincing blind guy. He says, "Oh, is that you? I didn't recognize your voice at first. Glad you like it. Look, I gotta go. Good luck with it."

He tries to walk around me, but I push the cane aside. "Hey Billy, wait up. You know, speakin' of luck, I been thinking lately that luck ain't just luck. I'm thinking it's more like karma. You know what karma is?"

"No, and I really gotta go, so maybe some other time, huh?"

"Where you going? Maybe me and Bouncer, you remember Bouncer, he's sittin' right there in the car by the way, maybe we can give you a ride."

"Thanks, but I'll walk."

"Where you going?"

"Just, you know, some errands."

"Hop in. We'll drive you."

"No, really, I -."

"I said, get in the car."

"Anywhere around here is good," Billy says. He's acting more and more nervous, sweating and fidgeting with his cane while Bouncer and me got him squeezed between us in the front seat.

I put my arm around his shoulders. They're boney and sharp. He smells of old cigarettes and gin. I pull him close and talk into his ear. "Any place in particular? I want to do right by you, Billy, since you gave me such a good deal on that truck." I'm watching a bead of sweat dribble down his temple, and I just have to smile. "You look hot, man. Want me to roll down a window?"

"Just let me out at the store. Up there on the corner." He starts to point with his cane, but then lets it slip down between his knees.

"That one? Right there?"

"Yeah."

"Wow, I mighta missed it. Hey Bouncer, pull over 'round the corner. Me and Billy are going to the store."

The car slows, pulls around the corner, and stops just past a fire hydrant. Billy lunges for the door, but I ain't budging. "Hey, Billy, did I tell you the good news? Seems a guy, I think his name's Carl, right Bouncer?" Bouncer is smiling almost too much to nod. "This Carl's gonna give me nine hundred bucks for the truck. How about that? Sold it. In just one day, and I double my money. Sweet, huh?"

Billy stops struggling for a second and turns his sunglasses at me. "Nine hundred?" he says. "Carl?"

"Yup. He's got the truck right now. Taking it for a test drive, then to his mechanic. If it checks out, he'll be back with the money. It'll check out fine, right?"

"He took the truck?"

"Sure. Why not?"

"No reason. Look, I better get going," then he makes another dive for the door handle. "Good luck with it," he says.

"Hey, like I said, it ain't luck. It's karma. You understand karma, Billy?" Now he's trying to climb over me. Maybe he thinks he's going out through the window. "Whoa, there Billy. I'll come with you and we'll talk some more about karma. Bouncer, you wait here. Keep the motor running. Maybe we'll take Billy for a ride, later."

I climb out, turn around and pull Mr. Kingsbury out of the car by his collar. He starts toward the corner, heading for the store, but I turn him around and take him down an overgrown, garbage strewn, dirt pathway that leads to the alley in the back.

Ten minutes later, I'm back in the car. "That didn't take long," says Sonny B. "Where's Kingsbury? Should I call an ambulance?"

"No, he saw the light." I flash a roll of twenties at him, "Four hundred eighteen dollars and eighty-six cents. Only thirty bucks short." I guess I can live with a thirty-dollar Stupid tax."

"You just gonna let him get away with it?"

"What am I gonna do? Bust his balls? Ain't worth it to tarnish my karma for a lousy thirty bucks. He appreciates that, too. Believe you me."

"Oh? So, Blind Billy is a big believer in karma now, huh?"

"Yeah, I explained it to him. I told him, 'You do good things for people, like giving me my money back, you get good karma, and then good things will happen to you. You do bad things, like, you don't give me my money back, you're gonna have bad karma. That means, bad shit's gonna happen to you, such as, I might break you like a shotgun, throw your ass in the trunk of Bouncer's car and take you out to Atlas Auto Wrecking, where Carl is waiting to talk to you, about your karma.

Low Ray

Low Ray was down to one leg again, and if I had any sense, I would have shut my mouth and kept on walking. But, when I saw him that morning, leaning against the trashcan down on 12th Street, it was obvious he was, once again, shy one flipper. He'd lost it more than once. The first time was in Viet Nam, and the way he tells it, "It hurt like hell." Since then, he'd lost quite a few legs, so many, in fact, that he'd started naming them. The latest one was Darlene, because it was too short and he had to put a high-heeled shoe on it so he could walk straight.

"Hey Ray, how's it going?" I asked, planning to walk on by.

"Oh great," he said. "Never better. Just great…fucking great." He threw me a look as he slid down the trashcan and bounced his backside on to the sidewalk.

"Um, did you lose your leg again?" I asked him.

"No, I'm having it re-chromed and polished so it'll go with my tux when I'm out dancing at the Ritz fucking Carlson." He looked at me and slapped his empty pants leg against the garbage can

"Sorry," I said. "What happened? Did you leave it somewhere? Can I – "

"Couple of goddamn roofers took it," he said.

"Roofers?"

"Couple of goddamn roofers, in from Montana. Named Ritchie James and Jimmy James, they said. We were playing cards down by the park and they brought out some beer and this jug of Early Times. Next thing I know, I'm waking up under the bench and Darlene and the roofers are gone. Goddamn roofers stole her. That be some low-down shit, man."

"Why would anyone steal a false leg?" I asked him.

"Hell, they can sell 'em to one-legged guys, fool. Where do you think I got that one?"

"I don't know. I thought you got it from the VA. Being as how you're a vet and all."

"Are you kidding?" he said. "I'm still on the goddamn waiting list to replace the one I lost three years ago."

"You bought Darlene off the street?"

"Yeah, man, eighty bucks," he said. "And it was crap too. It was off a white guy or something. Fucking wrong color, all pink and shit. And wearing that goddamn spikey heel shoe was a pain in the ass."

"Yeah, that never looked very comfortable."

"No shit, man. Hurt like hell," he said. "I think it screwed up my back."

"What are you gonna do? Where do you go to get a leg?"

He gave me a look from under his eyebrows and said, "Ikea."

"Look, smart ass," I said. "You want me to help you out or what? How about a crutch? You want me to go get you a crutch or something?"

Low Ray looked at me for a minute, his eyes drilling into mine. Then he said, "How about you get me a baseball bat and you and me go looking for Ritchie and Jimmy James. Get that bitch, Darlene, back."

"You know where they are?"

"No, but I know what they're driving."

So now we're cruising around town in Ray's rambling old septic tank of a van, "Low Ray and The Bomber – Pest Eradicators" emblazoned on the sides, looking for a couple of roofers driving a blue Pontiac with Montana plates.

When Ray was sober, he and his cousin, The Bomber, had a small business exterminating household pests. It wasn't a business they enjoyed or engaged in to any extent. But they had their own van with their names on the sides and the tools of the rat catching trade rolling around in the back. In that part of town, between the local rats, skunks, and roaches, there was enough business to keep them off welfare and on back door terms with most of the flop-houses, diners and greasy spoons in the neighborhood.

Unfortunately for Ray, the Bomber was on a short vacation that weekend, a guest of the county, across the Bay in San Francisco. He'd gotten a little frisky and pulled three nights, on a D and D charge. Bomber had a fondness for "drunk and disorderly." That's why Low Ray was hopping around town, playing cards and drinking with strangers, and why I got stuck with the job of helping him track down two roofers, and the high heel wearing Darlene. When I stepped on the brakes in that roach wagon, and heard the metal grinding on metal, I told myself for the hundredth time, "Get yourself a library card Stan, and stay off the streets."

"Hey Stan, look over there. I think that's them." Ray was pointing at two guys coming out of a liquor store.

"That ain't them," I said.

"No, I think it's them. Look, they're getting in that Pontiac."

"That's not a Pontiac, Ray. It's a goddamn Toyota."

"But, it's blue. That's them Stan. I recognize 'em."

"God dammit, that's Tommy Chan and his brother, Mel. They sure as hell ain't no roofers from Montana, and they ain't got but four legs between the two of 'em, Ray. I counted."

"Looks like the guys..."

"Ray, did you make up the whole roofer story? Are you going bat-shit on me here?" I looked over at him and noticed he'd turned a bit sheepish and was rubbing his stump. I gave him a serious look, "Ray? Where's Darlene? Just tell me, Ray."

"Stole. Someone stole her," he said.

"Did you maybe, misplace it somewhere? Were there ever any roofers?"

"They was roofers! Goddamn roofers. I'm telling ya. We was playing cards and they brought out this jug. Told me it was Early Times, but I think it was shine or some shit they cooked up, man. Some nasty shit, too. I lost about a day and a half." He looked out the window and said, "Wouldn't'a happened if The Bomber was there."

"Okay, look, it's time we re-examined our plan." I smelled burning brakes as I slowed down, turned onto Oak Street and headed for the park. "And, if you don't mind me saying so Ray, the stench in this van of yours is melting the wax in my ears. I gotta get some air." I looked across at Ray in time to see him popping open a beer. "Where the hell'd you get that?"

"Under the seat. Want one?"

"Not here, Ray. Christ, put it down before a cop sees us and we both end up in the shit." He took a long pull before settling the can between the seats.

"We're going down to the park," I said. "If I can hold my breath that long. Jesus Ray, what the hell is making that stink?"

"It's the bodies, in the back. If Bomber was here, he'd'a got rid of them. They start to go off after a few days, but I don't notice it so much anymore."

I reached out my hand. "Give me a beer. Now! Christ, long as I'm driving a van full of dead bodies, I might as well be drinking while I'm at it." As Ray put a warm beer in my hand I looked at him, "They're rats, right?"

"Yeah, mostly."

"Mostly? What the hell else? There ain't no dogs back there are there? I couldn't stand if there was a dead dog back there."

"No dogs, or cats, that I know of. They's mostly rats and mice, maybe a gopher or a skunk, but probably not a skunk. You'd know it if there was a skunk."

I turned and looked into the back of the van and as my eyes adjusted to the darkness, they focused on what I recognized as a lumpy pile of black trash bags, sliding around on the floor. It was too dark, thankfully, to see if they were leaking. I pulled the van into the parking lot and drove to the dumpsters in the back. "Get out, Ray, we're unloading this shit. Now!" Then I remembered he had only one leg and he wouldn't be any help disposing of fifty pounds of dead rodents.

"We can't just dump them, Stan," he said, and tossed his empty can out the window. "It ain't right. We gotta dispose of the carcasses according to the rules, or we could lose our license," he said. I heard the 'fst-pop' of another beer can opening.

"The rules? There's rules for getting rid of dead rats?"

"Shit yeah. There's rules for everything. Why do you think I still got 'em?"

"I was wondering that."

"Waiting for The Bomber to get out. He knows the rules."

"Kinda seems to me the first rule would be to wait until dark, then heave 'em in the dumpster," I said. "Christ, they stink."

"Oh no. You can't do that, man. They're full of poison. You just dump 'em and some dog or cat will come along and chow down and then you got a dead dog on your conscience."

"Shit, I guess you're right. So how do we get rid of them?"

"They gotta be incinerated. But we gotta wait until the Bomber gets out. He's got the license. They're pretty sticky about that."

"Well, hell, we got the van, with the "Pest Eradicators" on it. Ain't that good enough?"

"No, they need to see the license. Plus, we gotta pay a fee. We have to wait for Bomber. Want another beer?"

"Yeah shit, give me a beer. Gotta get something out of this crummy day." I looked at him, fumbling around under the seat again. "How can you just sit there, drinking beer and breathing this stinking shit-rot air?"

"You're right." He tossed me a beer and said, "We oughta get outta here. Hey, you hungry?"

"Hungry? Are you serious?

"'Cause I got some cheese in the back. We could make a sandwich."

"Now I'm really gonna be sick. Jesus, I'm gonna go sit under a tree. You can stay in here if you want," I said and climbed out of the van and headed across the lawn to a bench.

Ray called after me, "Hey, I'm sitting here, brother, because I only got one fucking leg 'cause I lost the other one in Nam, man. Fighting for your freedoms!"

He had me there. If I'd only walked on past him, sitting on his ass by the trashcan, he'd be lounging in the sun, and I'd be down at the library, checking out a book with my new library card. But no, I had to take pity on the bum.

I turned around and headed back to the truck. "Okay, what do you want me to do? And don't mention cheese again."

Ray tossed another empty out the window and popped a fresh one. "Just drive me down to Little D's diner. Donny owes me for a job and he'll float us lunch. I'll stand you a hamburger and then you can split."

"What about your leg? You still only got one leg, man."

"There's a mission, over Frisco. Donny knows the number. Sometimes they got legs and shit. They give away shoes, man, one at a time."

"You got legs there before?"

"Couple times. They ain't the best, but what the hell?"

"Alright, look. We'll go see Donny. We'll get the number and call the place. If they have a leg, I'll drive you over to get it. Then we're done. I ain't wasting any more of my life driving around in this stinking van, looking for a couple of goddamn roofers who might just be on their way back to Mars anyway."

"Hey man, they're real. They took Darlene, man, and if I find them, they gonna pay." And another empty beer can sailed out the window.

The smell of cooking hamburgers and frying bacon greeted me as I pushed through the back door of Little D's. Donny turned from the griddle when he heard the door open. "Stan? What are you coming in the back for? Margaret's over it, man. She ain't mad at you anymore. You can come in the front."

"Glad to hear it, D. But, I got Low Ray out back, in his van. Figured you wouldn't want him mingling with the customers."

"You got that right. Christ, I can smell him from here."

"Might be me. I been sitting in that damn van with him for an hour."

Donny leaned toward me and took a sniff. Then he wrinkled his nose. "Yeah, it's you," he said. "I can guess why he's here."

"He says he did a job for you a couple days back, and you might stand us some burgers."

"Really? That's what he wants?"

"Well, he's also lost his leg again."

"That's what he said?"

"Yeah. He says you know of a place in Frisco where he might get him another one."

"Yeah, matter of fact, I do," he turned and laid a slab of cheese on one of the burgers. Then he yelled through the pass-through to the diner, "Hey Margaret, was that one or two cheese?"

"No cheese, Donny," Margaret yelled back.

"Ah shit," he said, and started trying to scrape the melting cheese off the meat. "God dammit. Shit." Then he turned to me. "Looks like I'm cooking an extra cheese burger. You want it?"

"Thanks Donny, but I kinda lost my appetite lately."

"Yeah, Low Ray will do that to you." He tossed a new burger on the fire and set some buns on the heat. "So, he's lost his leg again, huh?"

"Didn't lose it, D. It was stolen. Couple roofers got him drunk and stole it."

"Really? Stolen, huh? Couple roofers?"

"Yeah, from Montana, he said."

"Montana? Ha! That's Ray all right. Well they don't call him Low Ray 'cause he's got a high I.Q." Donny poked at the meat again. "He thinks I might know where he can get a leg, huh?"

"You're the first one he thought of."

"Does he care what color it is?"

"Last one didn't match. I'm guessing he's open."

Donny nodded his head. "Yup. I think I know where there's one." He flipped the new burger and grabbed a couple plates.

"He said there's a Mission you might know of."

"Oh, he don't have to go to no Mission."

Margaret appeared at the pass through and yelled, "How're those burgers, D?" Then she saw me standing behind Donny, did a half turn, batted her eyes and said, "Well, hey Stan, how long you been back there, sweetie? You know, Big Guy, you're allowed in the front door again. I forgive you." She tossed some hair and said, "I ain't mad no more. Fact, I kinda miss ya." Then she pushed her breasts together, checked her cleavage and went back to work.

Donny smiled and said, "Jesus, Stan, I'd say you're more than forgiven. I think I just saw a pretty solid offer bouncing off Margaret just then."

"Later D," I said. "The leg. We gotta get us a leg. You know where we can get one?"

"Yeah."

"Where?"

"Right there." He turned and pointed his spatula at the big two-door refrigerator standing in the corner.

"In there? You got a leg in the fridge?"

"Not the fridge, fool. Down there," he pointed toward the floor in the corner.

I was looking at a big air vent, down along the baseboard in the corner next to the fridge. "In there?" I asked.

Then Donny tapped me on the shoulder and handed me a screwdriver. "Open it up," he said.

There was one screw holding the hatch in place. When I loosened it, the door fell into my hands. I pushed it aside, and saw a dirt-covered, garbage-strewn, crawl space that went back into darkness under the floor and below the walls of the building next door.

I didn't see it at first. But then, as my eyes adjusted to the dark, I saw it lying in the dirt, a high-heeled shoe, attached to a leg that disappeared back into the shadows.

Donny was sliding burgers onto plates and tossing bits of lettuce and tomatoes around them. He turned and said, "I called Ray and The Bomber a few days ago to come down and deal with my rats. The idiots showed up just at lunchtime and parked that putrid stink wagon right in front. Then they marched through the dining room carrying a bunch of traps and boxes, with 'Danger! Rat Poison,' printed all over them, complete with skulls and crossbones. They told Margaret, and everyone else in the place, that they're here to kill the rats. The customers just loved it."

He tossed the plates onto the pass-through window. "They're up Margaret!" he yelled, then turned back to me. "You know, those two, I tell ya, if brains were dynamite, the two of them together couldn't work up a good sneeze."

"Jesus," I said. "I'm starting to wonder how they ever outwitted any rats."

"Yeah, well, they ain't at the top of the profession," he said, then went on. "So, I kicked them out and told them to get that stinking truck out from in front of my place. Then, like a fool, I told them to come back at closing time, around nine o'clock, park in the alley and I'd let them in the back door."

"They were both more than half-lit when they showed up," he said. "Christ, The Bomber's breath would'a killed any poor rat he happened to come face to face with. But at least they were here, so I showed them the crawl space, and told them to just pull the door closed when they left. It'd lock automatically behind them. Simple, right?"

"So, they're supposed to lay the traps and poison, and come back in a few days for the bodies?" I asked.

"Yup. I come in the next morning and the fridge has been raided. There are empties all over the kitchen and there's Darlene, sticking out of the goddamn crawl space. From the smell, I thought the fool had poisoned himself and was dead in there."

"Darlene was sticking out of the hole?" I asked.

"Yeah, I figured Ray, being the little one, was the guy who climbed down under the floors and laid the traps. While he was down there, The Bomber musta started looking around the kitchen and found my stash of Johnny Walker that used to be up on that shelf over there. By the time Ray crawls out, Bomber is blasted and Ray, not bothering to re-attach Darlene, goes to work trying to catch up."

"Uh-oh."

"Yeah, right. During the party, they also ate all my ice cream and a whole tray of meatloaf."

"Uh-huh, I'm getting the picture."

"I'm guessing they were opening my last bottle of Red Label when something spooked them and they took off in a hurry. The Bomber probably just picked Ray up and hauled him out to the van. They were so drunk they didn't close the trap door or even notice they were short one leg."

"Now, that all may sound very logical to you Donny, but you have left out the part about the roofers," I said. "Those dirty, rotten, thieving scoundrel roofers."

Donny looked at me for a second and said, "Brother, you been breathing the same air as Low Ray for too long. There weren't no roofers."

"Shit, I been carting that idiot all over town, looking for those goddamn roofers, and that leg. Goddamn thing's been down there the whole time. Now he's sitting out in the alley, hoping to get a free hamburger and a ride to Frisco to get a new leg."

"You're a good man, Stan. Bit of a fool, but a good hearted one."

"Did they ever get around to catching any rats?"

"Well, I haven't crawled up in there to see, but I'm doubtful."

We both turned when we heard a bump and a rustling from the back door. It swung open and Low Ray fell into the room in an almost visible cloud of putrescence.

"Well, look who's here," I said.

Ray scowled, and sat himself up against the wall. His voice came out with the force of a wheezing cigar smoker when he said, "What the hell's going on, you guys? I'm hungry, Donny. Stan, we gotta get going. Get me a new leg."

Donny looked down at him, shook his head and said, "Jesus, Ray, Stan's been telling me how those roofers stole your leg."

"Yeah, the bastards."

"You know, they were in here 'bout an hour ago. Looking for you. Big guys."

"No shit? Did they have my leg?"

"No, they said they were looking for you because you stole a whole bunch of their tools. They want their stuff back, Ray. Boy, are they pissed."

"I didn't steal nothing of theirs, man. They stole my leg. Got me drunk."

"Only time they mentioned your leg was when they said that when they find you they're gonna rip that som' bitch off you and whip your ass with it."

Ray dragged his good leg around, looked up and whined, "They said that?"

Margaret walked by the pass-through window and my head spun around. I looked into the restaurant and bumped Donny on the arm, pointed toward the front and said, "Shit, Donny, is that them? Those two guys that just came in? Christ, they're huge."

Donny spun around, looked through the window and said, "Holy shit, that's them. Christ, it looks like they're coming back here."

"Is that a baseball bat that one guy's carrying?"

Ray starts scrambling to get up. I turn to him, "Quick, Ray, hide! Get your ass into the crawl space. Hide! They're coming." Ray sat for a second, staring up at me, until I barked, "Move!"

He threw himself through the hole and slithered into the dark, his one leg wiggling behind him like the tail of a giant rat. I slammed the vent in place and Donny took his screwdriver, turned the screw and fastened it shut.

Then I heard Ray say, "Hey you guys, look, look. I found it."

I said, "Shut up, fool! They'll hear you." Then I turned to Donny and said, "What do we do if they come back here? They really look pissed."

Donny smiled and said, "Man, I don't know. What if they start swinging that bat around?"

"Hey, you guys," Ray kicked the vent.

Donny turned back to the vent and called, "Keep your mouth shut Ray. Stay quiet down there. The roofers are coming."

Cris Hammond

Stan's Mime

I never had much use for mimes. I wouldn't give two farts for one, to tell the truth. They annoy me. I sat next to one on a bus one time, all the way up from L.A. I thought the poor guy was just a mute. He kept knocking me on the shoulder, pointing at stuff out the window and then making all kinds of strange faces and hand signs. I put up with it as far as Salinas, then I pretended to fall asleep.

At the Greyhound station in Oakland, we're getting off the bus and this mute hands me a business card. He points at his phone number in Oakland. A phone number? What's this bum gonna do if I phone him up? Tap out Morse code? Then I look again and I get it. It says he's a professional fucking mime, available for parties.

Still, to be fair, there are a lot of guys out there who would benefit by not talking. Judges oughta be sentencing some guys I know to 90 days of mime school, just for the crime of running their mouth.

So, last week, when I saw that goddamn mime and the Easter Bunny, going at it on the sidewalk outside the Taco Bell, I was kinda amused. "Whup ass boys." I said to myself. "Let the best weirdo win." But then a damn parrot jumps up and starts screaming. The little thing was squawking and hollering obscenities in three languages. It was drawing a crowd.

There I was, watching this six-foot Easter Bunny kicking a guy in white face on the ground, and swatting at the parrot with a newspaper. So, being me, I stepped in. I grabbed the bunny by his ears and pulled him off the guy. Then this idiot in the bunny suit spins around and takes a swing at me. Which forced me to duck into my crouch and stomp on his foot a couple times, which sent him hopping off down the street.

I'd seen that bunny hanging around the block before. He'd laid claim to the corner by the ATM for his panhandling business. Normally I don't pay any mind to those guys, but I thought this one, using the Easter Bunny rig, basket and all, was setting a bad example for the local kids. So, I didn't mind being handed an excuse to send him on his way.

Now, I'm staring at this clown who looks like a pile of dirty laundry with his face painted all white, sitting on the sidewalk, getting blood all over the place. His nose is spouting and he's got a good-sized cut over his eye. He needs help. Plus, the bird is walking around in circles at his feet, bobbing his head and rolling his eyes. They make a pretty pathetic pair, him sniffling and the bird, mumbling, twisting his head around and rolling his eyes.

So, I pull that damn mime up and walk him down the block to Mariano's, where I know Sal's got a first aid kit. The bird rides along on his shoulder and nibbles at his ear.

"Here's the rules, Stan." Sal's got his arms folded on his belly. "The mime can stay, but get that filthy bird outta here!" Sal's not in one of his better moods.

"Come on Sal, it's kinda cute. And it's trained. Watch." I pick up a peanut from the bowl and toss it down the bar. "Fetch," I say. The ornery thing looks at me and says something that sounds a lot like "Bite me."

"Let's just forget the bird for a minute, Sal. This guy needs a Band-Aide or something. You got a first aid kit handy? Some ice?"

"Shit, now he's bleeding on the bar." Sal grabs a handful of napkins and tosses them across to the injured mime, who wads them up, shoves them against his face and drips blood across the room to the corner where he sits on the floor. "Why'd you bring him here, Stan? What the hell happened?"

"The Easter Bunny was beating the shit out of him, just up the block."

"The Easter Bunny?"

"Yeah."

"I don't like that bunny. He's a mean son of a bitch."

"No shit. Mimes can be a pain in the ass, but hell, that goddamn bunny, he was way outta line."

"I wonder what started it?" Sal asks.

"No idea."

"Gee Stan, you think it was something he said?"

I'm just getting the blood cleaned up when Sonny Bouncer comes through the door. He lays his one good eye on the mime and from deep in his chest rumbles, "What's going on in here. There is one pissed off bunny rabbit out there. Big som' bitch. And, Sal, there's blood on the sidewalk out front, leading in here. It's on the door too. What the hell's going on?"

Sal puts his hands on his hips, "Stan here, our own Captain America, stomped on the bunny's toes a few times."

"I saw he was limping a bit. Cussing too." Sonny turns to me. "You did that? What the hell you got against the Easter Bunny?"

"He was kicking the shit out of the mime."

He points into the corner and says, "That one?"

"Yeah."

"And you thought that was a bad idea?"

"It's complicated, B. But, that bunny prowling around out there makes me think I oughta lay low in here for a while, 'til things cools down. How about you stand us a round, and I'll tell you all about my morning."

Sonny responds quickly. "Sal, the usual's all around," he says. Then he turns to me. "So, you come around the corner and find the Easter Bunny is beatin' on some mime, and you can't resist jumping into the middle of it?"

"Yup, I saved him."

Sonny looks again at the guy sprawled in the corner, surrounded by bloody napkins. "So, you got yourself a mime. Gonna keep him?" Then he squints his good eye and says, "Hey, I seen that mime before. He's got a bird, talks, does tricks, right?"

"That's the guy. The bird's around here someplace," I say.

Sal picks up the two drinks, and glides down the bar on his rolling bar stool. He hands us our morning tea, then goes over and takes a close look at the mime on the floor. "Yeah, I heard about him from some guys in here last night. He's been doing his act around the neighborhood, picking up change. And the bird, yeah, the bird does tricks. Hangs upside down on his finger, eats sunflower seeds and shits on command. Filthy thing."

"He ain't filthy." We all turn to the mime. He's talking!

"Hey," I say. "You can talk."

"Of course, I can talk. I do talk. Just not while I'm working."

"Well, maybe you can tell me what that mess out there with the Easter Bunny was all about."

"I wish I knew. I was just standing there, doing my act, when that big asshole comes walking by... waddling by, I should say. The bottom of that bunny suit must be on springs or something, the way his tail bounces when he walks."

Sal and Sonny are gathering around while I ask him, "So, he's walking by and he just decides, out of nowhere, to start wailing on you? You didn't say something to him to piss him off?"

"I told you. I was working. Silently."

"What then? Did you fluff his aura? Does the glass wall trick? What?"

"I didn't get near him. He just suddenly turns around and yells, 'Cowboy!' or something. I don't know. Maybe the bird said something, pissed him off. He's got a pretty foul mouth sometimes."

"Filthy things," Sal says. "I told you."

"Ronald isn't filthy. He's just, he's had a rough upbringing."

"Ronald?" Sal asks. "It's called Ronald?"

Now he's got us all looking at the bird, who's busy cracking nuts down the end of the bar. The mime calls, "Ronald?" Then he makes a clucking sound, puts his finger in the air and waves it around. The bird just looks at him, like he's gone crazy."

"Tuck— oth—Ronald –tchic-tchik-tchik…" The mime is calling.

"Akk! Go to hell!" Says Ronald, and goes back to the nuts.

"I didn't teach him to say that," the mime says.

"Oh, I see," I say. "He hangs out in pool halls when you two ain't working?"

"No, he doesn't. His owner taught him to talk like that… and worse. That's why I've been taking care of him during the day."

"It ain't your bird?"

"No, he belongs to a guy who lives upstairs from me. He usually takes it with him to work, but sometimes, when he leaves it home, it screams all day and is a real problem. So, I told him I'd take the bird with me sometimes."

"You are a real prince, for a mime. Is this guy a juggler, or a unicyclist?"

"He's a wallpaper specialist."

Sal says to Sonny, "This is just getting weirder and weirder. Maybe I'll go wipe the blood off the door." He rolls back to the bar to get his rag.

Bouncer is choking on his drink, "What the hell's a wallpaper specialist? Shit, nobody uses wallpaper anymore."

"Some still do," says the mime, dabbing at the cut above his eye. "But nobody knows how, so they screw it up and they end up calling this guy. Calls himself Wally, as in, 'Wally the Wallpaper Guy.' He does it mainly to get laid. He says ninety percent of his customers are women. They're crying on the phone about their do-it-yourself job that's gone wrong. He goes over and saves the job, and them. They are very, very grateful."

"I've heard some lines before," I say. "But, 'Hey baby, just call me Wild Wally Wallpaper, I'll save you!' That's a new one."

"Ak! Oh Wally! Oh Wally!" The parrot is suddenly interested and talking. "Oh Wally. Kiss me! Akk!"

The bird has us all staring in stunned silence when the door is violently kicked open, and the enraged, wild-eyed Easter Bunny hops into the bar. He stands there for a moment, a huge, pear shaped apparition, round hips swaying, and bunny ears, lying broken and bent, on his shoulders. The mime dives onto his belly and crawls at full speed under the first table. Not fast enough to escape the eagle eyes of the giant bunny though. He extends one paw and bellows, "You, mime! I know now, it's you. Your ass is mine!" He starts pushing tables and chairs out of his way as he clears a path through the bar.

Sal's having none of this. "That's far enough bunny! Get your furry ass out of my place, or – "

"Or what? Look, I don't want any trouble from you. But I want that guy's ass." He's pointing at the mime, huddled under the table. Then he looks up and sees me. "And his ass too, while I'm at it."

Now, this hasn't got me trembling like a pup, since it's coming from a guy dressed up in a bunny suit. I've faced bigger guys, and maybe even dumber, but this was my first two-hundred-pound bunny. He was trying hard to scare me with his killer eyeball, but the blackened nose and the whiskers drawn on his cheeks just took the edge off it. I say to him, "Look, Bugs, or should I call you Thumper? This ain't your day to be a hard ass. Look, why don't you just sit down like a nice bunny, and we'll talk this out."

Then Sonny adds, "Yeah, we'll get you a nice carrot, or an egg. How 'bout we tear up some newspapers and you can make a nice nest?"

"You better just go, fella." Sal is making his way behind the bar, where he keeps the riot gear.

"Just give me the mime then, and we'll go outside and settle this. It's between him and me."

"That ain't gonna happen, Bugs. I pulled you off him once today. I ain't giving him back. He doesn't even know what the beef is."

"Hell he doesn't. He knows." Then he bends down and looks at the mime. "Don't you, you little shit. You know. You been screwing my wife!"

Sonny turns to me, raises his eyebrows, and says, "Wow, Stan, there's a Missus Bunny."

The rabbit takes a step toward Sunny, then thinks better of it and says, "What d'you guys care what happens to that god damn mime anyway? Why don't you stay the fuck out of it? It's between him and me. That's it."

"No, it's not as simple as that," I say. "You're forgetting someone."

"Who?"

"Ronald, the bird. Poor thing, he depends on that mime."

"Goddamn bird's in on it! Filthy thing, bird shit on the nightstand. Feathers in the sheets!"

"How do you know it was that bird?" Sal asks. "Coulda been any bird. None of them are house broken."

"I know it was that bird, because he said something to me that only a bird, sitting and shitting on my nightstand would know to say."

We all turn toward Ronald, who has been minding his own business, working at the nut bowl. As we stare, he seems to sense that he's become the center of attention. He cocks his head to one side and says, "Eat me. Ak!"

We look at the bunny. Sal asks, "Is that it?"

"No. But he knows what it is. He said it before." Then the bunny moves closer, bends down, puts his paws up on the bar, gets in the bird's face, adjusts his ears, and says in a squeaky, high voice, "Cowboy?... Cowboy?"

The bird rolls one eye at him, blinks, and squawks, "Ak! Giddy-up cowboy! Ak!"

"That's it!" The bunny is hopping around. "See? He even said it in my wife's voice. She screams that when she's – she's, well, in bed!"

I look at Sonny, then at Sal. They're suddenly very consumed with some patches of dust on the bar. Someone's gotta say it. I figure the bunny is already pissed at me, so, what the hell, I'm the one who asks, "Hey Bugs, how's the new wallpaper?"

He straightens up, turns on me and says, "What? How'd you know about the new wallpaper?"

"A little birdy told me."

Cris Hammond

The Dance of Venus

Have you ever watched things go from just slightly deranged to completely nut-squash crazy in the time it takes the ice to melt in your drink? It can make you wonder about where this world is headed.

It hadn't been one of my best days so far, and it wasn't even noon. It started out at 6:00 a.m., me dragging my aching carcass all the way to 150Th Avenue to go sit in polite rows on creaking folding chairs in the hiring hall for four hours watching everyone getting sent out on jobs but me. There was a time when the hiring bosses would fight to get me on a rig. Now days it seems like they're all dodging me and saying, "Send me anyone but Stan." Even Three-fingers Wilson got a job unloading paint over at Standard Brands.

That was just plain insulting, so I took off. I walked down to the cash machine for a little dough and it practically starts laughing at me, and tells me to go take a hike. So, I end up sweet talking Sal into putting my morning Jack on the tab. This doesn't bring on his brightest smile, but I'm his only customer, and he recognizes that my mood is worse than his, so he takes pity on me. And here I sit, feeling the burn of my first jolt of whiskey and wondering how this day could get any worse.

Then Venus walks in the door, and I have my answer.

Her real name is Emaleen, or Venus, depending on what day of the week it is. She was Venus on Wednesdays and Thursdays, Passion on the weekends when the big spenders came in, and Emaleen on Mondays and Tuesdays, her days off.

She wasn't hooking back then, officially. She was just dancing. Not that she didn't get offers, mind you. She was good.

She could do things on a fire pole that would stump a monkey. And the ten's and twenty's stuffed into her costume, which she made herself out of a piece of string, added up nicely by the wee hours in the morning. All of it tax-free.

Beautiful, talented, and a good earner, how could I not fall? I was in love, and I came real close to marrying her, but Sal saved me when he put down his rag one day, looked me in the eye, and said, "Stan, she doesn't even know you exist." I had to admit it was true. Venus-Passion-Emaleen had higher hopes for herself than getting tied to a semi-employed ex-trucker with gimpy hips and a bad knee. So, she broke my heart. That was a while back.

Four or five years ago, she began running around with a big Irishman I used to drink with at Mariano's called Leg Bone Delaney. Leg Bone did a little midnight auto repo gig and handled an insurance and protection scam with a guy named Windows Lariman. It wasn't a complicated business. Shop owners would start experiencing a rash of broken windows in the neighborhood. Windows and Leg Bone would show up and offer protection from such a rash, for a certain price. As long as they paid, their windows stayed put. Their territory was West Oakland, everything north of Broadway and west of 18th Street. They were doing all right until Window's unhealthy love of controlled substances got him dead one day, face down in a plate of pancakes over at Dino's place.

Without Windows' management skills, Leg Bone began to lose clientele. Shop windows that he was supposed to be protecting started getting broken. People said it was a gang of Chechens moving in. Pretty soon, Leg Bone would show up for his premiums, only to find out some other thug had been there before him.

The take was shrinking and it wasn't long before he realized he was being pushed out. He was out gunned, and he was just smart enough not to make a fuss. He and Emaleen disappeared from the neighborhood, but not before making one last round of collections, from what was, by that time, what the Chechens considered to be their turf. That was a mistake. They were none too pleased by this and put out the word on him. He hadn't been seen for these past four years. Neither had Venus- Passion-Emaleen, until the day she walked into Mariano's.

I don't recognize her at first. The silhouette, outlined in the doorframe, doesn't say Passion or Venus. But as the woman takes a few steps toward the bar, the walk begins to look damn familiar. She's wearing tight black pants that accentuate her dancer's legs, extra high heels, and she's carrying a paper sack, like she's come from the grocery store. She only gives me a quick glance as she walks by and settles a couple stools down.

I'm still trying to place her when she puts the sack on the bar and says softly, "You know, you shouldn't be drinking this early in the day." It's her voice. She has changed a lot, but it is still her voice, for sure. She looks up at Sal, pushes a strand of hair from her eyes, and says, "Hello Sal, I didn't know if you'd still be here. It's been a long time."

"Well, I'll be, it's… Oh damn, what day is it?"

"Just Emaleen these days, Sal. I quit dancing years ago. We'll have two vodka martinis."

Christ! Is Emaleen buying me a drink? Maybe she knows I exist after all.

Sal takes a beat, looks over at me, sitting here beaming, and says to her, "Sure thing, but, um, Stan usually drinks Jack Daniels in the morning, if that's all right."

"Who? Who's Stan?" she asks.

I wave my hand and say, "Me. I'm Stan."

She looks me up and down and says, "Do I know you?"

There goes that fantasy. Not to mention a free drink. I pull myself together enough to say, "You might remember me from a few years ago, maybe not."

She glances at Sal, and then turns away and says to herself, "I don't know. Some guy named Stan?"

Sal leans his palms on the bar, "So, Emaleen, will that be one martini and one JD?"

"No, just the two martinis," she replies. "With olives."

Sal straightens up and says, "You know, you don't have to order them two at a time. I'm not going nowhere. And we ain't running out of vodka."

"Oh, that one's not for me," she says. "It's for Leg Bone."

"He's here too? Well, it'll be good to see him again," Sal says. "Two vodka martys, coming right up." Then he rolls his eyes and goes to work.

I'm sipping in silence for a few moments, thinking about hitting Sal up for one more, when I feel her eyes on me. I take a breath, turn on the stool and say, "Haven't seen you around here for some time, Emaleen. How you guys doing?"

She fusses with her paper bag a few seconds, squares it against the edge of the bar and says, "We been living in Mexico, Baja really."

"You and Leg Bone?"

"Uh-huh."

"How are things with the old man? It was pretty hot around here for a while, after you two left."

"Yes," she says, as Sal sets the martinis in front of her, leans against the back bar, and folds his arms. Emaleen lifts one of the glasses by its stem, mumbles something I don't catch, and takes a sip. She puts the glass down and says, "We have to be careful. They're still looking for him, so... you know, the

Chechens. We gotta be careful. If they find out we're here…. well…"

Looking at her dry, stringy hair and her clouded eyes, it's clear that, although Emaleen has only been away for a few years, an amazing transformation has occurred. When she left here, she was a bright, beautiful, energetic woman. The person sitting next to me now, seems edgy, tired, a bit confused, and I'm beginning to think she's talking to a paper sack.

Sal straightens up and says, "Hey, Emaleen, you want I should put Leg Bone's martini on ice? Keep it cold 'til he gets here?"

Her eyes rise slowly to his. They linger there. Then, she reaches into her pocket and pulls out a grimy, wrinkled piece of paper, flattens it out on the bar, and slides it toward Sal. "He wants me to give you this. It's a little favor he wants to ask."

"No problem." Sal looks over at me, raises an eyebrow, then picks it up and squints down at it. I watch his lips move as he reads the meandering scrawl across the note. Then his face goes dark. "Is he insane? No way! No way, Emaleen. It ain't happening here. Not in my joint. Uh-uh!" He tosses the paper back onto the bar.

"Maybe I can help," I say and reach for it.

Emaleen grabs it, "No, it's gotta be Sal. Leg Bone said…"

"What is it Sal? What's the problem?"

"He wants me to scatter his damn ashes, here, in the bar. He's nuts!"

"Yeah, that's pretty dumb. But, if you think about it, it's kinda nice too, that he thinks so much of the place, and you."

"You don't get it Stan."

"I get that it's not very practical. I mean, what, you spread him, and then you gotta vacuum him up later, and what, dump him in the trash? But it's the thought. When he gets here just tell him it ain't practical. He oughta do it outside someplace."

"No, Stan. You really don't get it."

"You can tell him nicely…"

Sal puts both fists on the bar, leans toward me and says, "He's here."

"Where?"

Sal looks at Emaleen. "I'm guessing, in the bag."

Emaleen puts her arm around the paper sack and pulls it closer to her side, looks into the bag and says, "It'll be alright, honey." Then I see a tear start down her cheek.

"Forget about it Emaleen," Sal says. "You ain't spreading Leg Bone Delaney all over my place. Get it out of your head."

"But, Sal, when we were in Mexico, and he was sick, it was all he talked about; ending up here with his pals. I promised."

"Emaleen, there was a time I might'a considered spreading your ashes around here, Venus, or Passion, no problem. But Leg Bone? No. I got no need to be sweeping up bits of his teeth and bones from behind the ice machine for years to come."

All this is not setting well with Miss Emaleen-Venus-Passion, who I'm beginning to think, is a bit touched. As she looks at Sal, her face gets hard. I'm watching the muscles in her jaw and neck start to work as she climbs slowly off the barstool. She settles her feet, puts her fists on her hips, looks at the sack and says, "I told you. I told you…. Yes, Okay, I will." Then, just like Venus in her prime, snatching at a twenty, her hand shoots out and grabs the sack. Then she takes two steps back from the bar and plants herself.

I'm ready for a dramatic show of Passion and an angry exit, but she just stands there, stock-still, grinding her teeth. Then, slowly, she reaches into the bag.

Sal cries, "Oh no! No, you don't!" and he lunges across the bar. But she just takes one more step back, out of his reach. Her hand comes out of the sack and she's holding the mortal remains of good old Leg Bone Delaney, in a great big zip lock bag. She puts her fingers on the zipper. Sal's eyes get big. He barks, "Stan, grab her. Don't let her do it!"

In this one, I am firmly on Sal's side. I hop off my stool, jump forward and throw my arms around her, smothering her in a bear hug.

She's struggling and I'm holding her while she's moaning, "Leg Bone! Oh, Leg Bone. I won't let them take you."

Which is why, when the door crashes open and two gorillas roar into the bar, they level their pistols at me.

The first gunman says to his pal, "Grisha is right. We follow woman, we find man."

The second ugly replies, "Aga. He will be pleased." Then they both smile and one of them says, "You should not be coming back here Leg Bone."

This new development puts an end to my little two-step with Emaleen. As I move away from her, she stuffs her baggie back in the sack and cries, "Oh my God, Leg Bone, they found us." This doesn't help my situation any, but it puts a couple of big smiles on two Chechen thugs.

Number One lowers his gun toward my chest, and growls, "You steal our money. You pay."

At this point, Sal's spitting and puffing and looks ready to vault himself over the bar. He shouts, "Hey, that's not Leg Bone. You guys got it wrong."

"No, no, he's not Leg Bone," Emaleen cries.

"Who is he then, woman? You Leg Bone's woman. You dancing with him. He is your man, Leg Bone. We are not stupid peoples."

"But, he's not," she says.

"Ha! You just call him Leg Bone. He is Leg Bone."

"No, he's not Leg Bone. He's Steve, or something like that. He's nobody."

That's when I decide I'm not going to risk my life for this woman. "Hey, guys, I'm not Leg Bone. He's dead."

The gun barrel closest to me says, "No, not yet!"

At this time, I'm beginning to notice that ugly number two has begun to move around behind me, putting himself between me and the bar. He's got his gun up, but he isn't in the full-on shooter's stance anymore, not that he really needs it at this distance. I decide to change the dynamic slightly. "Okay, Emaleen, time to give him up."

"No! No, never!" she cries. Then she opens up the sack, looks inside and says, "Don't worry honey, I won't let you go."

The number one mug turns to me and says, "Why woman is talking to bag?"

"Because, you fucking idiot, Leg Bone is in there."

"In bag?" I can see he's taking a moment to process this. He doesn't seem to be able to decide which one of us is more crazy. I watch his eyes, shifting between Emaleen and me. Then he turns to her and says, "Give me bag."

"Never!" she cries, clutching the sack to her chest. Then she bolts for the door.

The Chechen is bulky, but he's quick. He jumps in front of her, grabs the sack and gives it a yank, spinning her around. Another tug and the paper sack is in shreds. They each have a death grip on Leg Bone. I'm seeing that dangerous look returning to her eyes but the Chechen seems to be enjoying his little dance with Emaleen, this slender, insignificant woman. He lowers his gun, straightens up his shoulders, digs his fingers into the plastic bag and says, "Give me this bag, woman." Then he smiles.

Emaleen drops her right leg back a half step then lets loose with a dancer's high kick to the cookies with such grace, precision and follow-thru, that she lifts that poor bastard at least six inches off the ground. While his eyes are still bugging out, and he's gasping for air, she gives him another one.

Bozo number two, standing behind me, is so engrossed that he doesn't hear Sal slide the police baton out from the rack where he keeps it above the sink. So, he is quite surprised when he feels the blinding pain that turns his knees to water when he's cracked across the top of the skull. He sinks to the ground and I can tell by his eyes that all he is seeing are stars.

Both of the goons are writhing on the floor now, and Sal and I are wondering if we've just been delivered from the clutches of the Chechen mafia, or if we've sealed our death warrants, when Sal looks over to Emaleen, down on one knee, gently cradling the baggie. In two beats, he also notices a rip in the sack, and a stream of Leg Bone, making a small pile on the floor.

"Emaleen. He's leaking," he cries.

Punk number One is on his back, clutching his goodies and trying to ventilate as the pain flows in waves over his whole being, turning his entire body to mush. Punk number Two is in the fetal position on the floor, crying and holding his head.

I watch Emaleen pull the baggie to her breast, then kneel down and, with one finger, she draws a heart in the ashes on the floor. Then, she slowly writes their initials inside it.

Both their guns are lying on the floor so I hop over and kick them back toward the bar. Now, it's definitely time for me to go. As I make my move toward the door, Emaleen stands up with Leg Bone in her arms, and starts to dance.

She's Venus again, and Passion, but this time, she is also Emaleen. She's in her own world now, moving to something gentle, but with purpose. Her movements are graceful and flowing but getting stronger and stronger. Her eyes are closed and her shoulders and arms stretch out as she spins around, and around again. The baggie is wide open now and Leg Bone is flying out around her in translucent clouds that fall in a gentle dust around the room.

Sal and I stand like two cows in a field, mesmerized. Emaleen has brought her man home, just as she said she would, and with her beauty and love, she is sharing him with us again.

So, bat-shit crazy it is, but, I gotta say, I've had worse days. Still, I can't help thinking, those goddamn Chechens are gonna recover, and I want to be miles away when they do. Might be time to go sailing again.

The Warm Water

Rescued

Two couples from San Francisco, Brian and Carol, and Carson and Jeanette, had chartered a top of the line, fifty-five-foot Beneteau sloop and were, no doubt, planning to spend a week sailing around the warm waters off Martinique, smooching, and making merry the whole time. When they filled out the forms, they also made it clear that they wanted to be known as "The Merrymakers." They stressed it three times. I was willing to bet money that they would show up wearing t-shirts that said, "The Merrymakers." It was my fate to be their hired skipper.

Going from a licensed hundred-ton ship's skipper, twenty years ago, to "Your Pleasant and Experienced Captain," was like going from washing down uppers with Jack Daniels and hauling 80,000 pounds of freight across country, to sipping Fresca and driving the elephant train at the zoo. Makes you wanta just smack somebody sometimes. But still, with my knees and back gone, the icy Pacific still growling out there, waiting for a second crack at me, and God knows how many Chechen gangsters after my ass, waking up without a hangover and loafing along under sail in the Caribbean wasn't such a bad gig.

The normal routine when people charter a boat is they fly in the night before and the charter company picks them up at the airport. Then they bring them to the hotel here at the base. It's all part of the package. The next morning, they load their provisions, we do an orientation, and then we cast off.

That morning, when I got to the office, prepared to meet my band of eager fun seekers, the jolly couples were conspicuously absent. Bastide, the cab driver we used for ferrying our clients from the airport to the base, was sitting slouched by the desk, without his usual glowing smile. I walked over, touched him on the shoulder and said, "Hey Bastide. How ya doing? You got our Merrymakers out there someplace?"

"No way, Stan," he said. "I don't drive them, no more."

I'd never seen him like this before. His booming laugh is the background sound of the whole dock most days. His island cool had definitely been heated up to a boil. "What's up my friend?"

"That man, Brian, he a bad, bad man."

"What'd he do?"

"He was yelling at me, man. He call me a thief," Bastide said and hammered a giant fist on the table.

"Why'd he do that?"

"He say they don't want to go to the base hotel. They want to go to Club Med. Alright, so that's where I take them."

"So?"

"So, now they gotta pay me. Thirty dollar. He got real mad, man. Calls me a thief!"

"What?"

"Yeah, he say I'm stealing from him 'cause he a tourist."

I couldn't believe this.

"I told him, I only supposed to take him to the base, man, not Club Med. They want Club Med? Fine. I gotta go all that way round the bay, thirty miles, out and back."

"He didn't get that?"

"No. He says he paid already, and he not paying me no more. Calls me a crook and says he gonna make sure I don't drive no taxi no more. Gonna get me fired. I told him, I own that taxi. I don't got no boss. How you gonna get me fired? Then he say, he a 'rich and powerful man,' and he gonna fix it so I don't drive no taxi on this island no more."

"He said that? He's a rich and powerful man?"

"Yeah. A rich and powerful man. Yes sir! He crazy…crazy, man. He rich. And me? Just a poor, dumb taxi driver."

"What an idiot."

"That's right. Stupid, and crazy too. Then, one of the women tried to give me some money, but I give it back. I don't need no money from no rich and powerful crazy man. And I don't drive them no place. No. I don't know how they gonna get here, man." Then he looked at me. "You taking them sailing today?"

"Yeah, The Merrymakers. All week."

Bastide looked out the window as a taxi pulled up. "That's them now. I'm leaving." He stood up and as he turned toward the door, he flashed me a half-smile. "You have a nice week, captain."

They did, in fact, have t-shirts printed: bright yellow ones with "The Merrymakers" emblazoned across the front, above a picture of a Disneyesque sailboat, crewed by four happy mice. My charges stood on the deck in front of the office, surrounded by an immense pile of baggage and looking like an unhappy bunch of sixth graders, waiting for the camp counselor to come out and tell them which tent they're in. They were anything but merry.

I took a deep breath, told myself I'd faced Point Conception in a gale and lived, then I went out to greet them. The women were struggling with the luggage, sorting and piling it all onto a couple of rolling carts. One of the men was standing to the side, lightly swaying on his feet, the sweaty pallor of a hard-won hangover on his fac. He looked slight and frail; age, hard to determine. He could have been seventy or ninety. He had red-rimmed, hazy blue eyes and thin, dead, hair. His hands shook as he lit a fresh cigarette off the butt of the old one. His bony torso set precariously atop a pair of skinny, white legs that looked like they would fold up at the first breeze. I guessed that this was Carson.

The other guy was short, and fat. He had salt and pepper hair, flabby cheeks and an overbite that made him look like an irritated guinea pig. I guessed him to be in his late fifties or early sixties. His Merrymaker t-shirt stretched right across his belly, changing the smiling mice into four grimacing gophers. He wore Hawaiian print Bermuda shorts, showing off dimpled bowlegs above a pair of flip-flops with the price tags still on them.

I couldn't help wondering, for the hundredth time, about the way the world works. How come these two clowns are out flying around the world, chartering luxury sailboats for elegant cruises around the Caribbean? While me, the smartest bastard I know, is down to playing Mr. Step 'n Fetch It, grabbing my forelock and doing as I'm told?

It's gotta be their women, keeping them in line. Sometimes I think I maybe shoulda made a little more effort to keep my old lady from taking off. But then, by the time I came home from six days on the road and found the plumber making another house call, I knew I had no say in the matter.

The guinea pig planted his feet and started barking at the women, "Where's our boat? Carol! Go get someone." I noticed that his overbite gave him an occasional lisp.

Carol was a slight woman with shoulder-length, strawberry blonde hair and sad, tired blue eyes. She wore a flowing kaftan that was slit up the side, revealing a very firm and tempting thigh. She stopped straightening the pile of bags and turned to the guy with the mouth. He pointed a finger at her. "Carol, put that down! Go find someone. Tell them we're here." He looked down the dock at the line of boats in slips.

I figured Chubby for The Rich and Powerful Man. It occurred to me that he would really benefit from a solid smacking around. Who knows? I'd be sailing with that punk for a week. Maybe before the voyage was over…would cost me my job, but some things are worth it.

The last Merrymaker, Jeanette, a tall, smooth blonde with full red lips, short-cropped hair and Audrey Hepburn sunglasses, touched Carol on the shoulder. "Come on. Let's go find someone."

Before they could get away, I walked over and introduced myself. "Hey there, ladies," I said. "Welcome to Martinique. You must be Carol and Jeanette…" I looked at the word stretched across Jeanette's t-shirt, "…of the Merrymakers?" She looked down and then up into my eyes, puffed out her chest and smiled.

"I'm Stan. I'll be your captain for your epic cruise around the island." I held out my hand and Jeanette pushed it aside, stepped forward and gave me a full-body hug, and a wiggle.

Once she'd released me, I took a breath and said, "Nice. Here, let me give you a hand with that stuff." Then I grabbed the last of the bags, threw them onto the cart and rolled it over to Anton, the dock captain, who had been watching the whole thing from his lounge chair in the shade. "Anton, will you take these bags on down to *Trillium* and stow them please? I think it's slip 28 or 30. Thanks." He took charge of the cart and ambled on down the quay.

"Hey!" It was Brian, stomping toward us. He walked like a gorilla suffering from piles. He pointed his bellybutton toward me. "You work here?" He looked back at Anton retreating down the dock. "Is that guy going to our boat? Which one's ours? It's supposed to be, like, fifty-five feet long or something. Right?"

I looked down at him, offered him my right hand and said. "I'm Stan. I'm guessing you're Brian?"

"Yeah, Brian, that's me." He looked me up and down, almost as if he was counting my buttons. Then, I watched his face while he hesitated, then decided. He tentatively put out his hand. It was soft and small, flaccid. His fingers made no effort to grip. I was tempted, but all I did was give it a pump, and let him go. He said, "You're our captain, huh? You been doing this long?"

"Well, really it's my first day. But it's supposed to be pretty easy. They told me to just keep the island on the right, and in about a week, we'll go all the way around it and end up right back here."

He squinted into my eyes for a few seconds, sucked on his teeth and cocked his head. He looked over at Carol, whose face went slack, and then back at me. "That's very funny," he said, and forced a smile that was warm, like piss.

"So, we're all here," I said. "Anton is stowing your bags. He'll have a crew here in a minute to load your provisions and top off your water tanks. So, what we should do now is go on inside and do the orientation and check out the charts. Afterward, you can go up to the street to the liquor store for any specialty items you might want. Let's try to cast off in an hour. Okay?"

"Sure thing, captain." Brian suppressed his lisp. He turned and grabbed Carson by the arm, almost knocking him over, "Come on, Carson. The captain has called a meeting."

I stood aside and motioned them toward the door to the air-conditioned office and conference room. Brian dragged Carson into the building and the girls followed. As they went past, Carol and Jeanette stopped in front of me, smiled at each other, then jumped to attention and popped a crisp salute. "Yes sir, captain," they said in unison. Then more smiles and two more hugs. I figured then that this cruise could be heaven, or it could be hell. But, I'd been through both and lived.

Within an hour of casting off, the routine had been established. While I was at the wheel, Carson was planted at the front of the cockpit, wearing a life jacket and clutching a glass of Chardonnay in one hand and a cigarette in the other. Aside from movements involved with drinking or smoking, he could have been a stuffed bear. Brian sat across from him, no life jacket, holding a tall glass of rum and nursing a smoldering cigar. Carol anxiously fussed around Brian, jumping whenever he barked, "Get me a lime! Isn't there any more ice? Not a wedge of lime, Carol! Dammit, I want a twist of lime. A twist. You know that."

Jeanette, tall and elegant, had poured herself into her pleasantly revealing bathing suit, put on a pair of sailing gloves and taken up a position on the lee side, winch handle at the ready, prepared to trim the jib or the main sail whenever I gave her a nod. She knew how to sail and enjoyed it.

When Carol wasn't waiting on Brian, I encouraged her to take the helm and steer for a while. She was reluctant at first, timid, afraid to make a mistake. But with a little gentle coaching, she started to get the feel of it. Her smile began to come back, and it was a nice one.

Carson, with his Chardonnay, and Brian with his rum, stayed pie-eyed from mid-morning on. Carson was pretty much catatonic and, aside from tipping over occasionally and spilling his wine, was not much trouble. Brian wasn't so easy. He'd wake up each morning about ten o'clock, whining about his hangover and yelling at Carol for his clothes, his toothbrush, his breakfast, and his rum, with a twist of lime, not a damn wedge. Once he'd gotten himself out of bed and into the cockpit, he'd light his first cigar of the day and settle in with his drink. He didn't know a boat from a barn door, but he had condescending and unshakeable opinions about everything that happened aboard.

"Oh sure, just when I get comfortable, you decide you gotta turn the boat around," he said when Jeanette and I got ready to do a tack. Tacking the boat meant that he would have to move his fat ass to make room for Jeanette to haul in the jib and trim it.

"Brian, why don't you try trimming that sheet this time?" I asked. "All you have to do is wrap that line around the winch and pull on it when I tell you."

"Isn't that what we're paying you for, captain?"

"Well, not exactly. I'm here to make sure you don't run the boat into the island and sink it," I said. "And to help Jeanette sail the boat, and also, to make sure some idiot doesn't fall off." I looked at him and added, "It happens."

On the third day, out we did the thirty-five-mile crossing to Saint Lucia and made for Rodney Bay to anchor for the night. The trip across was uneventful, except for the notable fact that Brian put down his rum and got onto his feet to help trim a sail. He wasn't able to figure out which way to turn the winch handle, and Jeanette had to bail him out. But the girls heaped praise on him anyway and he acted like a six-year-old who had just ridden a bicycle for the first time without training wheels. Then, he celebrated with a fresh brimming glass of rum.

We got to Rodney Bay as the sun was setting and began looking for a place to anchor for the night. Anchoring a boat can be tricky, especially when the anchorage is crowded, or if there is a current running. This one had both, and it was getting dark. The first two nights out, we had simply picked up floating moorings, which involved nothing more than driving the boat up next to one and tying a rope to it. This would be our first time actually dropping the anchor.

"Jeanette," I said. "Would you go forward and drop the anchor when I tell you, please?"

"I'll do it." It was Brian. He'd put down his rum and was hauling himself to his feet. "I'll drop that anchor. That's a man's job anyway."

I looked at him. A cylinder of ash from his ever-present cigar tumbled down his gut while he tried to steady himself against the cabin top. "Have you ever dropped an anchor before?" I asked.

"How hard can it be? I pick it up. I drop it in the water." He sucked on his teeth. "Jesus, if she can do it, I th-ure ath hell can." I wasn't reassured by his lisp, but it's true, it doesn't take a huge intellect or overwhelming sobriety to drop an anchor, so maybe he could do it.

"Okay, look, you go up on the bow. Release the brake on the windless and free the anchor chain to run. I'll pull us up to a clear spot between those boats over there and stop. Then, when I tell you, you drop it over the side and let the chain out until I tell you to stop it. Got that?"

"Course. I'm not an idiot. What's a windmill?"

"Christ! Never mind. Jeanette, will you go-?"

"I'll do it!" His voice was rising. "Just tell me how to do that thing with the windmill."

"Jeanette, maybe you could go with him and show him how to work the windlass?"

"She rolled her eyes and said, "Okay. Come on Brian." She stood aside as Brian, with a grunt, hoisted himself onto the deck and started staggering forward. Jeanette watched him take a few ragged steps then she turned to me and said, "What if he falls off the boat?"

"Tell him not to let go of the anchor."

"Good plan," she said.

I maneuvered *Trillium* into a spot between a sleek, white power yacht and a couple of sailboats similar in size to us, then I pulled the throttle back to slow her down. Brian was in position on the bow, puffing on his cigar, cradling the anchor against his belly and peering into the water. I put the bow into the current, took her out of gear and she slowly came to a stop. That's when the engine stalled.

"Okay, Brian! Let 'er go!" I yelled. He just stood there, looking down into the water. I yelled it again. "Brian! Drop the anchor!" Jeanette looked back at me and put her palms up in a shrug. Brian held onto the anchor and gazed, transfixed, into the water. "Drop it!" I yelled again as we began drifting backward on the current.

Finally, he looked back at me and I watched the glowing end of his cigar waving from side to side, saying "Un-uh."

"Drop the goddamn anchor, now!" I yelled and watched helplessly as we were picked up by the current and pushed closer and closer to that big, shiny motor yacht anchored behind us. Its crew was gathering at the rail to watch, cocktails in hand as Jeanette began hitting Brian on the shoulder.

"What's the matter? I cried. "Drop the goddamn thing!"

"Turd," he yelled and pointed down at the water.

"What?"

"There's a big turd in the water," he yelled. "Floater."

"Forget the turd! Drop the anchor!" I pleaded, groping for the ignition switch.

"Boat behind you," Carol said and touched me on the shoulder. "Big one."

"Drop the fucking anchor, you idiot!" Someone yelled from the yacht. One of the crew had put down his cocktail and was aiming a boat pole at us to keep us from crashing into them.

Now voices started coming from other boats, "Alors, monsieur, drop zee anchor," and "Better drop that thing, boy," and "Little turd never hurt   nothing. Drop it."

I had been frantically cranking the engine over, trying to get it to start, but it seemed the batteries were about to give out. We were bobbing about three feet from the gleaming side of the power yacht and Carol was swinging a boat pole around to fend us off, when the engine coughed, blew out a cloud of black smoke and started. I slammed it into gear, hit the throttle and yelled to

Brian, "Don't drop the --!" and heard a giant "Splash!" as the asshole dropped the damn thing.

"Bring up the anchor!" I yelled.

An hour later, safely tucked in for the night, and everyone supplied with large doses of rum punch, I figured it was time for a little pep talk with the crew. "So, okay, that was our first time anchoring. Good job everyone." I looked at The Merrymakers, sitting glumly in the cockpit. "It wasn't entirely without a hitch, though. What did we learn, for next time?"

Brian, who had been sulking in his corner, was the first to speak up. He pointed his cigar at me and said, "You need to make up your mind about what you want me to do." Then, as I was picturing him with a winch handle lodged in his head, his cigar dumped another inch of ash onto his shirt, and he said, "First it's 'Drop the anchor.' Then it's, 'Bring up the anchor.' You gotta make up your mind, captain."

"Aw, yes. I guess I did –."

"It's not his fault," Carol said, turning to Brian. "He told you to drop it and you didn't do it. Do you know how close we came to hitting that boat back there?"

Brian slowly turned to her and said, "I need a fresh twist of lime for my drink."

Carol's jaw muscles bulged. Then she picked the wedge of lime out of her drink, gave it a squeeze, and threw it at him. It landed on the top of his belly, settled into the pile of ash, and stuck there. From that moment on, that fifty-five-foot boat started to shrink.

That evening, the cocktail hour was spent in silence. Brian was sulking, slurping down glasses of rum, and staring at the island. Carol was silent as stone, eyes locked on the setting sun. Jeanette was noisily slicing cheese in the galley, and Carson had no idea where he was.

Those days I didn't carry a full bottle of Jack with me on my charters. I'd gotten the boozing down to where a hip flask would last me for a week, or more sometimes. Having important captain's duties forward, I fished my flask out of my kit and took it to the bow, where I could keep an eye on the anchor and watch the sunset, clear of the frigid atmosphere.

"Maybe it's time we got off the boat." It was Jeanette. She'd come forward with a plate of cheese and crackers to offer. "The guide book says there's a nice restaurant in the town. Antonio's Grill? It might do us good to go ashore, change things up a bit."

"Yeah, I know the place. It's good. Sounds like a good idea. I'll run you to shore in the skiff."

"Oh, you're coming too," she said. "Carol and I want to buy you dinner. You've been putting up with a lot. We want to thank you."

"That's very nice, but –."

"No, you're coming. We insist. I've already called and made reservations for five people. I'll get Carson dressed. Brian and Carol are getting ready as we speak." I pictured Brian and Carol putting on Kevlar body armor.

It was decided. Maybe this would break some of the ice that was forming among The Merrymakers. I'd have to take them to shore in the skiff anyway, so I might as well go along. My only real concern was getting Carson and Brian into, and out of, the dinghy without losing them overboard. By then, they were fully crocked, and could hardly stand.

Five people are the maximum the little skiff could hold. We put Carson and Brian in the center of the boat, where they'd have a hard time falling out. Carol sat next to me in the stern, and Jeanette was on the bow, ready to tie onto the pier when we came along side.

"Where is this place we're going to?" Brian lisped. "I want a good meal for a change. I'm tired of all that barbequed chicken and hamburgers and crap. I want a th-teak!"

"It's a nice place. Don't worry, Brian," Carol said. "You can have a steak." Then I heard her whisper under her breath, "and I hope you choke on it."

"And I want wine, too," Brian went on. "Good th-tuff. The th-tuff on the boat is crap. I want good th-tuff."

"It's a nice place, Brian," Jeanette said. "Stan's been there. He says it's nice."

"Here we are," I said as I slowed the skiff and let her glide up to the dock. Jeanette slipped the line over a cleat, and we were there. "Okay, everybody out."

Brian was seated closest to the pier. He looked at it for a second, sizing it up, then he lunged, like a walrus flopping onto an iceberg. He bounced a couple times on his elbows and belly, rolled over, got onto his hands and knees and, with a walrus-like bellow, hoisted himself onto his feet, where he stood, swaying and looking proud.

Jeanette stepped lightly out next, followed by Carol. They each grabbed an arm and lifted Carson bodily and set him, swaying on his feet, on the dock.

They were all safe and dry for the moment. But watching Brian try to climb the ladder from the dock to solid ground, I wondered what I'd do if he fell into the water. He couldn't possibly climb out on his own, and I didn't think I could lift him. But really, I wondered if I'd even try.

Antonio's was four blocks up the main street. Carol spotted the sign and set off walking. The Merrymakers quickly spread out along the way. I caught up with Carol and we pulled ahead. Behind us, Jeanette took Carson's arm and walked him, like an unsteady child, in our wake. Brian, grumbling and snorting, stumped along at the rear.

Carol looked cool and attractive as she moved gracefully down the street. She gave off a warm glow from her time in the tropics and her blonde hair seemed to shine against the sparling backdrop of the bay. She wore turquoise earrings that enhanced her tan and complemented the blue in her eyes. She had looked tired, almost sad, when I first saw her on the dock, back at the base. But something inside her had changed. The sun and the sailing had filled her with a new radiance, and when she smiled, I felt its warmth. Walking this close to her I sensed an almost physical magnetism, pulling me toward her. As our hips touched and I looked down at her, I saw that she had become beautiful. Her light cotton blouse and skirt bounced and flowed around her with each stride.

"So, Carol, you throw fruit often?" I asked when we were alone.

"Not often enough," she said.

"Is he always like this? I mean, people kind of cut loose with the rum when they come down here, but usually not like him."

"It's not just the rum. He's that way drunk or sober." She was quiet for a while. Then she looked at me and said, "He was nice, once, when I first met him. I don't know when it happened, exactly. He changed. He started pushing people around. Swaggering, drinking…now he's just mean, a bully."

"I'm sorry to hear that. I had hoped you'd just have to endure a few more days and then go back home, back to normal."

"Normal? God, I'm beginning to realize how pathetic and sad my 'normal' really is. No, when we go home, we'll just go home. Nothing will change but the scenery. But you'll still be here, in paradise."

"Oh yeah. I'm pretty much settled in."

"It must be wonderful living here, on the island, the sunsets, sailing whenever you like. I never sailed before, but I'm beginning to really like it, despite him. I wonder what it would be like..." She touched my arm. "Oh look, here we are."

We stepped into a well-appointed foyer where we could see an almost crowded dining room filled with tables set with multiple wine glasses on crisp, white tablecloths. A black-suited maître 'd stepped forward to greet us.

"Ah, hello Stan. Is this your group?"

"Hi Marco. It's the crew off *Trillium*, The Merrymakers."

"Aw yes, group of five, correct?"

I nodded my head. "The rest are right behind us."

"Would you like to be seated now, or wait for the rest of your party?" he asked as he pulled large menus out of a rack and nestled them under his arm.

"We'll wait for the rest," Carol said. "They're right behind us."

"Very well," he said. Then we all turned as the front door opened. "Ah, they're here—Oh!"

Jeanette and Carson were stumbling through the door. Jeanette was struggling to keep Carson on his feet while blood flowed down his leg from a gash on his knee. It was filling his shoe, so that when he walked, he made a squishing sound, and left bloody footprints on the teak floor.

"Does anyone have a rag, or a Band-Aid?" Jeanette asked. "Carson tripped and hurt his knee."

"I'll just go get – Oh my!" Marco exclaimed. We all pivoted around and stared back at the front door, which had just crashed open again.

It was Brian, one hand on the doorframe, swaying in his bow-legged gorilla stance. He took two steps into the room and stopped. He planted his feet like bean bags on the ground, reached out and touched the wall for balance, and proclaimed to all within earshot, "I pith-t my-thelf!"

"Oh my God! He did," Carol cried, and grabbed my arm. We all watched the evidence, spreading across the front of his pants and down his legs.

Brian giggled, patted himself on the belly a couple times and said, "Justh-t couldn't hold it. Had to go. Pith-t my pant-ths." He laughed again, fixed a deranged guinea pig gaze on us and smiled.

"How about that?" I said. "Look Marco, The Rich and Powerful Man just wet himself. Who'd'a thought?"

Marco turned to me. "What did you say?"

"The Rich and Powerful Man?" I looked innocent and raised my eyebrows.

"That's him? That's the Rich and Powerful Man?" He looked at Brian again. "Yes, yes. Fat, Stupid! That's him!" Then he turned and called into the kitchen, "Louie! Louie, come out here. That guy, he's here. The rich and powerful man, he's here."

Three men burst out of the kitchen. One of them said, "Is that him? Really?"

"Yes, it's him. Just like Baptiste said; fat, stupid."

"Did he just wet his pants?"

"Yes," I said. "It sure looks like the Rich and Powerful dipshit just peed his pants." Brian was beginning to take a few unsteady steps forward, fingertips tracing along the wall.

Louie made for the kitchen. "Come on. We gotta call Baptiste." He pushed through the swinging doors and disappeared, leaving the other two standing, glaring.

Marco grabbed my arm. "You better get out of here, Stan. Baptiste's got lots of family on this island. They don't like that guy. Get him away from my restaurant. Go now."

I put my arm around Carol and said, "How about you stay here for a while, lady? I'll take that mess back to the boat. You have a drink and I'll come for you in a bit, Okay?" She looked up at me, and smiled, but she was crying.

The next morning, as the sun was rising, we weighted anchor and left Saint Lucia for Martinique. Brian and Carson stayed in their bunks most of the way, oblivious to the world and moaning in pain. Carol and Jeanette donned their bathing suits and sunbathed on the foredeck as we made the passage across the open Caribbean. We were back at the base in La Marin by sundown.

The Merrymakers had decided that it was time to go home. They were on a plane the next day: all of them except Carol. She stayed with me. Now, every New Year's Eve, we drink two special toasts. I raise a glass to Larry's bladder, the reason I'm still alive, and Carol drinks to Brian's, the reason she's living here, with me, on the edge of warm water.

Cris Hammond

Singing in The Dark

A glimpse into the next collection

Cris Hammond

Angela's Gift

I'm sitting in my miserable little cubicle and, I swear, I am this close to lighting a match and burning the whole goddamn building down. If I could wave a wand or push a button and blow the place up, I'm telling you, I would do it. For the last nine years, I've been dragging my ass into the crappy lobby of the Great Western building on Bush Street where I stand meekly waiting for the same damn elevator. For a few moments, I let dangerous thoughts start to form, but then, the doors open, my fate takes over, and I force myself through that familiar fog. I step in and hit the same button that I push every time, number six.

My days drone on like that. Occasionally, for excitement, I get up from my chair and look over the cubicle wall, down the cubicle hall, past the cubicle fire extinguishers and the donut tray, and enjoy the view of the cubicles on the sixth floor of the building across the street.

Nine years in this dump and there's no way out. I got no degree and since the accident I can't pound nails anymore and I have two alimonies to cover. My life ended when I walked in here. At least I'm not one of those damn interns up front, working for free. There is a world out there somewhere. Not for us though. Not for the faithful, tethered employees of Barry Benson Temporary Staffing Services, Inc. We have goals to reach, no, we have goals to *exceed*!

I swear. I'm this close.

Margaret, Little Miss "Go Team!" has just trotted past, handing out the announcement of her latest "Team Building Event," scheduled for this Saturday. Can you believe it? Saturday. She's calling it Team Power, and she's got us all scheduled to meet at Barry's country club in Hillsborough for team building games, competitions, and a special challenge: create a new Barry Benson

Temporary Staffing Services, Inc. Mission Statement. The announcement says, "Get Ready For Some Fun!" The last time she did this, the mission statement that 80% of the people came up with simply read, "Our goal is to Make Barry Richer!"

Margaret pronounced it a great success at team building. She would. At thirty-years-old, she is the Marketing Manager and Vice President in charge of Team Spirit. It's a made-up title. Everyone knows she got it because she's blowing Barry, and probably his idiot son, Mike, my boss. Last week, someone left a gift-wrapped pair of kneepads on her desk. Now Barry has issued a reward for information leading to the firing of the perpetrator.

Here in the San Francisco offices of Benson Staffing, we are dedicated to shuffling resumes from the thousands of unemployed people hoping for temporary or part-time work. They call us recruiters, but we're really just shufflers. Once we've shuffled the resumes, we shuffle them again. It's all on line now, so we spend all day staring at our screens, looking for keywords and clicking our mouses, or mice, whatever. Then we try to look busy, shuffling some more.

Twice a week, it's Live Interview Day. That's when we meet and interview potential candidates whose resumes line up with some of our job listings. First thing, every Live Interview Day, Margaret stands on her small stool at the front of the main hall and delivers her standard pep talk. She encourages us to be Up and Positive, so that we impart the signature Benson Brightness to our eager job seekers. That's when I really wish I had a button, just inside the top drawer of my desk. I relish the thought of slowly pushing it, and "Poof!" she vanishes in a ball of flames and smoke, like the wicked witch of the west, never to return.

Today is another Live Interview Day. I can tell because there are live donuts on the donut tray.

My first candidate is someone named Angel Cappobianco. We're not allowed to ask their sex or age on the resume forms, so I'm not sure what to expect from Candidate Cappobianco when he, or she, arrives. The resume in front of me shows a work history going back quite a few years, but I'm having a hard time inferring an age here. Experience is cited in the hospitality industry, food and beverage, finance, transportation, and even some information management. But these are all check boxes on the digital form and there aren't any added notes in explanation. I'll just have to see who walks in the door.

"Your first is here. Shall I send her back?" It's Stephanie at the front desk. Her job is to sit there and smile at anyone who happens to stumble through the door. She's required to be Up and Positive, exuding Benson Brightness 'til she's ready to puke, poor thing. I think she drinks at lunch. "Yes please, Stephanie, send her on back."

"She's on her way. Be prepared."

Looking over the wall of my cell, I behold a woman of advanced age, barreling towards me hefting a shoulder bag about the size of a Toyota. She's bundled in a puffy, flowing coat and paisley scarf that would have been hip in the '60s. I'm sure I smell patchouli oil. A significant collection of charm bracelets dangle and clank from her wrists as she comes banging off cubicle walls, striding toward number 1-3-6, me.

"Oh, this is so nice of you to see me," she says as she drops her load and flops into the chair in front of my desk. My first impression, as she was rolling down the hall, was that she was at least in her late sixties, but sitting across from her now, I'm not sure. Her hair is silver but it's glossy and thick. She has the full cheeks and chin of a woman of those years, but her skin is smooth and unlined, and her eyes are a brilliant clear blue that almost sparkle. Hands of a young girl shake the charms back as she pulls a small portfolio from her bag. She's wearing no makeup.

"I brought another copy of my resume if you want it," she says and waves a paper at me.

"Thank you, Ms. Cappobianco, but that's not necessary."

"Oh, please, call me Angela."

"I'm sorry. It says Angel here on the form."

Her face breaks into a glowing smile showing perfect white teeth. "Oh, my goodness. No, my name's not Angel. It's Angela. People make that mistake all the time. But I'm sure it's my fault. Sometimes I forget to put the "a" at the end."

"Aw, I see." I make the correction on my screen while thinking, 'Christ, she can't even spell her own name?'

Then she says, "But you might decide I am an angel before this thing is all over." She winks at me and then does what appears to be a very well-practiced and coquettish hair toss.

"Maybe, but I'll just call you Angela for now. So, it's nice of you to come-"

"People always used to get me confused with the real Angel Cappobianco. Do you know him?"

"No, I don't think I do."

"Oh, now he was a real angel. He used to play sax down in the Fillmore. He played Smokey's, The Pink Elephant, oh, and Johnnie's Hi Times. All the places. He was the king of the district back in the day. I don't go down there so much anymore."

"Oh, really? No more hitting the night spots huh?"

"No. Do you know the song, Stairway to Heaven?"

"Yes. The Rolling Stones, right?"

"No, silly, Led Zepplin."

"Right." I'm starting to wonder; where did this person come from anyway?

"Well, when Angel played his sax, it was like that, you felt like you were going on a shining stairway right up to heaven. Sometimes I think Jimmy Page got the idea for that song from listening to Angel play his horn. Although he was probably just a child then, so maybe not."

"Well, that's interesting." I have to get her on track or this thing will drag on through lunch. "Now, shall we get started?"

"Oh yes. That would be nice." She wiggles down into the chair. "Oh, you know what? I saw some donuts on a tray in the hallway. Would you like me to go get you one?"

"No, thank you, Angela. Um, but, do you want a donut?"

"I better not. My figure, you know." This time I'm sure she winked at me.

"Maybe we should get to your resume." I clicked a few keys. "So, it says here that you have experience in hospitality, transportation, and also food service?"

"Oh yes. All that."

"But you don't provide us with any concrete details. Can you give me some specifics to round this out? Did you work in hotels? Restaurants?"

"No silly, I raised six kids. Do you have any idea how much they can eat?"

"My ex-wives have the kids."

"Of course, but just ask them. You'd be amazed."

"I'm not allowed…never mind. So, let's keep going. You checked the box that says you have experience at information management. That might be something we can work with. We have some jobs offered in info management. But I'll need details. What's your area of expertise?"

"Information management. I'm good at managing information."

"Like what, exactly?"

"I can keep a secret."

"That's not --."

"I'm keeping yours."

"I don't have any secrets."

"No? Who's Margaret?"

"Did I hear my name?" Margaret liked to eavesdrop on Live Interview Day to make sure we were being sufficiently Up and Positive. She's suddenly standing outside my cubicle, holding a tray of donuts. "Would anyone like a donut? They're fresh." She looks at Angela and says, "And who's this?"

"I'm Angela Cappobianco. And you must be Margaret."

"Guilty as charged." Margaret laughs so hard she almost spills the tray. "And how are we doing on our interviews this morning?" She favors us both with a grin. I make another silent wish for that button.

Angela was the high point of my morning. Actually, I could say she was the high point of that whole day, and the day before. The other candidates were more qualified for the jobs we had open, and by the end of the day, I'd ended up placing three of them. Made some more money for Barry, and Margaret put three stars next to my name on her goddamn Team Accomplishments chart. Three stars! Christ, how about a lollipop next time? Still, none of those people were as interesting or genuinely human, as Angela. The truth is, though, I'm pretty sure I'll never be able to place her. She just doesn't have the qualifications that our clients need these days. It made me doubly sad because it meant that I'd probably never see her again. Then my phone starts buzzing. "Do you have an interview scheduled today?" It's Stephanie through the intercom.

This is odd. It isn't Live Interview Day. "Nothing scheduled. Why?"

"That woman from yesterday is here to see you again. Angela? She says you wanted to see her."

"Really? Right. Sure, send her on back." Why not? A break from zoning out over resumes wouldn't be all that bad. A few moments later, Angela arrives in a flurry of bangles and scarves and flops down in the chair. Something about her makes me want to smile.

"Good morning, Angela. What can I do for you today?"

"Oh, nothing. I just stopped by to see how you are. You seemed a little upset yesterday when I left."

"That is so thoughtful of you. But really, I'm fine. It was just a long day is all."

"You weren't angry?"

"No, not at all. What made you think that?"

"I felt it and saw it."

"Well, I'm fine. Really."

"I brought you something, to perk you up." She reaches into her bag and pulls out a small box, gift wrapped and tied with a bow. She puts it on the desk and pushes it toward me.

"Wow, Angela, you are so sweet. Thank you, but you really shouldn't have."

"Don't be silly. It's something special, just for you. I've had it for simply eons, now I want you to have it."

"Oh, shoot. We're not supposed to take gifts from our candidates. My boss might think I'm being, you know, influenced?" It's been so long since anyone has given me a gift, I don't know how to process this. She even wrapped it, with a bow. With all my heart, I want to keep it, but I shouldn't. Reluctantly, I push the tiny box back toward her. "I'm so, so touched, Angela. But I can't."

"Oh, you don't have to worry. It's just a tiny, little thing." She smiled. "I know that I'm not good hiring material. I also know you would do your best, with or without any little presents from me."

"You can count on that."

"But, you'll be unhappy when you can't find me a job. And I don't want that."

"Angela -."

"So, I came by to tell you that I already have a job. And you don't have to worry. Okay?"

"You do? Well, that's good to hear, but -."

"So, you take the present and think of me when you use it." She pushes the gift back across the desk, gathers her things and stands up. "Now, don't be unhappy. I'm going to come by sometimes and check in on you. Hear?" She smiles, gives a little wave and heads off, leaving me happy and sad, and gazing at the beautiful little box.

There's no privacy in a room full of cubicles. You can tell when everyone's listening. The room is quiet, no tapping on keyboards. So, I take my little gift and head into the rest room. In a locked stall, I pull the ribbon and it falls away. The paper is exquisite. It won't tear. It seems to unfold itself and come away from the box inside without any creases or wrinkles.

The box is a hinged, plush, jewelry box. The kind wedding rings come in. This isn't looking like just some "little" thing Angela had had lying around. My heart is beating fast and my fingers tremble as I open the lid.

It isn't a diamond ring. It's a small, exquisite ball, the size of a large marble. Its surface is covered with intricate designs of inlaid enameling and opal, all outlined in gold and polished to a brilliant gloss. From its color and weight, it feels like it must be actual, solid gold. I pick it out of the cradle that holds it, and roll it around in my hand. There's no doubt about it. This is a treasure.

I know right away I can't keep it. It's priceless and Angela, employed or not, isn't in a position to be giving prizes like this away. This should go to her six kids, and god knows how many grand kids. It feels warm in my hand though, like it belongs there.

I admit that I hesitated to call her right away. I knew I should, but I put it off. "She'll be at work." I told myself. "I've only got a home number for her from her resume." That got me through the day, but by quitting time, I know I have to call her, now. I dial the number. It's disconnected. I get her home address off the resume, grab my coat and briefcase and set off to hand deliver the golden marble back to her, personally.

The address turns out to be a print and copy shop on Pine Street. Nobody there knows anyone named Angela Cappobianco.

Team Power day was "A laugh-a-minute fun fest of team building challenges and goal oriented projects designed to unify and motivate the Barry Benson Staffing Services, Inc. team to meet and exceed this quarter's benchmarks!" At least, those are Margaret's words. To the rest of us, it was a wasted Saturday, watching Margaret and Barry making goo-goo eyes and furtively trying to touch each other. In the three-legged race, they arranged to be tied together at the hip and managed to fall down, six times. Team Power.

Barry's addlepated son, Mike, who is endowed with the esteemed title of President of Barry Benson Staffing Services, Inc., showed up after lunch, fidgeting and sniffing and wiping traces of white powder from his nose. He was riding his brand new, metal-flake, Harley Davidson Fat Boy. He sat in the parking lot, revving the engine and telling everyone how much he paid for it before going into the clubhouse bar and downing three martinis. Then he came out and tried to get Stephanie to go for a ride with him. She wouldn't go, but Tracy, from Recruiting, did. They never came back.

After a weekend spent leaving phone messages for my kids and screaming at that son-of-a-bitch upstairs to turn his music down, it's Monday again, and life on the sixth floor is noticeably gloomier than usual. Margaret's glowing though. She's put together a whole bulletin board of photos from Team Power Day and it's hanging in the break room. A key component of the Team Building exercise was to divide us all into teams and then set these teams against each other in challenges and competitions, like the "Make a Funny Hat Race" and the "Left-Handed Water Balloon Toss." See, that's how we grownups learn teamwork. Team Power, Yea!

We were supposed to come up with names for our teams, like the Lions, or the Giants. We chose names like The Buttholes, The Dipshits, and the Addicts. Margaret got upset and went and told Barry. He made us change back to the Giants, the Lions, and the Orioles.

On her bulletin board, she had put together a "Results" sheet that showed which teams had won the most points, indicated by more of her stupid sticky stars next to each team's name. The winning team was the Bobcats, who were actually the Vomits.

The excitement of finding out which team has the most stars almost has us forgetting that it is, once again Live Interview Day. As Margaret walks into the room, carrying her stool for her regular pep talk, I wonder what would happen if I stand on my chair and call for volunteers to strangle her.

I have no interviews lined up today. Mike won't be happy, but for some crazy reason I keep thinking Angela might drop in so I'm keeping my calendar open. I was really disturbed when her contact information had all led nowhere. The golden ball was locked in my drawer and I want her to have it back. This morning I took it out and held it. It's beautiful, and she was right, it does make me feel better, watching the light sparkle on it, and rolling it slowly in my hand. I set it back on the desk in front of me. As Margaret begins her "inspirational" speech of the day, the ball starts to move. It rolls an inch to the right.

Weeks go by. Dreary, pointless weeks spent shuffling resumes in the Great Western building. Each one of those forms represents someone's desperate hope. They're looking for something to change in their lives. I get that. But they only see their own, individual page. I see hundreds of them, and I see them now for what they are, white flags, waved by an endless stream of sad, pathetic people. If they dropped off the earth, who would care?

Angela seems to have dropped off the earth now too. I'm surprised how much I care. I've called her numbers again, and gone by the copy shop a few times, but it came to nothing. I even Googled her. There was nothing for any Angela Cappobianco, but there were pages on Angel. He was indeed a legend in his time. He played sax and sat in with the best. His biggest years were the 20's and 30's though. At first I took them as clues to Angela's age, but the math didn't work out, so I figured there was part of the story I didn't have.

Two months pass, then, on another Live Interview Day, she appears. With no warning, she steps into my cubicle. She's wearing the same flowing scarves, billowing coat and patchouli scent. Stephanie hadn't buzzed me, and I hadn't seen her coming down the hall. I just feel a presence and look up, and there she is.

Her hair is shining and her smile is radiant. "Hi," she says. "I've been thinking of you. I thought I'd I better come by and cheer you up again."

"Where have you been?" I get up and spread my arms. We aren't supposed to hug candidates, but I'm going to anyway. My first impressions of Angela had been that she was pretty stout, but as I close my arms around her, she seems to shrink inside her coat. She is suddenly delicate and light, and surprisingly small. I look into her eyes and it's as if I am seeing a radiant young woman. I hesitate before saying, "You know, Angela, you're in big trouble."

"Oh, I know. I've been bad, but you'll forgive me, right?" She pats me on the arm, gathers her coat and scarfs around herself and settles into the chair. She's the Angela I know again.

"I've already forgiven you. But you walked out of here and didn't leave me any way of getting in contact with you. Why'd you do that?"

"I knew I'd be back. You need me. You've been angry, and sad now too."

"No. Angry? Me? No. Not really. I'm happy that you came by. I have your treasure for you. It was so very nice of you to give it to me, but I'm giving it back." I get the little ring box out and hold it out to her. She won't take it so I put it on the desk in front of her.

"You don't like it?" She tries to make a sad face, but I can tell she's smiling inside.

"I love it. It's beautiful. But it's too much for me. You should give it to your kids or grandkids."

"Well, maybe I will someday. But for now, you need it more than they do. It makes you feel better sometimes, doesn't it?"

"As a matter of fact, it does. It's funny, but, yeah."

She reaches out and touches my wrist. "You'll want it when the anger hits again. It will show you what to do."

"I'm really not all that angry you know."

"It's okay. You don't have to say it. But, anger can be so fun. Sometimes, if you act on it, let it rage forth, your dreams can really come true." She leans forward and her voice lowers to a whisper. "Don't be afraid to let yourself be happy." Then, she picks up the golden ball and puts it in my hand. "Now, you keep it."

"Angela, I can't."

"We don't say 'can't,' at Benson Staffing, do we! That's not Positive!" Christ, it's Margaret, lurking around the cubicle walls with her damned tray of donuts. She turns to Angela. "And who do we have here?"

"This is Angela. You met-."

"So nice to meet you, Angela. You can just call me Margaret." She offers her tray. "Would you like a donut? We have glazed, chocolate, and sugar-coated."

"Oh, no thank you, Margaret. That's very kind. But -."

Margaret cut her off. "We girls have to watch our figures, right?" Then she turns to me. "Now let's try to be a little more positive, shall we?"

"Right. Yes, Margaret; Positive and Up. Will do." My fist closes on the little jewel box.

Suddenly President Mike is behind her. "Hi, donuts? Yum! Munchies!-What's-going-on? Hi! I'm-Mike-Benson, President! What's-going-on? - Huh? - Who's-this?"

Jesus, he's been at the nose candy again. "It's –."

"Hi! I'm-Mike-Benson. I'm-the-President-around-here! You-can-call-me-Mike! Any-problems-you-have-with-this-guy, - you-tell-me.- My-office-is-upstairs! - I-have-windows!" Angela raises her hand, but he keeps on, "Got-a-new-bike! You-like-motorcycles?" He notices her raised hand. "What!"

Angela gently touches her nose, then she slowly points her finger at Mike and says, "Mr. Benson, Mike, I think you might have a little bit of sugar, just there, on your nose. Probably from a donut."

Margaret spins around and looks at him, "Mike! Can I see you a minute?" She grabs his arm and drags him off. He's still babbling as she shoves him toward his office.

"My, a bit of a sugar rush?" Angela asks.

"That's my boss. The owner's son."

"I know." She smiles and stands up. "Are we angry again?"

"It's best if I don't say anything more right now."

"Well, I'll just be off."

"Angela, please, take it back." I hold the box out to her.

She opens it, takes the golden ball out and puts it on the desk. "I'll just take the box. You don't need that any more."

"No. Angela, please."

"You still need the ball. Keep it near you on your desk. It will show you what to do." She turns to go, but stops and looks back to me. "Don't be cross with me, but I've left you another tiny little present. It'll be fun." Then she giggles and is gone. And so is the light.

Margaret was out of the office the whole following week. She and Barry were at a Team Building conference in Las Vegas. When they came back, they both had glowing tans and she had simply "loads" of ideas for team building and morale enhancement. The first big announcement was that Fridays would be "Dress Casual Fridays" from now on. For our first "Casual Friday," she and Barry wore their new "What Happens in Vegas, Stays in Vegas" t-shirts.

President Mike celebrated "Casual Friday" in a flowery Hawaiian shirt, shorts and flip-flops. He went through the whole sixth floor telling everyone he wouldn't be in the office for two weeks and passing out brochures for yacht rentals in the Bahamas.

Casual Friday wasn't the morale booster that Margaret had hoped. Despite the number of polo shirts and khakis spotted on the sixth floor of Benson Staffing that day, no one could say that morale was soaring. So, when Mike was spotted walking through the room, followed by Margaret carrying her stool, audible groans could be heard above the clicking of keyboards and mice.

"Everyone? Everyone? Can we have your attention? Everyone?" Margaret is threatening to pep us up. "We have some great news for you all. Very exciting! Everyone?" She turns to Mike. "Mike here has something to say that I think you'll all love. Mike?"

She steps down and Mike, flowered shirt, flip-fops and all, climbs onto the stool. As he runs his hands over his shaved head, and composes himself, I begin to feel the familiar rage. I take the golden marble from my drawer and put it in front of me on the desk. It looks beautiful and calm sitting there. Gazing at it, I can almost completely tune him out, but not entirely.

"…a great day for Benson Staffing," Mike is speaking. "…just learned that I have been accepted into the Young Presidents Association of San Francisco…. you probably have no idea how great this is for me…"

As he brays on, I try to focus my concentration on the little ball. It's beginning to work. I can feel an inner calm approaching. As I stare at it, the ball starts to roll. It seems natural that it should. It makes a little path around my coffee cup, past the keyboard, and my notepad, to the edge of the desk, and then it drops over the side.

I grab for it, but it slips through my finger, falls to the floor and rolls under my desk. I drop to my knees and crawl after it. In the dim light, I can see it. An undulating pink glow is emanating from the golden ball. As I reach out my hand, the pulsing grows stronger, brighter, more urgent. I can feel its heat, searing my fingertips. I want to pull back, but there's a power drawing me closer, getting stronger. The ball is moving, getting more and more agitated and it appears to be attacking something lying beneath it on the floor. As I get closer, I realize what it is.

It's from Angela, torn from her coat, a button. I reach out and touch it. Suddenly, a voice is pounding in my head. It's roaring, "This is what you asked for. You're angry! Let's have some fun! Do it!" Jesus Christ! It's Angela. She's inside my brain, commanding me with her tone and pushing me, driving me with her words. "The rage. The rage. It's so good. Let's have some fun. Push the button!"

"God damn them all to hell! Yes!"

The blast was spectacular.

The Paris Writers Club

For years, it didn't matter. Time would go by and I could look away, live my life as if it had never happened. Years of silence, nights of rest, days of sunshine and rain, just like anyone else. The past was fading. The memories were silent. It happened so long ago, that I'd forgotten where I'd hidden the gun.

It's been soft and still in the black swamp of floating things I can't look at. If I kept moving, I could leave it behind. But now it's back, lurking, just beyond where the darkness begins. I've got to do this. It's no longer possible to live this way. I can't sleep. When I close my eyes, the visions come in shattered images; exploding, blood-drenched flashes that blind and illuminate at the same time. I see panicked eyes, pleading, "don't."

Am I drowning, dreaming, or locked in a grave? I struggle to climb out, to escape, but my arms are pinned, my legs, leaden. I have to tell this. I have to open the grave so I'll know that he's still in it.

I'm not hiding in Paris. I wasn't hiding in San Francisco, or Oakland, or the ranch outside Wichita, or any other shit-hole I fell into on the road. It's just that Paris is where it caught up with me. When I blacked out on the Metro, that's when the panic broke through. I woke up in a strange woman's arms. "Sir? Sir, are you all right?" She was beautiful.

She was speaking English, asking me a question I couldn't answer. So, I just said, "I'm fine, fine. Just, I don't know, stress." Her arms felt so strong and yet, so tender. I wanted to stay there and disappear.

Cris Hammond

"But you just collapsed. You should get some rest or something. You don't look well." She helped me to my feet and held me for a moment longer. "You sure you're okay?"

"I'm – yes, I'll be alright. I just need to, um, deal with it. Thank you, for being so kind. But I'll figure it out. Thank you. My stop is coming up."

"You don't look good. Can I say something?"

"Sure, what?"

"Talk to someone? Talk it out, or maybe write about it. Sometimes that helps. I did it once. It gets it out. It really helped."

"Thanks. I'll…I'll do that." The doors opened and I stepped onto the platform and watched the car pull away, taking her with it. I never learned her name, but it started with her.

I'm sitting in an apartment off the Faubourg Saint Antoine. It's on the fourth floor of a 19th century building overlooking a small park, enjoying a sparkling glimpse of the Seine behind the ancient fortress of the Chateau Vincennes. Books line the walls and cover the floors. Silkscreen prints of Thai dancers hang next to paint-by-numbers pictures of bullfighters. Teresa, a recently published author, opens her apartment once a week to a small group of writers who bring their work, and some snacks, for sharing and friendly, gentle critiquing.

It's my second time here. I came last week to get a feeling for the place and the group, but I didn't bring anything I'd written. Today, I've come prepared with a few pages, the beginning of my story. The other writers in The Paris Writers Club are sitting around the tiny apartment, copies of my work in hand, ready to make notes and suggestions. They'll check the punctuation, and spelling, watch for words that are repeated too often, find places where more "color" or "verve" can be added. They'll make comments like, "Can we improve the sense of place? I'm not quite there." Or, "You lost me here on page three. Who's speaking?"

They will also check for holes in the story, things that don't add up or don't seem possible. I'm ready to smile and nod. I'll agree, "Great input. It helped a lot. Thanks," and I'll jot down notes.

The group is committed to helping everyone improve their work, polish their style, create riveting characters and drama. Someday they'll all get agents and publishers. That's what they're hoping for. Not me. I just want the terrors to stop. The truth has to come out or I'll go mad. I can tell my story in this room. They don't have to know it's the truth.

My pages have been passed around and now Teresa turns to me. She smiles and her look says, "We're all ears."

"Okay. It's my first time reading, so please bear with me if I stumble a bit." I'm nervous as I clear my throat. I begin:

"It was about twenty years ago, 1995 or '96. Our daughter was only nineteen. Just beginning life. Starting college. Learning to breathe her own air. She was happy.

Then she met him. He was a good-looking guy, curly blonde hair, blue eyes, six foot, nice car. He would come into Amilie's diner where she worked, and order coffee and sit and talk to her. Told her jokes, made her laugh. He said he was a contractor, building huge, luxury homes down in Silicon Valley. He claimed to have a degree in Biochemistry from Stanford, wanted to be a doctor. But he told her he'd put that dream on hold to do work with this hands. He wanted to build things. Once in a while, he'd bring her a flower.

He made her feel pretty. She fell. That's when she told us about him. She was so excited. "His name's Bruce and he's a little bit older, twenty-seven or twenty-eight, but that doesn't matter. We just connect, totally." And that was it. She didn't tell us about the degree from Stanford or other things he'd told her. Just the basics: "He's really cute, and he has his own contracting company. He builds houses. You'll love him."

She cut back on school and they moved into a tiny house together in San Francisco. It wasn't far from us, and my wife, despite her misgivings, was trying to be excited about the whole thing, so she went over and helped them unpack, bought them dishes, linens. "I don't like it, but I can't stop her. She's nineteen," she said. "And if I start freaking out, it'll only push her away. I want her close right now."

So, I filed the fact that she was still a kid in a sealed box and lodged it in a crawl space in the basement of my mind. Then I went over to help put up shelves in their living room.

It was a shabby, little one-bedroom house behind a stately Georgian Style brick building near Sixth and Lake, backing up to the Presidio. I parked up the street and walked through piles of dry autumn leaves, down to number thirteen. A narrow driveway led down the side of the building to a steep, overgrown back yard. Lisa's house, a cabin really, was perched on rickety stilts over a boarded-up storage bay. Stone steps led up the hill to a peeling, glass-paned door that once was blue. I hefted my tool bag, and started the climb. The sloping deck swayed under my weight.

The door was ajar, so I stepped in. I was in a small, dark room that smelled of mold and dust. I guessed it was the living room. Two dirty windows let in a dull grey light that shone weakly across a wood plank floor and cast soft-edged shadows on stacks of boxes and pillows.

From down a dim hallway at the back, I could make out the sounds of plates and dishes being stacked in the kitchen. "Hey, Lisa. That you? It's me," I called.

Piles of crumpled newspaper grabbed at my feet as I picked my way across the room. As my eyes adjusted to the gloom, I recognized the old couch that had been in our basement, and her last apartment. It was shoved against the wall and covered with a sheet. A worn-out chair that I hadn't seen before was next to it with a small table placed in between. On the table was a framed photograph. It was the first time I laid eyes on Bruce.

I walked over and picked it up. The picture's soft corners and yellowing edges told me it was cut from a newspaper. Bruce was tall, and broad shouldered. He had lots of blonde hair and he was wearing a tuxedo, striding down the steps of a church. On his arm, was a woman in a wedding gown.

"Hey, Dad. Thanks for coming. Want some coffee?" Lisa was shouldering open a swinging door and leaning out of the small kitchen, her arms full of plates.

"Yeah, that'd be nice." I put the frame back on the table and dropped the tool bag on the floor. "Need some help?" I said, and moved slowly toward her.

She was wearing her favorite jeans and one of my old Giants t-shirts that I thought I'd thrown away. Her dark auburn hair was tied back in a ponytail and she had a light sheen of perspiration on her forehead. She shoved a small stepladder out of the way and plugged in the coffee maker. "So, what do you think? Don't you love it?" she asked.

"Oh, yeah. Love it. I like the living room, great view of the trees. Nice neighborhood, too." Small talk. What I wanted to say was, "Who's the bride? Was he married before?" What I said was, "So, where do you want those shelves?"

We went back to the living room with our coffee and settled on the couch. While I stirred sugar into mine, she moved a couple boxes to the middle of the room and dragged out a small pile of wooden planks that we'd use for shelves. "So, Lisa, I have to ask you. What's with that picture? Is Bruce married? Divorced? What?"

She stopped, put the wood down and blew out a breath. She touched her hair and her eyes got sad, and then she reached over and in one quick motion, picked up the picture and shoved it into a box on the floor. She said, "He's a widower. She died. In Chicago."

"She died? How'd she die?"

"She was murdered," she said, and pushed the frame deeper into the box.

"What? Jesus. Who? What happened?"

"He thinks it was drug dealers. But they never solved it. He couldn't live there anymore. He doesn't like to talk about it. He gets really strange, upset, when I ask him about it, so I don't."

"But, the picture. It was sitting right there."

"I know. I thought he'd put it away. Sorry."

"Why would drug dealers murder his wife? Was she involved with drugs?"

"No! I don't know. That's just what he said. He really doesn't like to talk about it so I don't push him. He's just trying to move on, so I leave him alone. He's fragile right now."

"How long ago was it?"

"I don't know for sure, but a while. Let's, just - let's - can we work on the shelves now?"

"Right."

The shelves went up quickly. I located a couple of studs then anchored the shelf brackets to them with two-inch lag screws. I set the boards on top, and Bingo, she had shelves.

"Wow, thanks, Dad. You made it look easy. I just know it would have taken me all day to do that."

"Ah, it's no big deal. I'm sure Bruce could have done it in half the time," I said as I dropped the electric screwdriver back into my bag. "Or had one of his men do it."

"His men?"

"Yeah. Carpenters? Doesn't he have carpenters working for him? Building houses?"

"Oh, no. He's not doing that anymore. He's selling that business."

"Selling it? Really? I thought he was busy, tons of work these days. Why's he selling it?"

"It's kind of complicated. His back is all messed up and he keeps hurting it at work, so he decided to sell it. There's this guy who he works with who's going to buy him out, but there's some stuff that he's got to finish first and it might take a couple weeks or so. There's one house he's working on in Woodside, and two down near L.A. somewhere. He's down there now."

"Wow, sounds like a pretty big deal. What's he call his company?"

"It's just his name, Bruce Einholt Construction Company."

"Um-hm. Are they nice houses? Does he build them himself, on spec, or what?"

"I've only seen one, but it was really nice. He took me out there one Sunday. Nobody was working so we could climb all over the place. I'm not sure what 'on spec' means though. He just builds them, I think."

A month went by without much incident. My wife, Nadine, was dying to get them over for dinner so she could give Bruce a thorough grilling, but something always came up and they couldn't make it. Selling the business took a lot of time and he was going to L.A. at least twice a week. On the surface, things seemed normal, but I couldn't get the image of the murdered wife out of my mind. I went to the library and scanned old newspapers from Chicago, looking for anything about a drug gang murder. I found a couple stories, but nothing I could connect with him. More information from Lisa would have helped, but it was clear that the subject was out of bounds.

"Dad, can you do me a favor?" Lisa said when I answered the phone. It was mid-October, colder than I'd remembered it to be in years. I could actually see my breath inside the house in the morning. I hadn't heard from Lisa for almost a month. We'd left messages but stopped short of going over there. Unannounced visits don't often go over very well.

"A favor? Sure, honey, what's up?" I said, just glad that she was calling.

"Am I still on your insurance policy?" she asked.

"I'm not sure. I can check. What's wrong?" God, she better not be pregnant.

"Oh, it's not for me. Bruce's back is acting up and I was wondering if we could get some pain pills. Oxycontin or Vicodin or something."

"He doesn't have health insurance? Doesn't he need it to run his business?"

"No…I don't know. Anyway, he sold that business. He's buying another one."

"Did he hurt his back on the job? Maybe he can get workman's comp. Has he looked into that?" I asked. "He could make a claim."

"He didn't hurt it on the job. He hurt it when he was in the Army."

"In the Army? He was in the Army?" This guy's been around. "Okay, if he hurt his back in the Army, maybe he should go to the VA and see if he can get some therapy or coverage or something. You don't want to mess around with a bad back." I said, "I could maybe get a prescription for some pain pills, but that's no answer. He should get some real help for it."

"He can't go to the VA. I asked him and he said no."

"Why not?"

"He wasn't in the regular Army, Army. Something about some special thing he was in. It's really totally secret and he doesn't like to talk about it too much. I shouldn't even be telling you about it."

"Come on, what are you talking about? Are you saying he was some kind of secret Army spy or something? Lisa, that's nuts."

"He hurt his back on a secret mission, jumping out of a helicopter, okay? God, I promised I wouldn't tell you. It was in Iran."

"The hostage rescue thing? The one where they called it off because the helicopters crashed?"

"Yeah, that's the one. He totally screwed up his back when it crashed. He got a medal. But, I'm not supposed to talk about it because it's secret."

"It's not secret. It was all over the news."

"Well yeah, I know, but the guys who were in it were secret guys. It's all been erased. That's why he can't go to the VA, because his military records have been erased."

"Lisa, that sounds a little farfetched. Are you sure --."

"Dad, what's wrong with you?! Why do you always have to question everything? Can't you just believe me sometimes? I'm not stupid! God, Bruce was right. He said you'd think I was lying. Look! Never mind. I don't need your help." She hung up.

I stood there, staring at the phone in my hand. She'd never hung up on me before.

It was four days before Christmas when Nadine finally got them to come over for dinner. They'd begged off on Thanksgiving and this invitation seemed to be only grudgingly accepted. We were both a lot more than nervous. Nadine and I were relying on support from each other to stay pleasant, and not to ask a lot of questions.

From the street, I heard the distinctive downshift and engine whine of a high-powered Porsche coming around the corner. It stopped in front of the house and the engine revved a couple times before it shut off. They were here.

I opened the front door and watched them come up the steps to the porch. Lisa was in the lead, looking thin and tense, almost jittery, but making a real effort to smile and put on her "Merry Christmas" face. I put mine on and we hugged. "It's so nice to see you, honey. You look great," I said and turned to the man behind her whose face I'd only seen in his wedding photo. "This must be Bruce. Great to meet you in the flesh finally." I put out my hand. He had a firm grip, but his hand was damp. As he stepped through the doorway, I rubbed my palm dry on my jeans. We went inside.

We sat in the living room, picking at cubes of cheese and trying to get conversation going. "See that decoration right there on the tree? The snowflake with Bambi in it?" my wife pointed near the top of the tree. "We gave that to Lisa on her sixth birthday. Every year she'd put it on the tree as high as she could reach. It just got closer and closer to the top," she said. "After a while, we had to start getting taller trees," she laughed and looked at Lisa who was still looking uncomfortable.

Then Lisa sat up, laughed and said, "Bet I can put it right up there near the angel this year." She took the ornament off the tree and turned to Bruce and said, "Help me. Lift me up."

Bruce pushed himself off the couch and stood behind her. I watched him put his sweaty hands on my daughter's waist.

"Okay," he said. "When I count three, give a little hop and I'll lift you up. One, two, three!" She hopped up and he lifted and held her long enough to place the Bambi snowflake right next to the angel.

I kept a smile on my face as I watched him set her down, then fuss and straighten her blouse. "Wow," I said. "Looks like the back's better."

Teresa is perched on the arm of her sofa, holding a mug of hot tea. She makes a couple notes on the pages she holds, then she lays them gently on the table in front of her. Her pale blue eyes are deeply sincere and she has them locked onto mine to emphasize her point. "Thank you, that was really good. Good start. I'm intrigued to find out what happens next with this guy who I suspect is very seriously evil. Shall we open it up for comments?"

She turns her gaze to the other five people, seated around a small coffee table piled with bits of brioche and croissant, scattered among steaming mugs of tea. She swings her cup toward a man sitting across from her.

He takes the cue. "I liked it too. Good beginning, but I have some concerns." Craig is an American, about thirty-five, heavy set, with dark wavy hair and a manicured beard. He is working on a non-fiction biography of Ty Cobb, the baseball star. "I'm just a little concerned that Bruce claims to have a degree in Biochemistry from Stanford. I get that he's a liar. But, wouldn't a practiced liar keep his lies a little easier to believe? Know what I mean? I don't know if Lisa would believe him. Maybe you should change it to something like, I don't know, Civil Engineering? Also, if he's from Chicago, maybe he would say he went to Northwestern? Instead of Stanford?"

I nod my head and look down at my pages and scribble in the margin.

"Um, may I just say?" Eva had raised a finger. Her British accent lends all her comments an air of learned sophistication. Her novel in progress is based on her grandparents' experiences in World War II and a dark secret that threatened to ruin their lives. She is still bundled in the parka and scarf she's worn in from the cold. Her hair has purple tips and is shaved close on one side. She takes a breath and says, "It bothers me that the girl's parents would let their nineteen-year-old daughter move in with a guy she's just met. I just wonder if they wouldn't put up more of a fight?"

"I think it happens a lot in the US." Craig interjects. "Lots of people live together in college. But, I'm confused a little about the college. Is she in college and who's paying for it?"

"Good point, Craig. Thank you. I'll take a look at that." I pretend to make another note in the margin of my pages, and I'm thinking, "They're talking about the fucking writing, not about what really happened. God, she was only nineteen. She believed him."

It had been a dark and freezing week in Paris. My shoes are wet through from the rain, my toes burning from the cold when I come out of the metro stop at Faubourg Saint Antoine. I had been able to write more during the week, but it was getting increasingly difficult to keep up with the words when they came gushing out. The attacks were coming more frequently.

As I climb the steps to Teresa's flat, a sense of déjà vu rushes over me. A ghostlike dread grips my chest and the ringing in my ears becomes a pounding throb. Waves of nausea envelope me and I cling to the railing and gasp for air. "Not now!" I say aloud. "No attacks, not now. Breathe." The panic fades, its roar subsides, like a train into the distance.

And then it's back. The ringing in my ears rising to a screeching howl, sweat rolling down my chest and the images again, I can't keep them away. Explosions. I can feel the kick in my fist. I see his soft white hands in the air, as if that would stop me.

I'm getting scared. He's coming back. I can feel it. He's close. But he can't come back. He can't. Without a face? No. He'll never come back.

"Are you okay?" I open my eyes. Teresa is cradling her teacup and pointing her chin at me. She looks concerned. The others look away as I scan the room. They sip tea and shuffle their pages.

"Fine. I'm fine. Sorry. Shouldn't have had that extra coffee, I guess."

She looks into my eyes a second longer and says, "So, how was your week? Were you able to get some more work done? Want to read?"

"Sure," I say. "But I didn't really get to fixing some of the things you guys mentioned last time. I started, but I decided to keep going on the story and get it out. Polish it later. The more I can get down on paper, the better I'll feel."

"Isn't that the truth, right?" Teresa says to the group. Then she turns back to me. "Would you like to go first? I'm dying to hear more about Bruce."

"Okay. Again, I'm sorry if I stumble a bit. I'm not used to sharing like this. Um, last week I stopped with Bruce lifting the daughter up to the Christmas tree. Remember his back pain and all that?"

"Yes," Teresa says. "The parents are finally meeting the mysterious Bruce. Go ahead."

My hands are still trembling as my eyes strain to focus on the page and begin to read:

"I was in Delta Force." Bruce was finally talking. The silence hadn't been total. There were some coughs, offers of wine and chips. I thought I had really blown it and my daughter would hate me forever. But after some time looking stunned, Bruce opened up. "I was in a specially trained unit that did covert operations and secret missions."

"Bruce, you don't have to go into all this," my wife said as she wiped imaginary crumbs off the coffee table.

"He parachuted into Nicaragua once," Lisa added. "And El Salvador, right?" She looked at Bruce with her eyes wide, the way she does when she's making you feel special, and wants something. He nodded back.

"Wow, that sounds really hairy," I said. "I can see why you probably shouldn't be talking about the things that you had to do. How'd you get out of those places? You know, after your mission?"

"I had maps and coordinates, and equipment to find my way. Also, there were people on the ground who were in place to help get me to an airfield, and there would be a plane to take me out," he said. "Anyway, there's no record of any of this, so I should just leave it at that. That's the problem with getting into the VA and stuff. But yeah, the back's a lot better."

"Look, sorry about the pain pill thing. I just didn't understand. What are you going to do about it though? Can you get insurance?"

"Oh, yeah. I'm buying a business, car repair, Porsches, and it will have insurance that I can get on. But the back's really a lot better anyway, so…"

"Well, that's a relief," Nadine said. "You should look into that right away. You're too young to have to deal with back pain all the time."

"Did you say Porsches? I love those cars," I said. "I used to have one years ago, before we were married. Crashed it though."

"Well, we'll be working on Porsches and Volkswagens mainly, but other German cars too."

"Wow, you build houses, you fix cars. Like to work with your hands, I see. Plus, you get to drive them. Nice perk. That was a Porsche you drove over in, right?"

"Yeah, 911."

"Thought so. My dentist drives a Porsche. It's a 911, too. 911C I think. What's yours?"

"Same. 911C."

"Dinner time," Nadine said. She got up and headed for the kitchen but not without giving me the look that says, "Shut up now."

The evening wound to a close after an elaborate dinner, slaved over for two days by Nadine, and enjoyed largely in silence. We ended the evening with three coffees and one whiskey, mine. As we were walking Bruce and Lisa down the front steps and out to their car, I turned to Bruce and said, "Donde esta la biblioteca?"

"Huh?" he blinked and managed a confused look as he fumbled for his keys.

"Donde esta la biblioteca?"

"What's that? I don't understand."

"Donde esta la biblioteca? It's Spanish. It means, 'Where is the library?' Don't you speak any Spanish?"

"No. Where's the library? I don't get it," he said.

"Sorry. I get one little whiskey in me and I start showing off. Forget it." I said.

"Right, Dad." Lisa punched me on the arm as she went around and opened her door. "Come on Bruce, let's go. Bye Mom. Dinner was great. Love you." She slid into the car and closed the door.

Bruce opened his window and said, "Thanks a lot for dinner."

"Loved having you." Nadine gave a little wave. "Now you drive safe going home."

"Yeah, go easy on the gas pedal, man," I said. "That C-Class Porsche is a monster you know."

"I know. That's why I love it," he said and gave the engine a couple revs.

"Hey! Stop that!" I said. "Safe home you guys, bye."

Bruce put it into gear and the car moved slowly down the block and around the corner.

Nadine turned to me and frowned. "What was that 'biblioteca' stuff all about?"

"Wanted to see if he spoke Spanish," I said.

"Why? What's that got to do with anything?"

"You think if he was a Delta Force specialist, chosen to be parachuted into secret missions in El Salvador and Nicaragua, it would be kind of helpful if he spoke Spanish?" I said. Her eyes went wide and she put her fingertips to her mouth. "Also, there is no such thing as a Porsche 911C. There's an S, an SE, and an E. But no C. The guy's full of shit."

Teresa is dipping her teabag up and down in her cup. "Thank you. I like where this is going. But I have a couple of comments, or just a question?" She raises her eyebrows. "I wonder if we could hear more of what the wife is thinking? Maybe some dialogue between Lisa and Nadine. I would think the mother would be a little more concerned."

Ellen, an American journalist working on a screenplay, says, "Um, is there anything you can add here to make the Bruce character at least a little bit likeable? It might deepen his character and give us more reason to believe why Lisa has fallen for him so hard. I mean, she says he's fragile. Maybe you could expand on that. Show a tender side?"

"I see what you mean. Good idea. Yeah, I'll work on that." My fist trembles as I write my notes; "lies, lies, lies!!!"

I write all week. The words are coming out in a torrent. I read them back and sometimes they are nearly unintelligible. I have to make real sentences, phrases that make sense, and words that paint the images I don't want to remember. When I write them, I see it again and the nausea returns and the lights dance, flickering around my eyes. But, I haven't passed out this week. Maybe, telling the story, facing it, is really helping.

Today, Ruth brought homemade lasagna for us to share. Teresa made a salad, Eve and Craig brought boxes of cookies and I brought a bottle of wine. Empty plates and half-full wine glasses are scattered around the tiny room. Only Craig and I haven't read. So, Teresa spins a spoon on the table and it points to me. She nods. "Your turn."

I empty my wine glass and start to read:

"It was almost two months before I got the call. It was from a guy named Jerry Manifusco who owned a German car repair shop in Burlingame. He had some interesting questions.

"I'm calling about Bruce Campbell. He put you down as a reference," Jerry said.

"Bruce who?"

"Campbell. You used to work with him, doing construction? Knew him in Chicago? He put you as his reference."

"I'm sorry, I – reference for what?"

"A job. On his job application, he put you down as a reference."

"Uh, sorry. I don't know anyone named –."

Jerry interrupted me, "Christ! You don't know him? He said you were his father-in-law for Christ's sake. Shit, I knew it."

"He said I was his father-in-law? In Chicago?

"Yeah."

"He said my daughter was his wife in Chicago?"

"That's what he said, ya."

"Did he say what happened to this wife of his in Chicago?"

"Yeah, he did. I'm sorry about that."

"What kind of a job is he applying for?" I asked.

"Oh, I gave him the job a while ago. It's just a cleanup job, around the shop. It's simple stuff, cleaning up after the guys. That's why I didn't bother to call all his references."

"Why are you calling me now? What's happened?" I asked.

"Do you know this guy or what?" I could tell that Jerry was thinking he might be wasting his time.

"I don't know a Bruce Campbell, but I know another Bruce. Might be him."

"Well this Bruce might be a thief, or worse even."

"What's he up to?"

"Not sure it's him, but it looks like it."

"What?"

"Well, he started just working afternoons, cleaning up the shop, de-greasing the floors, replacing all the tools. He usually got out of here same time as me." Jerry paused. "But after a couple weeks, he said he was going back to some classes at Stanford and wanted to know if he could come in later, about seven, work nights, weekends. I figured it'd be okay, so I gave him a key and the alarm code."

"Uh-oh," I said.

"Yeah, right. That's when things started growing wings, and flying out the door. Just tools at first."

"I might know this guy."

"Now I'm getting invoices from my suppliers for parts and tools I never ordered. None of it ever showed up." Jerry's voice was getting tight. "I figure it's gotta be him."

"Did you ask him about it?"

"Yeah, I asked him. Son-of-a-bitch threatened me. Said he was some kind of Green Beret, trained to kill, and he would break my back if I gave him any shit, and he could kill me and nobody would do anything about it, because he was Delta secret force, protected by the government or some shit."

"Jesus."

"Turns out he's also threatened one of my mechanics. The guy is pretty freaked out."

"What's he look like?" I asked, and Jerry proceeded to describe Bruce Einholt. "I know who this guy is, I think. I didn't know he'd threaten people though."

"Might be the drugs. I'm pretty sure he's doin' it or selling, or both. I'm about to call the cops. Thought I'd call you first. See if this guy is as crazy as he seems. If he's a vet and all, well –"

"Drugs? What. Wait, do me a favor and hold off on the cops until I can come down and we can talk." I said. "Where's your shop?" Jerry agreed to hold off for a day and gave me an address in the South Bay.

"Um, can I break in here a second?" It's Nita, the poet. "Um, I wasn't here last week, so maybe I'm a little lost, but if this man, Jerry, suspects one of his employees of stealing, why doesn't he just fire him?"

"That's a good question, Nita." Teresa turns to me. "You say that Bruce threatened Jerry. Maybe we need to hear more of that here. What do you think?"

"Interesting. I see what you mean," I say, and put my head down to make a note. Then I say, "But, maybe this Jerry doesn't want to just burn Bruce right away. He hired him after all. Must have liked him at some level anyway. I'll work on it though. Thanks."

"In the US, it isn't always that easy to just fire someone." It's Craig. "Especially if you're going to also accuse them of stealing. You could get your ass sued, man."

Eva looks surprised. "Really? I guess I didn't realize that about the U.S. Maybe you might want to just mention that here, just to kind of let us know some of the other forces at work?" She likes to end her sentences on an up note, like a question.

I write a note to myself in the margins. "What the fuck do they know about it?"

Teresa turns to me. "Do you want to go on? It looks like you've got three or four more pages?"

"Sure, if you don't mind? I'll go fast."

"Go ahead."

I continue reading:

"It wasn't a big place but it was clean and the work was humming. Three lifts and six bays, all filled with Porsches, Volkswagens, and BMWs. He had six mechanics who looked like they were factory-trained guys, not just cleaned-up shade-tree mechanics off the street. The sounds of hydraulic torque wrenches and ball peen hammers echoed off the metal walls and fourteen-foot ceilings. Jerry was a short brick of a guy. Swarthy thick cheeks covered with a roughly hacked, three-day beard. His hands were black, but his shirt, with a patch that said "Jerry" on the chest, was clean. When he grabbed my hand to shake it, I didn't feel flesh. I felt oak. He tried to be cordial, but his smile was cold, and forced. He motioned me to follow him into his office.

He shut the door and pointed at a chair that looked like it had gotten lost from a '60's breakfast set where the kids carried forks in their back pockets. I sat on a Bosche Parts catalogue, rather than on what was left of the seat.

"Okay, do you know this guy?" he started right in.

"Yeah, I do," I said.

"What the fuck's going on? Bruce Campbell? Bruce Whatever. Is the guy a thief or what? Why shouldn't I just call the cops and fuck 'im?"

"The name I got is Bruce Einholt. Look, I only know this guy because my daughter's messed up with him. She's nineteen."

"Oh Christ." Jerry rubbed his jaw and it sounded like sandpaper on concrete.

"What do you think he stole from you?" I asked. "Parts? Tools? If you give me a list or some idea, I'll go to their place tonight and look around. See if I can find any of it. If I do, I'll bring it back and you'll be okay. Then you fire the shit-ass and we're done."

"What about the drugs?" he asked.

"I was gonna ask you about that. What drugs?"

"Look, we got customers here. They come in and leave their cars. We write down the mileage, for the guarantee, you know. Well, lately I been noticing some cars going outta here with too many miles on the clock. Not huge, forty, fifty miles extra. But it ain't right. He's taking them night running."

"He's stealing cars and joyriding? What's that got to do with drugs?"

"Couple days ago, in a Porsche, I found some shit I didn't like. A spoon. Not a coke spoon. Found those before. This is a Porsche and Beemer shop. It's normal. But this was a cooking spoon. That's H. My customers ain't into that stuff."

"Shit."

"Shit is right." He pushed his chair back from his desk and pointed a finger the size of a head bolt at me. "If that fucker is muling heroin, or even doing it in my customers' cars, I'll have his ass."

"Okay, look, Jerry. Just hold off for one more day, please. If that's what he's into, I gotta get my daughter out of there before the cops come in. Just, give me a chance to go in there tonight and see what I can find. If you call the cops and they go roaring in and bust him for drugs, all your shit will be gone with him. They'll seize it and it'll be gone. If I can find your stuff, I can get it out before the cops come in. Let me get my daughter away from him before any of this shit starts flying around. Once she's safe, if I find anything that will bust his ass for coke or heroin, I'll put it on the fireplace mantle and call the cops in on 911. I want this motherfucker out of my daughter's life, forever. I want him gone. Can you keep him here tonight until eight or nine? That'll give me time to see what I can find."

He looked at me and his fist came up and grated concrete again. "I got a kid," he said after a while. "She's twenty-one now. She got mixed up with a bum like this when she was younger. I should'a killed the bastard. I wish I had. I hurt him, but not enough. She's still messed up." He looked down and opened his desk drawer. Then he closed it again. "I'll keep him here. Get your daughter out of there."

On the way back up to San Francisco, I called my wife. "Hey, it's me."

"How'd it go? Is it as bad as I think?" Her voice was tight and she sounded small and frightened through the lousy cell connection.

"It's pretty bad. I'll tell you all about it when I get home, but I want you to do something."

"What?"

"Call Lisa and tell her you want to take her to dinner tonight, and a movie. Just you and her. It has to be tonight." I said.

"What's up? What are to going to do?"

"This mechanic guy says that Bruce has been stealing from him. He's got a whole list of stolen tools and parts and stuff that he thinks Bruce took. I'm going to their place tonight to look for it. If I find it, we'll call the cops and get him busted."

"Jesus. I can't believe this is happening. Do you think Lisa knows about this? She's living with a thief and they're hiding stolen stuff in their house? I don't believe it."

"I'll be home in a half hour. Just make sure you and she go out tonight. Go to a movie or something, anything. Just make sure she's out of the house. I'll see you in a little bit." I closed the phone and tossed it on the seat next to me. "Shit-fuck-and damn!" I hollered and slammed my fist into the dashboard.

"Drugs?" Nadine's voice split the air in the kitchen like a hatchet thrown against a wall. "What are you telling me? He's dealing drugs?"

"That's what I want to find out. I'm sure he's a thief, though."

"God, how'd this happen?" Nadine's voice rose to almost a wail. "We never should have let her move in with that creep."

"She's nineteen. She's an adult. Remember? Maybe, if this gets nasty, she'll see what he is and leave. I mean, all that crap about him being a secret Delta Force assassin? She still believes that stuff. If we say it's bullshit, she just gets mad at us and closer to him. But if he gets arrested and all this stuff starts coming out, and from the cops, not from us, maybe she'll finally see him for the lying psycho that he is. But it can't come from us."

"Okay. I'll take her to a movie and a late dinner or something."

"Good. That should do it."

"Be careful, please," she said. "What if Bruce comes home? What if he catches you in there? Is he dangerous?"

"I doubt he's dangerous. I'm sure all that Special Forces, 'trained to kill' stuff is all in his head."

"Still, he's big, and he's strong. What if he catches you and he really is dealing drugs? I don't want you getting hurt."

"Jerry said he'd keep him working at the shop tonight. He's gonna wait for me to call before he lets him go."

"Take the gun."

"What?"

"Just in case anything goes wrong. Take it, please."

A nine-millimeter Smith and Wesson weighs just under two pounds, fully loaded. This one used to belong to my father. He left me the gun and a 1979 Volkswagen Bug when he died. The car didn't run and had outstanding tickets, the son-of-a-bitch. There was no holster for the gun, but there was a plastic bag full of bullets. He'd shown me how to fire it one time when he was drunk and thought he'd take out a wall in his apartment. Open things up. Let in some light. He wondered why I didn't ask him to come live with us in his last years.

Two pounds doesn't seem like a lot, but the shape is awkward. You know you're carrying a Smith. It affects the way you walk.

Lisa had locked the place up when she left to meet Nadine, but the hinges on the door were so sloppy that all I had to do was lift on the handle, give it a nudge, and the thing swung open.

It was a dump. I could tell that Lisa was trying to make it livable, but it was still a dump. Dishes were stacked in a kitchen too small for cooking, but at least they were clean. There were two piles of clothes on the couch, which was covered with what looked like an old tablecloth. One pile was definitely dirty.

I had my list from Jerry. I was looking for a hydraulic floor jack, three new sets of metric socket wrenches, a compressor, and a set of pneumatic torque wrenches, for a start. It only took a second to see that none of that stuff was lying around in the living room or bedroom, so I went back outside and climbed down under the house. I turned on my flashlight and the beam fell on a bright red, hydraulic floor jack. Bingo. Jerry will be pleased.

I went back upstairs to look for the other stuff, which I really didn't want to find. There was nothing obvious sitting out on the counters or tables. It looked like Bruce drank a fair amount of beer and they liked Chinese food. I went through all the drawers and cupboards and found nothing interesting until I dug deep under the sink, behind a cruddy toilet plunger. It was a set of scales. One of those old kind with weights to counterbalance whatever you were measuring. The weights were in grams.

Then I found it and my stomach turned; a razorblade and a small mirror with shadowy lines of white powder, in a drawer by the bed. That bastard.

My phone rang. I fumbled to flip it open and tugged on the antenna. "Jeez, you scared me." I said.

"Oh God! It's awful!" It was Nadine. She was hysterical, screaming. "It's Lisa! She's not – They're taking her away! She isn't conscious. They're taking her to the hospital. Oh, this can't be happening."

"What are you saying? Where are you? Nadine, talk to me."

"She went to the restroom. I waited but she didn't come back so I went to see. Oh God, she was on the floor, in convulsions! She's not conscious and they took her in the ambulance! Her nose. Oh, she was bleeding."

"Where is she? Which hospital? Talk to me, please."

"Saint Mary's. Oh God!"

"I'm on my way."

Tubes, electrodes, electronic heartbeat, green lines on a screen. One tiny, translucent hand is on top of the sheet. Blue veins. Stabbed. My baby lies there, broken. Her eyelids flicker, but they don't open. I touch her cheek. She doesn't feel me here. I want to scream. I wish my hands were claws, so I could slash through his chest and pull out his heart and crush it, like he's crushed mine. Instead, I clamp my eyes shut, control my breathing and ask, "What happened?"

"They think she snorted heroin, laced with something." Nadine's face was a contorted fright mask. "He gave it to her, didn't he!"

"Yes. It was him." I said.

"That was a close one." The doctor had just walked in. "Luckily you found her in time and she didn't have too much. I want to keep her here for at least a couple days though. There was something mixed into it that we haven't pinpointed yet. Something corrosive. The police are going to want to talk to her, too. Where'd she get it?" He was looking at me.

"God, if I only knew." I said. "We had no idea that she was involved with that stuff in any way. She's never -." I turned to Nadine. "Did you know she was into that shit?"

"Oh my god, no." Her eyes were beginning to well up.

His eyes locked onto mine for a second too long. "Well, you'll want to have a heart to heart talk with her in the morning when she comes around." He turned to go. "If you want to stay here tonight, just tell the nurse and she'll bring you a more comfortable chair and a blanket."

"Thank you." I said as he walked away. Then I turned to Nadine. "I've got to take care of something, but I'll be back in a little while. You stay here. Call me if you need me. I won't be long." She closed her eyes and nodded.

I flipped open my phone when I got back in the car. "Jerry. It's me. Is he still there? Good. You can send him home now. Yeah. Just tell him you're through for the night and send him home."

In the little cabin, I racked a round into the chamber of the Smith and Wesson, turned the lights off and sat down in the old chair to wait. I realized that I was looking forward to this.

It's still winter in Paris but I'm beginning to sense that the clouds are thinning. The sky that was so dark, for so long is turning almost luminous. Soon it will be blue again. I no longer walk the streets and see faces glaring at me as if there was a hideous stain splashed across my face.

The fits are gone. No blackouts. No terrors. Bruce is gone. Still interned under the dirt in the forest, this time I know he'll stay there. I'm not frightened anymore. I've found a way to keep the memories in their places, buried deep, with the bodies. I'll just write about them. Read them to the group. They'll think they're just stories, fiction. And the bodies will stay buried, all of them.

"So, do you have something you want to read this week? Something dark, and shocking?" Teresa smiles and blows on her tea.

"Actually, yes, I do. It's a new thing, still coming out, so please, bear with me."

As I look around the group and smile, I feel another black weight begin to float away from my secret soul, and I take a breath. I know that this is how I can live with the ghosts. They don't terrify me anymore. They make good stories and the group loves hearing them. They're smiling as I start to read.

"Even standing here on the platform with the train rumbling and groaning toward me, I can still hear it echoing in my head; the sharp, hollow crack of the bat against her skull. She didn't scream, or cry out. It was just a short moan that nobody heard. It was her fault. She wouldn't stop talking. She wouldn't shut up. Always asking questions, staring at me, like she could see inside me. She denied it, of course. But she knew. Just like the others. And she would have told someone."

Cris Hammond

About the Author

Cris Hammond is an artist, writer, cartoonist and entrepreneur, currently living in Paris. His comic strip, *Speed Walker, Private Eye,* appeared daily in over 150 newspapers across the U.S. His oil and watercolor paintings of ships, the sea, and rural France, have been shown in galleries across the nation. Mr. Hammond has contributed to special effects teams of George Lucas' Industrial Light and Magic, winning Academy Awards for films such as *Star Trek III & IV, Innerspace, and The Abyss.*

In 1994, he took a life-changing detour into the corporate world. Eight years later, he left that world with a new determination, to paraphrase Boz Scaggs, *"to get up and make his life shine."*

So, he sold his house, bought a canal barge in France and set off on a fifteen-year journey through the canals and rivers of the country. The voyage has taken him and his wife through over 1500 kilometers of inland waterways and rewarded them with a floating home on the water in the heart of Paris. His first book, *From Here to Paris,* is an inspiring and hilarious memoir of that adventure. It is available on Amazon.

Short Pours, The Stan Chronicles is his second book. It is a collection of fictional short stories, with a lively touch of memoir sprinkled throughout. The inspirational spark for the stories has come largely from the author's life, lessons learned and friendships, old and new. But, they are fiction. I swear.

To stay in contact: mailto:cris@crishammond.com

www.ingramcontent.com/pod-product-compliance
Lightning Source LLC
Chambersburg PA
CBHW071302250626
47159CB00004B/1281